MURDER AT TRAITORS'
GATE

IRINA SHAPIRO

Copyright © Irina Shapiro, 2024

The moral right of the author has been asserted.

Ebook ISBN: 978-1-80508-180-7
Paperback ISBN: 978-1-80508-182-1

Cover design: Debbie Clement
Cover images: Arcangel, Shutterstock

Published by Storm Publishing.
For further information, visit:
www.stormpublishing.co

# ALSO BY IRINA SHAPIRO

# PROLOGUE

It had been rainy and overcast all evening, but, just before midnight, the clouds parted to reveal a nearly full moon. It silvered the ancient castle and lit Harry Thayer's way as he walked along the rampart of St. Thomas's Tower, his hands in his pockets, his cap pulled low. He'd arranged to meet Tim Hutchins at midnight, a time when everyone was in their beds and the boys would not be seen. Harry felt a pang of guilt at betraying his father's trust and hoped he'd never discover what Harry was up to, but he couldn't say no to Tim, both because he was afraid to lose Tim as a friend and because he didn't want to stop. The thrill was addictive, and the possibility of being caught added a layer of danger that Harry found difficult to resist.

His hand in the pocket of his coat, Harry caressed the gold watch, then fingered its thick chain. It was a thing of beauty, and solid gold too, judging by its weight. Tim would take it to his fence tomorrow, and then they'd split the profit sixty–forty. Sixty to Harry, who lifted valuables off unsuspecting visitors to the Tower of London, and forty to Tim, who disposed of the stolen items. Tim wasn't happy with the percentages, but Harry took the most risk, so it was fair, Harry decided as he gazed out over the moonlit river. He hoped Tim would get there soon so he could hand over the watch and go home.

Harry leaned further into the embrasure when he saw a solitary rowboat approaching from the direction of Tower Bridge. It was cold on the river, and the only people out at this time of night were the hardened men and women who harpooned floaters with the intention of robbing the bodies before they either washed up on the bank or floated out to sea, their valuables lost forever.

Instinctively taking a step back so as not to be seen, Harry watched as the boat approached the entrance to Traitors' Gate. No one went there anymore, and there was talk of bricking up the entrance for good if the proposed plans to build an embankment ever went through. Harry pulled his cap lower and flattened himself against the stone parapet, his gaze never leaving the boat. There was something odd about the occupants, and Harry was in no doubt that he'd be in danger if spotted. The man on the oars was a dark shape, his hat pulled so low that Harry could see nothing of his face. His shoulders were tense, and his arms moved rhythmically as he guided the rowboat toward the gate. The other man reclined in the prow, his face upturned, his arms strangely limp. He wasn't wearing a hat, his coat hung open despite the December chill, and his face was unnaturally still, his eyes reflecting the moonlight in a way that was distinctly eerie. His mouth was slightly open, and, when the boat drew closer, Harry suddenly realized that what he'd taken for a dark cravat was actually blood-soaked white fabric.

The man rowing maneuvered the boat as close to the gate as he could manage, climbed out, and tied the rope to a post before grabbing the other man beneath the arms and heaving him onto the stone lip. Having seen enough to know he most definitely shouldn't be there, Harry crept along the parapet until he reached the stairs, where he nearly collided with Tim.

Tim opened his mouth to speak, but the look in Harry's eyes must have forestalled him, and he followed Harry down the stairs in silence. Neither boy spoke until they were safely away from the tower and on their way to the Yeoman lodgings, the tied accommodation assigned to the warders. Harry's father thought himself fortunate to dwell within the walls of the fortress, but at times, Harry longed to live outside the gates, like other boys his age. Having forgotten all about the loot until then, Harry pushed the stolen watch into Tim's hand as soon as they reached Harry's door, and watched Tim disappear into the night. Deeply shaken by what he'd seen, Harry locked the door behind him, took off his shoes, and crept to his room on silent feet. He climbed into bed without bothering to undress and pulled the counterpane over him. He lay there shivering, certain that, come morning, all hell would break loose.

# ONE

## TUESDAY, DECEMBER 14, 1858

It was absolutely freezing, but a pale winter sun hung in a cloudless blue sky and the river sparkled playfully, looking for all the world like a magical waterway rather than a dumping ground for rotting refuse and London's many dead. At least a dozen boats could be seen in the vicinity of the Tower of London, ranging from dinghies and packet boats to lumbering barges and a sleek clipper that appeared to be heading out to sea, the sails snapping in the wind.

No one paid any attention to the weather-beaten rowboat that pulled up before Traitors' Gate. Their collars turned up, their hats pulled low, and their noses pink with cold, the occupants could have been mistaken for eccentric tourists from abroad, curious to see the famed Traitors' Gate, or perhaps even writers or historians working on some obscure article few would ever read. But Inspector Sebastian Bell had little interest in either sightseeing or history, unless it was very recent and had resulted in a brutal murder.

He crossed his arms and huddled deeper into his serviceable black coat and dark blue woolen muffler as he fixed his gaze on the ancient gate. His companion, Colin Ramsey, warm in a beaver hat and a caped greatcoat, held the oars firmly in his gloved hands but once they had come alongside the entrance was no less transfixed, his lips tightly pressed together, his eyes narrowed against sunlight glinting off the water. What they were looking at wasn't just a weathered old portal that had served as a gateway to death in centuries past. Their attention was on the body that hung suspended from the grille by a large, sturdy meat hook, the metal wrapped around the victim's neck. The victim wore a dark suit and polished shoes, and, although there was no obvious sign of a wound, his cravat and shirtfront were rust-brown with dried blood.

A young policeman waited on the other side of the gate. He stood on the stone steps to keep his shoes dry from the river water that pooled beneath the gate at high tide, and stomped his feet to keep warm. A Yeoman warder, who didn't appear bothered by the cold, was next to the constable, glaring at the corpse with obvious distaste, and a second policeman, a burly fellow with ginger hair and a face shaped like a potato, descended the steps and waved to the two men in the boat. Sebastian raised a hand in greeting, his gaze finally sliding away from the corpse.

He turned to Colin. "Have you seen enough?"

Colin nodded. "It's always helpful to see the body in situ, but don't ask me to draw any preliminary conclusions until I examine the remains more closely."

"You may take him down, lads," Sebastian called out. "Have the body brought to Mr. Ramsey's mortuary in Blackfriars."

Although not a full-time police surgeon, Colin Ramsey lent his services to Scotland Yard for a very reasonable fee. One advantage of engaging his services was that the postmortem was performed quickly and competently, and Colin, who fancied himself a criminologist, volunteered his opinion free of charge. It was a bonus most inspectors resented, but Sebastian welcomed Colin Ramsey's insights and trusted him above all others to unlock the secrets of a dead body. Unlike the staff surgeon, Mr. Fenwick, who treated both the policemen and the bodies he autopsied with equal contempt, Colin Ramsey was a friend, and one of a handful of people who understood something of Sebastian's past and recent struggles.

"Well, go on," Sebastian prompted the constables, who seemed paralyzed with indecision.

"Yes, sir," Constable Meadows replied with obvious reluctance. The constables would have to wade into frigid knee-deep water to take the body down—unless the warder could offer a more practical solution that didn't involve waiting for low tide, but he didn't seem in any rush to suggest alternatives.

Once they finally overcame their reservations and moved cautiously toward the gate, Sebastian turned to Colin. "We should go back," he said.

Colin, whose elegant hands rarely wielded anything weightier than a pen or a surgical scalpel, lifted the oars and began to row back to shore. Sebastian felt awful for putting his friend to the trouble, and thought that he probably should have asked one of the constables, but he had wanted Colin to see the body in situ. Sebastian would have gladly rowed them out himself, but he was still recovering from an injury he'd sustained in the line of duty and couldn't risk undoing six weeks of convalescence by putting such strain on his shoulder.

"What do you think?" Colin asked when Sebastian failed to share his observations. His breath came in vaporous huffs, and his face and neck were a mottled red from the strain of rowing. "The poor devil," he added under his breath as he took a final look at the corpse. "What a way to go."

"I know him," Sebastian said.

"You do?"

"You've met him as well," Sebastian reminded Colin, "only you might not have noticed. Your attention was engaged elsewhere at the time," he added with a knowing smile.

Colin looked confused. "I don't recall meeting him. Who is he?"

"Jacob Harrow."

"The journalist who reported on the Highgate Angel case?" Colin exclaimed. "Of course. Now I remember." He nodded, having apparently recalled the particulars of the investigation and Jacob Harrow's role in identifying the killer.

"He doesn't look like someone who died by hanging," Sebastian observed.

"No, he doesn't," Colin agreed. "His eyes aren't bulging, his tongue isn't protruding, and I didn't notice any scratches on his neck even though his hands are unbound. Of course, the post-mortem will tell us considerably more."

"He may have been stabbed," Sebastian mused. "That would account for the blood."

"A definite possibility."

"The meat hook was a nice touch," Sebastian added. "Double-sided with equally large hooks on each end."

"Is that unusual?" Colin asked.

"A bit. It's wide enough to fit around the neck. Must be used for large game, since I haven't seen many like it."

"Do you make a habit of examining meat hooks?" Colin inquired with an amused grin.

Like most surgeons, he wasn't overly disturbed by the sight of violent death and treated most cases as an intellectual exercise rather than a gruesome end to human life, but that didn't mean he was devoid of sympathy or compassion. Once the victim was dead, he or she was beyond earthly pain, and the only service Colin Ramsey could offer them was to help apprehend their killer. To get them justice was to give them a voice and have that voice be heard one last time in a court of law, where someone was sure to be listening.

"No, but I will start paying attention to them now," Sebastian replied.

"Who reported it?"

"A passing boatman spotted the body early this morning and alerted one of the warders when he came ashore. The warder informed the Chief Yeoman Warder, who in turn summoned the Lieutenant of the Tower, who apprised the Constable of the Tower, who sent a message to Scotland Yard."

"Ah. Now I understand the reason for the delay," Colin said.

"Will you have time to perform the postmortem today?"

"I will begin as soon as the body is delivered," Colin promised. "I should have the results by midafternoon."

Sebastian nodded. He'd hoped for as much and was grateful to Colin for his diligence. Dr. Fenwick would have made him wait, if only to remind him who was in charge, at least until the body was closed up again and the doctor had been recompensed for his services.

"What about you, Sebastian? Perhaps you should have a rest," Colin suggested. "You're still recuperating, after all."

"Thank you, I'm quite all right. I'd rather get started."

"I wouldn't know where to begin," Colin said, shooting Sebastian an admiring glance. "There's no way to track down witnesses, if there were any, and, given the location of the body, I doubt anyone even noticed anything. I'm surprised the boatman spotted the body. He must have passed quite close to the Tower."

"That's what puzzles me," Sebastian said. "Someone went to the trouble of hanging Harrow off Traitors' Gate, not an easy feat, considering the logistics. It could not be done during the day, given the number of people on the river at any given time, and the Tower is closed at night, leaving only the employees and their families on the premises. Harrow must have been brought by boat and hanged at night. But the killer wanted the body to be discovered. If not, why go to the trouble of rowing out to the Tower and staging such a gruesome display?"

"You think it was a message of some sort?" Colin asked.

"It would have to be. Why hang a body on Traitors' Gate unless you want to make it clear that the man was a traitor?"

"A traitor to whom? His country? A friend? A lover?"

It wasn't a question Sebastian could answer, at least not yet. He had interviewed Jacob Harrow in connection with the Seaborne case and had found the man to be unpleasant, venal, and self-serving, but Sebastian knew nothing of Harrow's personal circumstances or his life outside the offices of the *Daily Telegraph*. He did recall that Harrow had worn a wedding ring, so his wife would have to be identified and informed of her husband's death. Sebastian felt sorry for the unknown woman and, despite his dislike of the victim, felt pity for the man. Unpleasantness wasn't a crime, and no one should suffer what Jacob Harrow had obviously endured in his final moments, but the murder said something about Harrow's killer, and whoever it was had been vicious and daring.

"Impossible to say at this juncture," Sebastian said, "but the manner of his death gives me a starting point."

"Does it?" Colin asked.

"I will speak to the Chief Warder, then call at the offices of the *Daily Telegraph*."

Jacob Harrow had been employed by the newspaper since his return from Crimea, where he had not only fought in the war but had also reported on both the military positions and the grievous conditions at the front. He had earned the respect of the public with his unflinching honesty and harsh criticism of the men who'd sent countless soldiers to their deaths in poorly planned and often disastrous campaigns. Harrow's telegrams and letters to the newspapers had been signed only with his initials, to protect him from certain court-martial, but, once he'd returned and resigned his commission, he had been able to lay claim to his work and publish his opinions freely. His editor at the *Daily Telegraph* should be able to tell Sebastian something of the man and point him in the direction of Harrow's next of kin.

Colin breathed a sigh of relief when they finally approached the shore and the owner of the boat, who'd been handsomely paid for its use and had been cooling his heels for over an hour, pulled it onto the bank. Sebastian stepped out onto the muddy ground and headed toward the steps that led to the street. Colin caught up with him, after wiping the mud off his boots. His forehead glistened with perspiration despite the cold, and his breathing was ragged as he trotted up the steps. He would need a few minutes and a hot drink to recover from the unexpected exertion.

"When would be a convenient time for me to call?" Sebastian asked as the two men stopped before a street vendor and ordered two mugs of tea.

Colin took out his watch and consulted the time. "Say two o'clock?"

Sebastian nodded, but his mind was already on the questions he intended to ask and the answers he hoped to receive. Sometimes asking the right questions made all the difference, especially in a murder inquiry, and he already knew that, if the grotesque display of the body was anything to go by, this case would prove tricky.

Having finished his tea, Colin tipped his hat and walked off, his head bent into the wind, his shoulders squared. Sebastian headed in the opposite direction, striding toward the Tower of London.

# TWO

It took Sebastian some considerable time to skirt the outer wall and arrive at the Tower's main entrance. He got there just in time to see the police wagon depart, the body of Jacob Harrow stowed in the back. He was met at the gate by the Chief Warder, Mr. Thayer, a stout fellow with a ruddy face and shrewd dark eyes that peered from beneath bushy brows. His chest was puffed out with self-importance and, although the man was polite, Sebastian got the distinct impression that he wasn't overly fond of the police and had little desire to help.

"I am to escort you to the office of the constable," Mr. Thayer said, and set off at a trot.

Sebastian didn't know who held the position of Constable of the Tower now, but until only a few years ago it had been the Duke of Wellington. That was someone Sebastian would have liked to meet, and preferably not in the course of an investigation; but now wasn't the time to indulge his fantasies about coming face to face with his boyhood hero.

"Name?" Sebastian asked.

Mr. Thayer shot Sebastian a look of ill-concealed contempt. One might think he had just asked who sat on the throne or who the prime minister might be. He supposed the constable was as important to the Chief Warder, if not more so, since the constable ruled the Tower's self-contained kingdom.

"Stapleton Cotton, *1st Viscount Combermere*," Mr. Thayer replied, enunciating the title just in case Sebastian wasn't sufficiently impressed with the exalted personage he was about to meet.

"Thank you, Mr. Thayer. I look forward to making his acquaintance."

They walked the rest of the way in silence, and Sebastian took the opportunity to study his surroundings. He'd visited the Tower of London only once, when he was a boy and the family had come from Suffolk for Queen Victoria's coronation. All he could recall of that occasion was rowdy crowds, public drunkenness, and his sense of frustration at not being tall enough to see anything of the procession. Had he been younger, his father would have sat him on his shoulders, but Sebastian had been nearly ten, so all he'd got to see were people's backs and the occasional elbow aimed at his head. He might have had more fun had his brother Simian been there, but Simian had been ill and remained in Suffolk with their grandparents, glad to stay on the farm and avoid braving the crowds.

The only thing that had made the trip to London truly memorable was the visit to the Tower of London. Sebastian's father had been a great one for history. He had regaled Sebastian with stories of Londinium, first established by the Romans, and William the Conqueror, who had built the Tower to showcase his strength. Sebastian couldn't recall the names of all the kings and queens who had been held at the Tower, either to be released or to meet a grisly end on a scaffold, but he remembered the boy princes who'd disappeared without a trace, their fate having captured his childish imagination. He had enjoyed seeing the fortress but, after several hours of exploring grim buildings dotted by beady-eyed ravens and sidestepping Tower

Green, where so many had lost their heads, he'd asked his father if they could go to the zoological gardens at Regent's Park.

Sebastian could still remember his excitement at seeing the menagerie, and the cherished memory nearly brought tears to his eyes. He had hoped to take his own child to see the animals someday, but that was not to be. His son slept beneath the cold earth with his mother, his family innocent victims of Sebastian's ambition and one man's desire for vengeance. As he followed Mr. Thayer into the Constable Tower, he willed himself to clear his mind of personal feelings. He was here because a man had been murdered, and he had to focus on the case.

The constable sat behind a massive desk, his office a memorial to those who'd come before him. A gilded portrait of the Queen graced one blood-red wall, and there were several paintings of the constable's predecessors and polished ceremonial weapons displayed around the room. The constable was considerably older than Sebastian had expected. He had to be in his eighties, although his clear gaze and erect bearing were that of a much younger man, probably due to decades spent in the military. His thinning white hair was neatly trimmed and combed to cover his balding pate, his moustache waxed into points. The constable wore his uniform as if he were about to go on parade, and his pale blue gaze, when it swept over Sebastian, was far from welcoming.

Sebastian was not invited to sit but left standing before the constable's desk like an errant schoolboy, a lack of manners he resented. He might not bear military rank, but he was an inspector of the Metropolitan Police and deserved the respect due a man sworn to uphold the law.

"How can I help you, Inspector Bell?" the constable asked.

"I would like permission to examine the crime scene and question the Tower staff."

The viscount leaned back in his chair and looked at Sebastian as if he had just said something so profoundly idiotic that it didn't even warrant consideration.

"Inspector, the crime scene, as you call it, is an ancient and historically significant gate, the bottom of said gate submerged in water. I don't know what you hope to find, but feel free to look as long as you don't cause any further damage. I have charged Lieutenant Constable Bowles with questioning the men, and no one has seen or heard anything, so I don't think further inquiries are necessary."

"Who was first on the scene?" Sebastian asked, refusing to back down.

"Chief Warder Thayer followed by Lieutenant Constable Bowles. No one has been permitted to enter St. Thomas's Tower since the body was discovered except your men and Mr. Thayer, and no one has come forward with any pertinent information. You may speak to the Chief Warder, but once you're finished here you must conduct your investigation from Scotland Yard. If anything pertaining to the case comes to light, you will be sent for."

"Thank you, sir. Good day."

The viscount inclined his head in acknowledgement and watched Sebastian walk to the door, his gaze boring into Sebastian's back.

Mr. Thayer was waiting for Sebastian outside, his attention fixed on a bird wheeling above the White Tower.

"I'd like to ask you a few questions, Mr. Thayer," Sebastian said.

"Very well."

"Is there somewhere we can talk?"

The sun had disappeared behind a thick cloud, and it had grown considerably colder, the chill wind penetrating the worn wool of Sebastian's coat and turning the stones beneath the thin soles of his boots to ice. His shoulder was aching, and he rolled it gently to relieve some of the discomfort and caught

Mr. Thayer looking at him with obvious impatience. Since every employee of the Tower came from a military background, they clearly viewed Sebastian as an outsider and seemed to feel no obligation to offer him assistance, more so because the body had been outside the gate, not inside the compound. Still, they couldn't openly refuse to help the police, and why would they? They were all on the same side, the side of law and order.

Mr. Thayer considered the request for a moment, then said, "Come with me."

He led Sebastian toward the residential block, where the warders and their families lived. The accommodation was surprisingly spacious and looked to be comfortably furnished, not at all like the barracks Sebastian had imagined when walking past earlier. A plump woman of middle years smiled at him warmly, took his things, and invited him into the parlor.

"You look chilled to the bone, Inspector," she said when her husband introduced them. "It's always so much colder by the river. Even the high walls can't keep out the wind. Do sit down by the fire, and I'll make you a nice cup of tea."

"Thank you, Mrs. Thayer. That's very kind," Sebastian said gratefully. He was cold, and the dull pain in his clavicle gnawed at him like an infected tooth.

"Not at all," she said, and left the men to it.

Mr. Thayer removed his hat and set it on a sideboard, then sat across from Sebastian and stretched his legs out toward the fire. Sebastian didn't expect friendly banter from this taciturn man, so he dove right in.

"Who reported the body, Mr. Thayer?"

"I told you. A passing ferryman."

"Did you take his name?" Sebastian asked, and hoped his irritation wasn't obvious.

"No."

"Why not?"

Mr. Thayer smiled ruefully. "To be honest, I didn't believe him, and by the time I returned he was gone."

"Why didn't you believe him? Are passing ferrymen known for indulging in daft pranks?"

"The idea just seemed preposterous, and the fellow did reek of spirits."

"What did he say, exactly?" Sebastian asked.

"He said he was rowing past and saw a dead body hanging off Traitors' Gate, suspended by a meat hook."

"Did he see anyone else in the vicinity?"

"He didn't mention it."

"What time was this?" Sebastian inquired.

"We unlock the gates at dawn. The ferryman arrived about a quarter past seven."

"What did you do?" Sebastian asked after Mrs. Thayer had delivered the tea tray and set it on a low table between the two armchairs. She also brought a plate of ginger biscuits that filled the room with a wonderful smell, and poured the tea for the two men, before leaving them to talk.

"I went to investigate," Mr. Thayer said. He took a noisy sip of tea and reached for a biscuit, which he dunked into his cup, then shoved into his mouth whole.

"Did you see anything that might be important?"

"Just the body, which had its back to me. I could see the hook, though, so I knew then the ferryman had been telling the truth."

"Was there anything beside the body?"

The warder shook his head and reached for another biscuit. The man frustrated Sebastian with his lack of initiative, and it took all his considerable resolve not to say so. How had Thayer attained his high position without showing some ambition? Or maybe that was the reason. He did what he was told and didn't stick his nose where it didn't belong. The body had been outside the gate, so as far as Thayer was concerned it wasn't within his bailiwick. Perhaps if the body had been found inside, the response would have been more enthusiastic.

"It was clear he was dead," Thayer said once he had swallowed his second biscuit. "There was no sense getting my feet wet searching for clues."

"Did you not think it might be prudent to have a closer look?" Sebastian asked irritably, unable to tolerate the man's lassitude any longer.

"Inspector, we lock the gates at sundown, which is around four o'clock at this time of year. The body was not there yesterday. Someone would have seen it if it were. This means that whoever did this was not someone inside the Tower, and the victim is not one of our own. Therefore, the murder is the jurisdiction of the Metropolitan Police." Mr. Thayer drained the rest of his tea. "I'm sorry, but that's all I can reasonably tell you. Now, if you don't mind, I must return to my duties."

The warder pushed to his feet, and Sebastian followed suit. A boy of about thirteen brought Sebastian's coat, hat, and muffler, and cast a timid glance at Thayer before disappearing behind a door.

"My son, Harry," Mr. Thayer said with obvious pride. "It's time for his lessons."

"He looks like a fine boy," Sebastian said. He thanked Mrs. Thayer for the tea and headed toward the gate where the body had been hanging.

Just as Mr. Thayer had said, there was nothing to see. With the body gone, the gate looked as it must have for centuries, the murky water of the Thames lapping at the wooden partition and rippling in the wind. Even if anything of note had been left behind, it would have been washed away when the tide came in, the evidence would now either be resting at the bottom of the river or have been carried off on the current.

Sebastian sighed with frustration and walked away, feeling none the wiser.

# THREE

By the time Sebastian arrived at the offices of the *Daily Telegraph*, it was half past eleven and the newsroom resembled a council of war. Black-suited journalists were smoking, almost to a man, calling out comments and questions to each other and scribbling furiously, the nibs of their pens scratching against the paper as they hurried to make their deadlines. Even though they were doing little more than putting words to paper, there was an atmosphere of urgency and suppressed excitement, as if their every word had the power to change the world and the lives of the people that inhabited it. And perhaps it did, although not always for the better.

"Inspector Bell, if I'm not mistaken?" a young clerk inquired as Sebastian headed toward the large office at the back. They had met during a previous investigation, and the clerk clearly remembered him. Sebastian couldn't recall the man's name, only that he was a very junior employee. "How can I help?" the clerk asked as he trotted after Sebastian.

"I need to speak to the editor-in-chief."

"You must make an appointment," the clerk pleaded with

him. "You can't simply turn up. Mr. Lawrence is a very busy man."

"I'm here on police business," Sebastian said. "He'll have to see me."

"But Inspector," the clerk tried again.

"Don't worry," Sebastian reassured him as he reached the door. "I'll make certain he knows you did your job."

The young man still looked nervous but stepped aside and looked on as Sebastian knocked on the closed door.

"Come," a hoarse voice called from within.

Sebastian had never met Marshall Lawrence but knew the man by reputation. He was intelligent, unapologetically ruthless, and had a nose for a good story, an instinct he'd honed while working at the *London Illustrated News* as a staff reporter. Marshall Lawrence understood the value of sensationalism and the importance of timing. He also remained strictly behind the scenes and did not seek attention for its own sake.

The man behind the massive, paper-strewn desk had to be in his sixties, possibly even early seventies. Even seated, he was clearly tall and still in fine physical form. A fringe of short gray hair encircled his bullet-shaped head, and Sebastian was sure that the rheumy blue eyes didn't miss a thing. A monocle was perched on his narrow, patrician nose as he studied an ink-stained sheet of paper with an expression of ill-disguised disgust. Whoever had written that piece was in for a stern reprimand and possibly even a loss of wages. Marshall Lawrence looked somewhat surprised to find a stranger walking into his office but set the article aside, removed the monocle, and studied Sebastian with an air of mild curiosity.

"And you are?" he asked.

"Inspector Bell of Scotland Yard. Your man out there did try to stop me from barging in," he added, recalling his promise to the young clerk.

Marshall Lawrence ignored that last bit and fixed his gaze

on Sebastian. His curiosity appeared to have been replaced by grudging approval. "You're the chap that sent Adelaide Seaborne's murderer to the gallows and brought down a corrupt MP and his dissolute son."

Sebastian inclined his head, and the editor gestured toward the guest chair. Sebastian removed his hat, unbuttoned his coat, and unwound his muffler, then hung his things on the coatrack and settled in the proffered chair.

"Am I to assume you have a story you wish me to print?" the editor asked.

"As it happens, I would rather you held off on printing the story I'm about to tell you."

"Oh? Why is that?"

"Because I'd like a chance to investigate the case before you cause mass panic."

"Mass panic is good for business," Marshall Lawrence replied with a sly grin. Sebastian was in no doubt that the man was deadly serious.

"Not *my* business."

The editor opened a monogrammed cigarette case, extracted a cheroot, lit it, and took a deep drag. "All right. I'm listening."

"Jacob Harrow was found dead this morning."

The editor's shock was obvious, but he didn't interrupt and waited for Sebastian to continue.

"His body was left hanging on Traitors' Gate, suspended by a meat hook."

"I certainly hope there's more to this story," Marshall Lawrence said when Sebastian paused. "The headline is intriguing, but I need more of a *hook* to pique the readers' interest." The man's scheming smile put Sebastian in mind of the serpent in the Garden of Eden.

"There is more, but until I discover who murdered him and why I would like to keep it quiet."

"So, what do you want with me, Inspector?"

"I want to know something of the man. Was he prone to ruffling feathers?"

"Unless a journalist publishes his mother's favorite recipes or offers gardening advice, he's bound to ruffle someone's feathers, but I must admit that Jacob Harrow had been playing it safe of late."

"Why?" Sebastian had a fairly good idea but wondered just how much Harrow's editor knew of the journalist's dealings with Jonathan Wright MP, who had been feeding Harrow confidential information and was now languishing in Newgate Prison on charges of slander.

"I suppose coming home from Crimea and settling into family life put out the fire in his belly."

"Might someone he'd eviscerated in one of his wartime articles have wanted revenge?" Sebastian asked.

Marshall Lawrence shook his head. "Not at this stage. Murdering a journalist who hadn't mentioned the war in years would do nothing to clear their name or ease their conscience."

"Perhaps Jacob Harrow was working on a new piece that would level fresh accusations against someone who'd rather kill than face another scandal," Sebastian suggested.

Marshall Lawrence shook his head. "Harrow had no interest in writing about the war. In fact, he recently turned down a story brought to him by someone he'd known in Crimea."

"What sort of story?"

"I don't really know," Mr. Lawrence replied, his lack of interest evident in his demeanor. "Something about an abuse of power at the highest level. Harrow met with the man, Captain Hadley, and took down the relevant details but had decided not to pursue an investigation into the allegations. The public has lost their appetite for the debacle that was the Crimean War, and Harrow had told the man as much."

"Did Captain Hadley approach anyone else?"

"Not as far as I know. He saw the wisdom of letting sleeping dogs lie," Mr. Lawrence added with a dismissive wave of the hand.

"What about the individuals Jacob Harrow vilified based on Jonathan Wright's information? Might they wish to revenge themselves on him?"

The editor shook his head. "They were vindicated by Wright's arrest and conviction."

"Jacob Harrow wasn't charged. Some might think he evaded justice."

"Jacob Harrow was the mouthpiece, not the source. If someone had him murdered, I highly doubt it was one of our esteemed MPs."

"When was the last time you saw Jacob Harrow?" Sebastian asked, his notebook at the ready.

"Last night. A few of us went to the Portland Club after work, to have a drink and try our luck at cards."

"And how was Mr. Harrow's luck?"

"Enviable. I believe he won fifty quid."

Sebastian made a note of the sum, then turned his attention back to the editor, who was quick to put forth his own theory.

"Clearly robbery wasn't the motive, or the perpetrator would have left him where he fell. This savage act was meant to send a message that had nothing to do with money."

"I wholeheartedly agree," Sebastian said. The answer had to lie in Harrow's past, quite possibly something that happened after he came back from Crimea. "How did Jacob Harrow come to work at the *Telegraph*?" he asked.

"Harrow came to see me shortly after he'd returned from Crimea. Given the insightful and often scathing articles he'd sent in from the front, I was happy to have him. Dissent and verbal lashings invite debate and retaliation in print, and, in turn, result in a surge in circulation. Increased visibility is good for business."

"How did you know he'd written the articles sent from Crimea?" Sebastian asked. "The byline always read *J.H. War Correspondent*. Could have been anyone."

"Mr. Harrow brought the articles he'd written with him. He had every single one, and they weren't clean transcripts that could have been copied from the papers and passed off as his own. There were notes in the margins, crossed-out words, and rephrased paragraphs. Hiring J.H. would be a coup for any paper. I wasn't about to allow him to walk away and apply to another publication."

"Was there anyone who took issue with your newspaper offering him a platform?" Sebastian asked.

"Of course. Once it became known that Jacob Harrow was J.H., there were several individuals who wrote to me, demanding that Harrow be dismissed."

"Anyone in particular?"

"The letters were anonymous."

"How convenient," Sebastian said.

"Despite their outrage, many of these men acknowledged, albeit in private, that they were in part liable for the heavy losses we'd suffered in the Crimea and did not care to have their names bandied about. They might have won their case in a defamation trial, but ultimately they would still come out the loser, since their every failure would be exposed by the defendant as proof of his innocence."

"Was there anyone who did bring a charge of defamation against Mr. Harrow once his identity was revealed?"

Sebastian was sure such a case would have been extensively covered in the papers, but he'd been in such a state of impenetrable grief after his wife Louisa's death that he had largely withdrawn from the world and had spent his days in an opium-induced haze. Not a circumstance he wished to discuss with the editor of the *Daily Telegraph*, who might use the information in one of the many articles meant to chastise the police service. The newspapers frequently stoked public outrage and derided overworked, underpaid, and greatly outnumbered police officers who risked their lives to bring order to a vast metropolis that sprouted criminals the way the Hydra grew new heads.

"There was one plaintiff. Captain Hugh Pickering. He brought a case of defamation to the High Court, but the charges against Jacob were dismissed."

"Based on what?"

Marshall Lawrence gave Sebastian a searching look, seemingly surprised that he wasn't aware of this already, but Sebastian dismissed the silent reproach. Even if he had read about the case at the time, he could hardly be expected to recall the details.

"Based on the testimony of two fellow officers, who testified that Pickering had exceeded his authority and knowingly sent his men to their deaths in an ill-conceived gambit to distinguish himself before his superiors."

"Where can I find this Captain Pickering?" Sebastian asked.

"At Highgate. He shot himself the day after the verdict."

"Did he have anyone who might wish to see him avenged?"

Marshall Lawrence made a show of thinking. "I really couldn't say. My interest in Captain Pickering ended the day he died."

"When was that?"

"September 1856. Don't you read the papers, man?"

Sebastian ignored the question and made a note of Captain Pickering's death. If the man had relations who held Jacob Harrow responsible for the captain's death, then they might consider seeing him hanged on Traitors' Gate a fitting end.

"Was there anyone else who might have wished to revenge themselves on Jacob Harrow?" Sebastian asked, hoping that another name would spring to mind, but Marshall Lawrence shook his head.

"I'm sure Mr. Harrow received his share of poison pen letters, as does any reporter who dares to speak the truth, which is why so many resort to pussyfooting around the facts or writing about horse races and reporting society gossip. Our justice system does not protect free speech in the press, Inspector, since the burden of proof is on the defendant rather than the plaintiff in a case of slander. Too many good men have been sentenced to prison or worse for having the courage of their convictions."

"So, it is your opinion that Jacob Harrow was murdered as retribution for something he had said in print?"

Marshall Lawrence scoffed. "I don't credit opinions, Inspector Bell. I work with facts, and the only fact you're in possession of is that Jacob Harrow is dead. Everything else, including your assumption that he was murdered, is pure supposition at this stage. Now, if you don't have any other questions for me—"

"Did Harrow seem worried or frightened last night?" Sebastian asked.

"No. He was his usual oblique self."

"Oblique?"

"He wasn't the sort of fellow who liked to talk about himself," the editor explained.

"Do you have the Harrows' home address?" Sebastian asked. He could sense Marshall Lawrence's mounting impatience and knew that he had only a few more minutes until he was shown the door.

"Ask Mr. Leslie—the young man who tried to prevent you from barging in here," he added with a sardonic smile.

"Thank you," Sebastian said, and stood to leave, but Marshall Lawrence forestalled him.

"Unless you promise me an exclusive interview about the case tomorrow, I will run the story this evening."

"Will you resort to printing falsehoods?" Sebastian asked. "You said the facts were insufficient."

"The information is only false if someone can disprove its veracity. Until then, it's news."

"I don't expect to solve the case by tomorrow," Sebastian said. Even if he did, he saw no reason to give Marshall Lawrence a helping hand.

"No, but your reputation precedes you, Inspector, and I am sure you will have the results of the postmortem and a working theory by end of day. That will be enough to titillate the public until you have a suspect in custody. And repeatedly getting your name in print is no insignificant thing, not if you hope to gain the notice of your superiors and advance your prospects."

Sebastian ignored the veiled bribe. No doubt Marshall Lawrence had friends in high places who could help him rise through the ranks, but he wasn't fool enough to imagine that such support wouldn't come without a price, and he had no intention of becoming indebted to any man. If he advanced in the Metropolitan Police, it would be on merit, not favors granted by those who'd expect to collect.

"I'm sorry, Mr. Lawrence, but I'm not at liberty to discuss the particulars of the case."

"Suit yourself. Now, I'm a busy man, Inspector Bell, and I think I've given you enough of my valuable time."

"Thank you, sir," Sebastian said, and walked out of the editor's office.

Mr. Leslie wasn't difficult to locate since he was hovering just outside the door. Sebastian asked for Jacob Harrow's address, then spent the next half-hour speaking to Harrow's colleagues. Their responses were similar in nature and frustratingly brief. Amiable enough, intelligent, a bit arrogant and vainglorious, but overall a decent chap. No one knew of any threats or potential enemies, and everyone was equally shocked to learn that Jacob Harrow had been murdered.

Sebastian did discover that Captain Hugh Pickering's mother had died shortly after the trial, and he had become unpopular with his fellow officers over the lawsuit since a number of them had been called to testify and the trial had shone an unwelcome spotlight on their own activities during the war. According to Mr. Cooper, who'd covered the trial and Captain Pickering's subsequent suicide, no one except the captain's housekeeper had attended the funeral. Sebastian would have to verify the information, but it seemed no one would care enough to avenge the man's death, especially at this late stage.

Frustrated by the lack of useful information, Sebastian adjourned to a nearby chophouse. It was too soon for the post-mortem results, and he didn't think he should call on Jacob Harrow's widow until he had more information to share with her. The poor woman would be distraught to learn that her husband had been murdered. The least Sebastian could do was offer her some answers about his final moments.

# FOUR

Sebastian presented himself at Colin Ramsey's house at two o'clock, as agreed. Colin's young housemaid, Mabel, opened the door and smiled apologetically when a reedy female voice called from the parlor, "Is that you, Mr. Melville? I'll have you know I'm still smarting from that time you beat me at croquet. Do come in and say hello."

"I'm sorry, Inspector," Mabel whispered as she took his things. "Mrs. Ramsey is having a bad day. If you could just pop in and say hello?"

"Of course," Sebastian replied, and followed Mabel to the parlor.

One of the reasons Colin had decided to convert the cellar into a mortuary was so that he could be home to look after his mother, whose mental faculties seemed to be deserting her at an alarming rate. Gemma Tate, who was a nurse during the Crimean War and had become a dear friend, had referred to the condition as a softening of the brain, which was sometimes brought about by aging and at other times by trauma the individual couldn't seem to recover from. Mrs. Ramsey's symptoms had set in after the sudden death of her husband and, although she still had lucid moments, the condition seemed to be progressing, necessitating constant care and vigilance in case she decided to go off on her own.

Anne Ramsey sat by the window, her hair curled as if she were a young girl and her cheeks stained with rouge. Her mind seemed to have found refuge in the past, and she spent her days lost in a world she could no longer inhabit, happy only when she could avoid reality.

"Good afternoon, Mrs. Ramsey. It's a pleasure to see you again," Sebastian said.

"It's kind of you to call, Mr. Melville," Mrs. Ramsey said. "Would you care for some refreshment? I believe there's cake," she added coyly.

"Thank you, but I'm rather pressed for time," Sebastian said. "I only wanted to stop in and say hello to Colin."

"Pfft," Mrs. Ramsey said dismissively. "All he does is hide in that cellar. And there's that strange odor. I do declare, I have no idea what he does down there, but it can't be healthy. It's high time he was married. A man needs a loving woman to look after him. And how is your dear wife? Was she not in a delicate condition the last time we met?" Mrs. Ramsey lowered her voice conspiratorially, since such things weren't openly spoken of in polite company. It seemed that, despite calling him by the wrong name, she still managed to remember Louisa, or perhaps Mr. Melville's wife, whoever she was.

"Really, Mother," Colin exclaimed as he came into the room. He adored his mother, but on this occasion he couldn't manage to hide his vexation.

Mrs. Ramsey looked taken aback, uncertain what she'd done to upset her son. At least today she still recognized that Colin was her son. There were days when she thought he was his late father. Colin looked like he was about to explain, then took one look at Sebastian and seemed to change his mind. Anne Ramsey would not retain the information, given her inability to focus, and would probably ask Sebastian after Louisa again the next time they met. Having to explain that Louisa and the baby were gone did not make them any more dead, but speaking the words still caused Sebastian unbearable pain and made him feel as if he'd lost them all over again.

"It's all right, Colin," Sebastian said quietly. "She means no harm." But he felt heartsick and wanted only to remove himself from Mrs. Ramsey's presence. "Please excuse me," he said, and made his way down the narrow stone stairs that led to Colin's cellar mortuary. Mrs. Ramsey was right about the smell, though. It was appalling.

Aside from performing postmortems for the police, Colin also taught private pupils in his mortuary. Surgical students rarely got the chance to practice their skills and were expected to learn by watching surgeries in the operating theaters at London's many hospitals. Some were interested in a more hands-on approach and preferred to learn by doing, a privilege they were willing to pay for since it was considerably cheaper than relocating to Scotland, where the medical schools sourced cadavers by less-than-honest means. Colin did not permit his students to perform a postmortem on a victim of violent crime, but he did allow them access to the body once he was finished, if the victim had no kin to claim the body and the remains would wind up in a pauper's grave by way of the dead house.

"I'm sorry about Mother," Colin said once they were alone. "She seems to be getting worse. You have no idea how maddening it is to watch her decline and to not be able to help."

"The mind is an unexplored country," Sebastian said, quoting something he'd heard.

"Well, perhaps it's time someone explored it," Colin grumbled. "Mother is in good physical health, but she can barely remember what day of the week it is or what she did yesterday. Half the time she believes I'm still in the schoolroom, and the other half she thinks I'm my father."

"Have you thought of hiring a nurse? It's a lot for Mabel to manage."

Colin nodded. "I was hoping to put it off a little longer, but I believe you're right. The time has come. I will speak to Miss Tate next time I see her. She might be able to offer some advice." He sighed. "Anyway, enough about me. We have a murder to solve."

He shut the door behind them and invited Sebastian to join him next to the table at the center of the room, where the remains of Jacob Harrow awaited, his hips modestly draped with a linen towel, his chest mercifully closed. When he was expecting his students, Colin didn't bother to close up the bodies or replace the organs he'd removed, instead leaving them in ceramic bowls on a wooden counter for easier access. The clothes Colin had removed from the body were folded neatly, awaiting inspection, and the victim's personal possessions were stowed in a painted cardboard box that must have contained a present or an assortment of marzipan before it migrated to the cellar and was repurposed for more grim uses.

"Did Harrow have his purse on him?" Sebastian asked.

"Robbery was most definitely not the motive," Colin replied, clearly eager to share his own conclusions. "Jacob Harrow was still in possession of his purse, watch, wedding ring, and cufflinks."

"I didn't think this was a robbery gone wrong," Sebastian agreed as he opened the box and examined each object in turn. The watch was solid gold and bore an inscription inside the lid.

*With Love, M.L.*

In his conversations with Jacob Harrow's colleagues, Sebastian had discovered that Harrow's wife's name was Emma, so the watch couldn't be from her—unless M was short for Em, but that seemed a bit farfetched. The purse contained nearly sixty pounds, which was consistent with what Marshall Lawrence had said about Harrow walking away from the gaming tables with substantial winnings. There was nothing remarkable about the thin wedding band or the onyx and gold cufflinks, but, taken together, Jacob Harrow's possessions would have fetched a tidy sum if pawned.

The clothes would have sold for a pretty penny as well, especially if someone had managed to get the blood out. The fabric was of the highest quality, the stitches even and neat, the trademark of an experienced tailor. The shoes were beautifully made and almost new, the soles hardly worn. Sebastian wondered what had happened to the man's hat and gloves, and if he might have had a walking stick. He didn't think the killer had any interest in selling the items to a rag-and-bone man, so it was likely he'd discarded them along the way, or left them at the original crime scene. At this stage Sebastian thought of the killer as a man, since a woman, no matter how strong, would have had a hard time getting the body up on that gate, unless she had an accomplice.

Setting Jacob Harrow's clothes aside, Sebastian turned to Colin. "What did you discover from the postmortem? Did he suffer before he died?"

"Yes, but the suffering wasn't prolonged," Colin replied.

"Thank God for small mercies," Sebastian said. The sight of the meat hook had put him in mind of horrors he didn't care to verbalize.

The two men took up their positions on either side of the body, and Colin pointed to a narrow slit on Jacob Harrow's chest. "The cause of death was a single stab to the heart. The weapon was narrow, double-sided, and possibly curved, and death would have been almost instantaneous."

"Was that the source of the blood down his shirtfront?"

"Yes and no."

"Can you be more specific?" Sebastian asked.

Colin used his thumb to pull down Jacob Harrow's chin, and Sebastian peered into the mouth cavity.

"His tongue is missing," he observed.

"Precisely. Someone cut out his tongue, most likely with the same instrument and almost certainly before he was dead, hence the profuse bleeding. The killer then administered the fatal wound before hanging the victim from the gate."

"Are you certain Harrow was dead before he was hanged?"

"There are no signs of asphyxiation, so yes, he was dead by the time he was hanged."

"Was there anything else of importance?"

"There's evidence of a struggle, and I would venture to guess that the assailant brought Harrow to the ground and sat on his chest, pinning his arms with his own legs." Colin pointed to areas of bruising on the victim's arms and face.

"See here?" Colin went on, directing Sebastian's attention to Jacob Harrow's jawline. "There are fingermarks, one on the right and four on the left. At some point, the killer used his left hand to hold Harrow's face still."

"Would he not have needed both hands to remove the tongue?" Sebastian asked.

"I should think so. One hand to hold the tongue, the other to slice it off at the base. But perhaps this happened before the killer had decided on that course of action."

"You mean it was a spur-of-the-moment decision to remove the tongue?"

"Impossible to know," Colin replied. "I would have liked to see the severed tongue. It would tell me something of the killer's mindset."

"How so?"

"Well, if he used some sort of tool to grab the tongue and pull it out, then it would indicate that he'd come prepared. If he used his fingers, then it was likely a more spontaneous decision. And if the edge was ragged, it would indicate that his hand might have shaken, or that the victim had thrashed about. A precise cut would show resolve and experience."

"Can you not tell by looking at what's left?" Sebastian asked.

Colin shook his head. "It's a fairly clean cut, but difficult to tell for certain without seeing the rest of the tongue. I wonder what he did with it."

"You keep saying he," Sebastian pointed out. "I happen to agree with you, but I'd like to hear your reasoning."

"I can't see a woman behind this attack. For one, she would have to be a giantess to overpower a man of Jacob Harrow's size and strength and then hoist his dead body high enough to get the head into the hook. For another, this sort of brutality is more traditionally associated with men."

"Still, it's not completely impossible, is it? Perhaps there was more than one assailant."

"Perhaps," Colin agreed. "A woman may have been used to lure Harrow to wherever he was killed, and the man might have done the killing. Perhaps the man pinned down the victim and held his face in place while his accomplice removed the tongue. It's also possible that the second person was also a man, or that there was only one assailant to begin with. There's simply not enough evidence to say either way. I wonder where the tongue is."

"Floating along the Thames if it wasn't eaten by fish. Or a dog, if it was discarded in the street," Sebastian replied. "Anything else you can tell me?"

"There are several old scars, a historic fracture, and a scar on his abdomen from a bullet wound, but it was well healed so not relevant to the victim's death. I expect he was shot in Crimea. The fracture is considerably older, from when he was a child or an adolescent. Probably broke his arm climbing a tree or fighting."

"Is that all?" Sebastian asked, his gaze fixed on Jacob Harrow's pallid face.

Harrow didn't wear an expression of suffering, but that didn't mean he hadn't died in agony. Sebastian's mouth soured as he imagined having one's tongue cut out while still alive. Such an act would not be performed randomly and spoke volumes about the motive, as did the choice of location for displaying the body. Sebastian might have pegged the murder weapon as a standard-issue dagger for British soldiers, but the daggers were straight and the weapon used had been curved, so that ruled out a military connection, at least on paper.

"Any idea where he might have been murdered?" Sebastian asked as he forced himself to tear his gaze away from the victim's slack mouth.

"Not a clue. There's muck in his hair, but his clothes are clean, which tells me he was down on the ground and was still wearing his coat at the time of the attack."

"How long has he been dead?"

"At least six hours at the time of discovery, but the body was left out in the bitter cold, so it's a rough estimate. Might be significantly longer."

"So, someone approached Jacob Harrow after he left the Portland Club last night. It might have been someone he knew or a complete stranger. The person either abducted or lured the victim somewhere where they wouldn't be seen and proceeded to overpower him and cut out his tongue. Once the killer was ready, he stabbed the victim through the heart and waited for him to die. He then disposed of Harrow's hat, gloves, and possibly a walking stick, and transported the body to the river, where he loaded it into a boat and rowed out to Traitors' Gate.

He would have to have had the meat hook ready, or perhaps he came upon it along the way and had a flash of inspiration. The killer hung the body and vanished into the night. Does that sound about right?"

"Yes, it does," Colin said.

"The hems of the trousers are muddy but didn't appear frozen when we saw the body, which would indicate that they were never wet."

"What are you suggesting?" Colin asked.

"His legs must have been bent at the knee when he was on the ground, and then the body was probably loaded into the boat on the riverbank and then pulled out directly onto the stone lip beneath the gate, which means the body was brought to the Tower at low tide."

"The body was shielded from the worst of the wind," Colin said, "so it is possible that the trousers were wet and then simply dried, but if it were me I would certainly wait for low tide to avoid getting soaked. The killer would have been near frozen by the time he got back if he got thoroughly wet."

"If it were me, I'd murder Harrow by the river, so as not to transport a corpse through the streets of London," Sebastian mused.

"If it were you, you would have gutted him in some alley and wouldn't have bothered with the theatrics," Colin replied.

"True, but the killer obviously had a message he wished to send, and it has been received. He believed Jacob Harrow was a traitor who needed to be silenced."

"But whom did he betray?" Colin asked.

"That's what I need to find out. But first, I must break the news to Harrow's widow. Not a task I relish."

"The poor woman," Colin said. "Although she must suspect that something has happened to her husband if he never came home last night."

"Perhaps she wasn't expecting him."

Not everyone's marriage was a congenial one or made up of only two partners. At this stage, Sebastian knew virtually nothing of the man, and it was entirely possible he'd kept a mistress and had been on his way to her place when he'd left the Portland Club last night, which would introduce several new angles. Now that Sebastian knew about Jacob Harrow's death, it was time to learn more of his life, and one person who could help him instantly sprang to mind—Gemma Tate. Not only had she been in Crimea at the same time as Jacob Harrow, but she had also known him personally and had read the articles that had brought Harrow to the attention of the public.

Sebastian smiled at the thought of Gemma. Since the investigation into her twin brother's murder, she had become a cherished friend and was the only person in his life who knew the unedited truth of what had happened to the man who'd murdered Sebastian's wife and son. He hadn't told her right away—it had taken time to work up the courage to share his most damning secret—but Gemma had listened and understood and had not judged Sebastian either for unwittingly putting his wife in danger or for taking justice into his own hands when the law had failed him. Telling her had been unexpectedly freeing and surprisingly healing. Perhaps he had needed to unburden himself and having trusted the right person had made all the difference, and, although he still craved the oblivion of the pipe, he had found the strength to resist the urge and hoped he'd never find himself back in the clutches of addiction.

Despite the grim reason, Sebastian looked forward to speaking with Gemma. He hadn't seen her in nearly a fortnight, since she had vacated the house she'd shared with Victor. She had moved into a boarding house in Birkenhead Street that was conveniently located near her new place of work, the Foundling Hospital in Gray's Inn Lane. Sebastian would have liked to see Gemma's new lodgings but was certain the landlady wouldn't permit him inside. Any respectable boarding house for women

jealously guarded its reputation and would not allow a
gentleman caller on the premises, not even in the parlor and not
even if he happened to be a policeman. There had to be a public
house or a tearoom where Sebastian could take Gemma if she
was at home and had time to speak to him. But as much as he
longed to consult her, he had to call on Mrs. Harrow first.

# FIVE

The Harrows resided at Ashburn Gardens in South Kensington, a surprisingly fashionable address for a mere newspaperman. The white stucco townhouse with black railings and a black-painted front door was identical to its neighbors and in good repair, at least at first glance. A uniformed maid opened the door to Sebastian's knock and gave him a bullish stare, her demeanor radiating distaste. Both her features and her manner were uncommonly off-putting, and Sebastian wondered if Mrs. Harrow had deliberately hired an ill-favored servant in order to prevent her husband from taking an interest in a young woman living under his roof.

"What do you want?" the maid asked belligerently.

"Inspector Bell of Scotland Yard to see Mrs. Harrow." Sebastian held up his warrant card to demonstrate his credentials.

"Mrs. Harrow is not receiving."

"This is not a social call."

"Then perhaps you should have called at the tradesman's entrance," the girl retorted.

"What's your name?" Sebastian asked.

"Judith," the maidservant replied cautiously.

"How would you like to spend a night in the cells, Judith?" Sebastian asked pleasantly, as if he were inviting her to tea or for a stroll in the park.

"On what charge?" Judith challenged him.

"Obstructing a criminal investigation."

The maidservant blanched and immediately stepped aside, clearly deciding she didn't fancy the idea one bit. She stood there, staring at Sebastian, her mouth hanging open, then seemed to remember herself.

"After you announce me to Mrs. Harrow, bring her a glass of sherry. She's going to need it," Sebastian said.

The maidservant nodded and disappeared into a room on the right. Sebastian listened carefully but didn't hear any noise coming from either the upstairs or the kitchen, which was sure to be in the cellar. Perhaps Jacob Harrow's finances stretched to only one servant, which wasn't enough for a house this size.

The maidservant emerged a few moments later, gestured for Sebastian to go in, and hurried down the corridor. Since she didn't take his things, Sebastian removed his hat, shrugged off his coat, and draped it over his arm before entering. The drawing room was well proportioned and tastefully decorated in shades of mauve and cream. Heavy velvet curtains with gold-braid tassels hung at the two windows, and the furniture looked expensive and virtually unused. There was a painting of a country scene above the mantel and a vase of hothouse flowers in an oriental vase on a walnut sideboard. A thick Turkey carpet covered the floor, and a roaring fire blazed in the hearth. This was not a household that economized on frivolities or coal.

A young woman sat before the fire, her gaze fixed on the leaping flames. Gold ringlets framed her heart-shaped face, and, when she turned toward Sebastian, he noticed that her eyes were the deepest shade of blue. She offered a small smile of welcome, but her shoulders were hunched, and her arms were crossed before her, her fingers clutching at the fringed silk shawl that was draped over a gown of dove gray. The young woman made no move to rise, nor did she offer any words of greeting.

"Mrs. Harrow?" Sebastian asked.

She nodded. She didn't invite him to sit, but to loom over her would not do, so Sebastian placed his coat over the arm of the settee and took the chair across from Emma Harrow. She pretended to stare into the fire, but Sebastian thought she was fully aware of his every move and was bracing herself for bad news.

"Mrs. Harrow, I'm Inspector Bell of Scotland Yard," Sebastian began.

"He's dead. Isn't he?" Emma Harrow asked. Her voice was barely audible, but there was conviction in her tone.

"If you mean your husband, then yes, he is."

"How?"

"He was stabbed." Sebastian thought it was kinder not to elaborate. She'd learn the particulars soon enough, but for now he wanted to spare her the horror of her husband's final moments. Learning that she was now a widow was bad enough. "Mrs. Harrow, I'm very sorry for your loss, but I do need to ask you some questions."

Emma Harrow nodded, her gaze still fixed on the leaping flames. She was remarkably composed, but then it seemed she had been preparing herself for bad news. "I don't know anything," she said at last.

"Then this won't take long. Why did you assume your husband was dead?"

"Because he didn't come home last night. Jacob would never not come home. He went out sometimes, but he was always back by midnight. He knew I'd be waiting for him."

"Is there someone you suspect?" Sebastian asked.

Emma Harrow shook her head.

"Was your husband upset or worried about anything in recent days?"

"Not that I know of."

"Did he think someone meant him harm?"

"If he did, he would never tell me. He didn't like to worry me, but people don't like journalists, Inspector, because they often tell a truth no one wants to hear. Anyone he'd written about might have held a grudge."

"Was your husband working on something new?" Sebastian asked.

"He was always writing, but I don't know what he was working on. He didn't discuss his work with me because the subjects he explored were generally unpleasant. When we got married, Jacob promised that he'd shield me from the world, and he tried to do just that."

Sebastian couldn't help but feel sympathy for the fragile woman before him. Her shield had been torn away, leaving her completely exposed to the horrors that lay beyond. Jacob Harrow may have had his faults, but his wife seemed to have loved him and felt safe under his protection. Sebastian hoped she had someone who cared for her to turn to, because she would need unwavering support as the details of her husband's murder began to emerge. Even if she had never read a newspaper in her life, she'd still hear the headlines if she so much as ventured outside and know that Jacob Harrow had been mutilated in life and humiliated in death.

"Mrs. Harrow, did you know your husband was shot some years ago?" Sebastian asked. He didn't know if she had seen the scar. There were some couples who'd never seen each other unclothed, disrobing only under the cover of darkness. Perhaps the revelation that her husband had been shot had come as a shock and Sebastian had just upset the grieving widow further. In truth, he wasn't even sure why he'd asked the question since the wound was years old, but it seemed important to understand the context.

Emma nodded sadly. "Yes, Jacob was shot in Crimea, during the Battle of Alma in September of fifty-four."

"Was he treated at the hospital at Scutari?" Sebastian asked.

"Yes, I think so. Jacob didn't like to talk about that time, and I didn't press him."

"He wrote extensively about his experiences in Crimea though. Do you have the articles he posted to the London papers while at the front?"

"Anything to do with Jacob's work is in his study. He keeps —kept," she corrected herself, "the study locked. It was his dream to write a book," she went on miserably. "He was a great admirer of Charles Dickens and wanted to author a novel that would receive worldwide acclaim. He'll never write it now." She angrily wiped the tears that slid down her cheeks with the back of her hand, then remembered her manners and used a handkerchief to dab at her streaming eyes.

"Do you have a key to the study?" Sebastian asked.

"Yes, but you can't go in there. Jacob would not like it."

Sebastian decided to drop the subject for the moment and circle back later. "How many servants do you employ?"

"We had three, but Jacob fired his manservant last week, and Mrs. Warren, that's our cook, left on Friday, on account of her arthritis. A new cook was meant to start on Monday, but she never arrived." Emma sniffed. "We had to make do with Judith's cooking."

"Why did your husband sack his valet?"

Emma looked momentarily confused, as if she had no idea, but then seemed to recollect the reason. "Jacob said he wasn't very good at his job and asked too many questions."

"What sort of questions?"

"I don't know. He never said."

"Can you give me the man's name?"

"Ellis Baylor."

"And do you know where he might have gone?"

"No idea. I had little to do with the man, I found him coarse," Emma replied.

"Can you tell me anything else about your husband's final days?" Sebastian asked.

Emma Harrow shook her head and returned her gaze to the fire. The woman was either naturally incurious or so distraught that she couldn't manage to gather her thoughts long enough to answer his question. More than anything, Sebastian wanted to leave her in peace, but the time to ask questions was immediately after the murder, when the subjects were off balance and might reveal something they would later decide to keep to themselves, either because it was incriminating or because they wanted to protect the memory of their loved one.

Emma turned to face him. "Inspector, I've answered your questions. Please..." Her voice trailed off, and Sebastian knew he wasn't going to get much more out of her, not that she'd told him anything even remotely useful.

"Mrs. Harrow, do you have family who can see you through this difficult time?"

"I will go to my parents. I can't bear the thought of being here on my own." For the first time, Emma Harrow looked resolute. "When can I bury my husband, Inspector?"

"The body will be released in a few days. If you would provide me with your parents' names and address, I will notify you when Mr. Harrow's remains are ready to be collected by an undertaker."

"Thank you, Inspector. My parents are Mr. and Mrs. Jonas, and they reside at three Elm Tree Road, St. John's Wood," Emma replied.

It was obvious she wanted Sebastian to leave so she could give in to her grief and begin to make plans for her departure, but he couldn't go just yet.

"I will go in just a moment, but I need to ask you a few more questions. It's important," he said, and Emma Harrow nodded dejectedly. Now that she thought she was about to be shot of him, she might answer truthfully in order to expedite his departure.

"Did your husband have any close friends? Someone he might have confided in?"

"I have never met any of Jacob's friends, but I believe he was close to Godfrey Price, Harold Wise, and James Harrow. He corresponded with them regularly."

"Do they not live in London?"

"James Harrow is Jacob's cousin. He lives in Essex with his mother. And Godfrey Price and Harold Wise knew Jacob in the war. They wrote quite regularly, at least once a month."

"Were there any close friends or acquaintances located in London? Did he ever invite anyone to dine?"

"Jacob was a very private person. His experiences in Crimea had left him wary of people's motives. We rarely entertained."

"And when you did?"

"We only ever invited my parents," Emma said.

"What about your husband's parents?"

"Jacob's mother died when he was a boy, and his father passed shortly before we met."

"Did your husband ever mention Captain Hadley?" Sebastian asked. "I believe they knew each other from the war."

Emma shook her head. "I've never heard that name. Why do you ask?"

"Captain Hadley had a lead on a story."

From the expression on her face, Emma Harrow clearly knew nothing about her husband's work, so Sebastian decided to move on. "Mrs. Harrow, I need to speak to Godfrey Price, Harold Wise, and James Harrow. Can you kindly provide me with their addresses?"

"James lives in Brentwood. I don't know where the others live."

"But surely, if your husband corresponded with them regularly, there must be an address book or letters he kept."

"Everything is in the study." Emma Harrow began to cry softly again. "I can't bear to go in there. Please don't ask it of me."

"Perhaps the maidservant—" Sebastian began, but Emma shook her head.

"No. Jacob's papers must not be disturbed."

Sebastian could pull rank, but that would be unnecessarily cruel. He'd find another way to obtain the information he needed.

"You have my deepest sympathy, Mrs. Harrow," he said.

"Thank you," she whispered. She appeared to be emotionally shattered, and Sebastian hoped she would seek out her parents sooner rather than later.

He took his things and left the drawing room. He wasn't overly surprised to find the maidservant hovering outside. She'd probably been listening at the door the entire time.

"I told you to bring your mistress a sherry," Sebastian reminded her.

The maid opened her mouth to sass him but then seemed to recall his threat about spending the night in the cells and hurried into the room.

"Can I get you a sherry, madam?" Sebastian heard her ask Emma Harrow before he let himself out into the lavender twilight of the December afternoon.

# SIX

Birkenhead Street was a far cry from Ashburn Gardens. The redbrick houses were featureless and grim, the people who made their home there too focused on survival to be concerned with civic pride. The loss of employment or the death of the main breadwinner could result in circumstances that would force them to move into some of London's worst slums, and they were keenly aware of what that would mean.

The boarding house where Gemma had taken a room looked somewhat less bleak. The window frames and door weren't scarred or peeling, and the step was cleanly swept. When Sebastian knocked, a bombazine-clad woman in her forties opened the door. Her gently silvered hair was scraped back into a bun and covered with a prim cap, and her gaze was worthy of the most highly trained detective at Scotland Yard. She likely needed no more than a moment to take Sebastian's measure and decide whether she would speak to him or shut the door in his face.

"How can I help you, sir?" she asked when she was satisfied. It was reassuring to know that he didn't look as disreputable as he felt.

"Inspector Bell of Scotland Yard to see Miss Tate."

The woman's eyes widened in horror, and Sebastian belatedly realized he'd just made a grave mistake that could cost Gemma her new home. He hurried to correct his mistake and reassure the landlady that Gemma wasn't known to Scotland Yard for her criminality or an association with anyone who might soon find themselves at the end of a rope, and he was there to consult her on a matter of some urgency that only she could help with.

"Miss Tate was very helpful during a previous case," he added for good measure.

Given the landlady's furrowed brows and the tightening of her already thin lips, Sebastian knew that he'd blundered again and cursed himself for a fool. *Why would any respectable woman get involved in a criminal investigation?* her gaze seemed to ask.

"I seek medical advice," Sebastian amended. "Miss Tate is an experienced nurse."

The landlady looked dubious but nodded slightly. "Gentlemen are not permitted on the premises, Inspector. I will inform Miss Tate that you're here, and if she wishes to see you she will meet you outside."

"Thank you, ma'am," Sebastian said with as much humility as he could muster.

He stepped away from the door and positioned himself a few yards away so as not to appear threatening. The door remained firmly shut for a long while, and Sebastian was beginning to doubt that Gemma wished to see him when she stepped outside. The warmth of her gaze and the sincerity of her smile told him everything he needed to know, and he found himself grinning back, his heart lifting at the sight of her. Gemma wore a short black cape and matching bonnet over a gown of unrelieved black, since she was in mourning for Victor. The garments were somber and unfashionable, but they did little to take away from her natural beauty, her lovely green eyes, chestnut hair, and creamy complexion a welcome counterpoint of color.

"Sebastian," Gemma said as he took her gloved hand in his and brought it to his lips. "It's been too long."

"You look well," Sebastian replied, still smiling. "Everything all right?" He cast a glance toward the boarding house and noted the twitch of the net curtain at the window. The landlady was watching.

"As well as can be expected," Gemma said.

"Is there somewhere we can talk?"

"There's a coffeehouse two streets away," Gemma said. "It's not the Savoy, but it's relatively clean, and they make decent coffee."

"Have you eaten supper?" Sebastian asked.

"Not yet. Supper is included with the rent and is served precisely at seven. I believe today it's boiled fowl and salad," Gemma replied unenthusiastically.

"If you'd prefer something a little more appetizing—" Sebastian began, but Gemma shook her head.

"I'm afraid I have an early start tomorrow. Besides, Mrs. Bass won't let me in if I stay out past curfew."

"Curfew," Sebastian repeated, as if this was the first time he'd ever heard the word.

"I don't mind, really," Gemma said as they set off toward the coffeehouse. "I have little reason to stay out past nine o'clock."

Sebastian nodded approvingly. A woman on her own should not be abroad in the evening, especially in a neighborhood such as this and during the winter, when darkness came early. Gemma Tate was not the sort of woman who might attract the attention of someone seeking a spot of company for the evening, but her beaded reticule could tempt a cutpurse.

The coffeehouse was a utilitarian room crammed with a dozen square tables. The walls were painted dark green and appeared almost black in the pools of feeble light the oil lamps cast into the nearly empty space. Perhaps in someone's imagination the shade was meant to remind the patrons of a forest in full leaf, but on a winter evening the murky color made for an oppressive atmosphere. Having ordered a pot of coffee from a lanky youth with adolescent spots, Sebastian turned his attention back to Gemma.

"Are your lodgings satisfactory?" he asked.

His room at Mrs. Poole's still looked exactly as it had the day he'd moved in. There were no personal possessions aside from clothes, a shaving razor, and a few books, most of which had been purchased for him by Gemma from a used bookstall near St. Paul's during his convalescence. And his cat, Gustav, who spent his days hunting mice, and inevitably left Sebastian an offering for when he returned home. Sebastian had one framed photograph, taken of him and Louisa on their wedding day, but he'd never set it out and kept it safely hidden in his linen drawer. He still couldn't bear to look at it, even after all this time.

Sebastian hoped that Gemma had made her room feel more welcoming, though, and had set out the photographs that used to be displayed on the mantel in the home she'd shared with Victor. It would make him feel better to know that Victor and their parents were there to look out for Gemma, if only from a faded photograph. And he hoped she'd taken the lovely watercolor that used to hang in the dining room, and which she'd said reminded her of summers spent playing in the park with her twin when they were children.

"The lodgings are adequate," Gemma replied with her usual forthrightness. "A place to lay my head after a long day. And it's nice not to have to worry about meals. Uninspired as they may be, the food is filling and plentiful."

"And your new situation?"

Gemma smiled sadly, and Sebastian could tell that she

didn't want to talk about the orphans. The Foundling Hospital was not a hospital in the usual sense. It was an orphanage for children whose mothers had met certain criteria. These were not prostitutes, whose children were often left to die in the streets or at baby farms where unscrupulous carers fed them laudanum to keep them from crying or asking for food. These were women of good character who'd fallen prey to unscrupulous men or disgraced themselves and their families. But their children were given a chance, which was more than most orphans could hope for. Gemma worked in the infirmary and was charged with looking after children who'd fallen ill or were injured.

"Is it not what you expected?" Sebastian asked, and was relieved when Gemma smiled.

"In Crimea, when I finally went to bed after my shift, the faces of the patients we'd lost that day floated before my eyes, and I felt as if I had lost a battle and would almost certainly lose the war. I know we saved many men, but it was those we couldn't help that stayed with me." Gemma's gaze was soft, and her smile widened. "When I go to sleep now, I recall the little faces of the children I helped that day. There are some who are gravely ill, but most come to the infirmary with bellyaches, sore throats, and scraped knees. And to be able to make them feel better and send them on their way gladdens my heart."

"And those who are seriously ill?" Sebastian asked.

"Some will recover. Some won't. But at least they won't die in some foreign hospital, surrounded by strangers. I might not be able to help every child, but I can offer them comfort and companionship in their time of need. And in the more extreme situations, I give them a spoonful of Godfrey's Cordial to help them sleep."

"Godfrey's Cordial?"

Gemma sighed. "It's also known as Mother's Helper. In essence, it's a tincture of opium, but for those children who are in terrible pain it's a way to escape their suffering, if even for a short time. I don't approve of dosing children with opium, but sometimes that's the only option I have left. I want to spare them suffering and the certain knowledge that they're dying."

"I'm sure they value your kindness."

"A bit of kindness is all those children can hope for. Most dream of their mothers coming back to claim them, but from what I hear that almost never happens. But there have been a few children who have been reunited with their parents, and that gives the rest a glimmer of hope."

Sebastian nodded in understanding. There were thousands of orphans in London, and most knew nothing of their origins. Some banded together with those who grew up alongside them and they looked after one another. Others perished from cold and hunger. The best they could hope for was that they would reach adulthood and have a chance at a life of their own. Most of them never dreamed they would be reunited with the parents, who'd either died or abandoned them, so the children at the Foundling Hospital were considered lucky.

"And how are you, Sebastian?" Gemma asked. "Has your shoulder been paining you?"

"I'm well," Sebastian hurried to assure her. "And investigating a new case."

"It's really too soon," she protested. "You must look after yourself."

"If I don't return to active duty, I'll lose my mind," he replied, but he was secretly pleased by her concern for his well-being. "Gemma, I would be grateful for your help with this case."

"You have it," she replied without a moment's hesitation. "What would you have me do?"

Sebastian hated to disappoint her, but he had to be honest. "I don't need you to do anything, but I would like to ask you a few questions."

"Am I a suspect?" Gemma joked.

"The only thing I suspect you of is being more knowledge-able on the subject than I am."

Sebastian waited until the waiter had set down the pot of coffee, a jug of cream, and a bowl of sugar and departed. Gemma poured them both coffee, and they fixed it to their liking.

"Jacob Harrow has been murdered," Sebastian said once he had Gemma's undivided attention.

"Jacob Harrow?" Gemma echoed, her shock obvious. "Where? How?"

If it were any other woman, Sebastian would have spared her the grisly details, but Gemma was a nurse and had seen injuries far worse than a severed tongue and a knife wound. He told her all of it, leaving nothing out, not even the historic injuries. Gemma listened carefully, then raised her cup to her lips and took a sip of coffee.

"How can I help?" she asked.

"Jacob Harrow's wife confirmed that he was shot in Crimea. I thought he might have been in your care at Scutari."

Gemma shook her head. "I never met Jacob Harrow during the war, which is not to say that he wasn't admitted to the hospital. There were so many wounded and so few nurses and doctors. It was chaos, especially after a battle, when the wounded numbered in the hundreds."

"Can you tell me about it?" Sebastian asked gently. He didn't want to upset Gemma or force her to relive experiences she would rather forget, but he needed to understand what it was like and what sort of bonds existed between the people who had survived the conflict.

Gemma nodded and sighed, a faraway look coming into her eyes. "I thought I understood what I'd signed up for, but nothing could have prepared me for what I was forced to endure. Scutari was hell on earth," she said quietly, her anguished gaze coming to rest on Sebastian. "No words can adequately describe the suffering of the wounded or the wretchedness of the staff. The conditions were appalling. There weren't enough beds and no running water or sufficient light. Patients were dumped on the floor and left to lie in their own waste, blood, and pus for days on end." She shuddered and wrinkled her nose, as if she could smell the reeking ward and see the agonized faces of the wounded. "Many men never regained consciousness, so we never learned their names. It took their loved ones months to realize that their husbands, brothers, and sons were dead."

"Did no one keep a record?" Sebastian asked.

"Miss Nightingale tried to keep an account, but it was an impossible task. And she had more immediate concerns, such as the lack of medical and cleaning supplies. There was so much blood. We never seemed to be able to wash it off. And the rats," Gemma added with a delicate shudder.

"Rats?"

"They were everywhere. I can still hear their squeaking as they scurried between the wounded men, their eyes glowing in the dark, and their tails leaving tracks in the muck," Gemma said. "They were the stuff of nightmares. Even once I had returned home I would sometimes wake up screaming and beating at my arms and legs, terrified that the rats would gnaw at my flesh and sink their teeth into my bones."

Sebastian covered Gemma's shaking hand with his own and her voice trailed away, the haunted look eventually fading from her eyes.

"I can't begin to imagine what you have suffered," he said softly, once again amazed by her bravery.

"It was nothing compared to what the patients had to endure as they lay dying, their final hours on this earth so hellish they probably prayed for death. It's a wonder anyone survived," Gemma said. She shook her head as if she were trying to chase away the awful memories and took a gulp of her cooling coffee.

"I know how difficult it is to talk about that time, but is it all right if I ask a few more questions?" Sebastian asked. He felt terrible for reminding Gemma of the most harrowing days of her life, but she was his only unbiased source who had a tangible connection to the case he was investigating.

Gemma nodded. "I want to help," she said. "And speaking about the horrors I've witnessed is liberating in a way. It's like opening a window and allowing the bad memories to fly free."

"Then I'm glad," Sebastian said. "You can talk to me any time you feel the need to unburden yourself."

"Why don't we address your burden first," Gemma said, the corners of her mouth lifting in a half smile. "What do you want to know?"

"Did Victor know Jacob Harrow before meeting him in London? Did he tell you anything of the man when he found himself employed by the same newspaper?"

Gemma sighed, painful memories of her twin clearly distressing her further. "I didn't see very much of Victor in Scutari. I had one afternoon off, usually every other Thursday, but I was permitted to leave only if I could be spared. Victor would meet me if he was able and we'd go for a walk or find somewhere to have a cup of tea, but most of the time I simply went to bed. I was so exhausted that those few extra hours of sleep were the only thing holding me together from week to week."

"So Victor never mentioned Harrow?"

"Not that I can recall. And he didn't have all that much to do with him in London. They were acquainted, but I wouldn't call them friends. Why are you so interested in Crimea? Surely Jacob Harrow's death is not connected to the war. Or is it?" Gemma asked.

"I don't know, but I was hoping to learn something of the

man. I have spoken to his editor-in-chief, his colleagues, and his wife, and have learned precious little."

"Someone must have held a grudge against him."

"Yes, but who? The obvious assumption is that Jacob Harrow had revealed someone's secret, possibly in print, but the severed tongue could also be a misdirection intended to muddy the waters."

"Yes, I suppose it could be," Gemma agreed.

"Did you know Captain Pickering?" Sebastian asked.

Gemma's surprise at hearing the name was evident. "Not personally, but I recall the case. He committed suicide after he lost the defamation case."

"Might there be a connection? Someone who's been biding their time?"

Gemma took another sip of coffee, her expression thoughtful. "There was a younger brother," she said at last. "Reginald Pickering. He was fifteen at the time of the trial."

"Was he mentioned in the papers?" Sebastian asked.

"No. But Victor attended the trial and met Reginald in the courtroom. Reginald was very angry with the verdict; I do remember Victor mentioning that."

"I imagine he was even angrier about his brother's death."

"He was left alone in the world," Gemma replied. "I wouldn't be surprised if he was still nursing a grudge."

"Any idea where Reginald is now?"

"He would be seventeen, so possibly still at school. Do you think a seventeen-year-old could have carried out such an attack?"

"Yes," Sebastian replied without hesitation. "An angry adolescent is capable of anything."

"I do hope it wasn't him," Gemma said.

"A desire for revenge would certainly fit the facts."

"It would be difficult enough if Captain Pickering had died in Crimea, but to lose a brother to suicide is so much worse. Perhaps Reginald was unable to make peace with his passing."

"Death is death," Sebastian said.

Gemma shot him a knowing look. "Surely you don't believe that."

Sebastian sighed deeply. He supposed if he did that losing Louisa and the baby in childbirth or due to an illness would be easier to comprehend, although no easier to bear since they'd still be gone. But knowing that Louisa had died by an act of savagery, terrified and alone as her lifeblood flowed out, still gave Sebastian nightmares, and sparked crushing guilt. He was learning to make peace with the past, but there were moments when he was right back in that room, holding Louisa's cold body in his arms and wishing he would die too, so the three of them could be buried together.

"I suppose some deaths are easier to accept," he grudgingly admitted.

"A death on the battlefield is seen as honorable, the man revered as a hero by his family, even if he was an absolute cretin in life. Death by suicide is viewed as shameful and unlawful. It wasn't so long ago that a suicide would be buried at the crossroads with a stake through the heart. And if Reginald took it upon himself to avenge his brother's death, he might end up dying at the end of a rope, another young life squandered," Gemma said angrily.

"If Reginald waited more than two years to avenge his brother, then this murder would not only be premeditated but meticulously planned."

"It certainly doesn't sound like the emotional response of a hot-headed youth," Gemma agreed.

"No, it doesn't. This was very personal, and extremely intimate."

"What on earth do you mean by that?" Gemma asked, her eyes widening at Sebastian's description.

"To cut out a man's tongue, then stab him through the heart, one has to come face to face with the victim. The killer would see his victim's fear, feel his breath on his face, smell his sweat, and hear his pleas. He'd watch the victim choke on his blood, and the killer's fingers would be slick with it as he held the severed tongue. This was someone who derived pleasure from Jacob Harrow's fear and pain, a person who'd lusted after that moment of complete power."

Gemma nodded in understanding. "This was someone whose heart had been broken."

"Exactly. And I think Harrow may have broken a number of hearts, both male and female. Not necessarily in a romantic way, but this was a man who had the power to crush dreams."

"And now his poor wife's heart has been crushed. Will she be all right, do you think?" Gemma asked.

"I hope so. She is going to her parents' house."

"Where do they live? I can't help hoping it's some charming cottage in the country where Emma Harrow will be spared the horror of hearing the daily headlines and seeing the awful drawings of her husband's body."

"Elm Tree Road in St. John's Wood. Hopefully, her parents will offer her the sanctuary she requires to cope with her grief."

Gemma finished her coffee and set down the cup. She appeared to be deep in thought, so Sebastian gave her a moment while he finished his own drink. It wasn't too bad and had revived him somewhat. It had been nearly two months since he'd spent an entire day making inquiries and, although he hated to admit it, he was tired.

"Victor didn't like Jacob Harrow," Gemma suddenly said. "I hate to speak ill of the dead, especially a man who must have suffered terribly in his final moments, but Victor didn't trust him."

"Did he say what had led him to feel that way?"

Gemma exhaled sharply. "He said he couldn't square the

man who'd written all those impassioned articles at the front with the man he'd come to know in London."

"Did he have any theories regarding this about-face?"

"People often expect an author to be the person they are on paper, but what they don't understand is that quite often their words are simply a work of fiction. They have a talent for stirring their readers' emotions and offering them the understanding they long for, but that doesn't necessarily mean the writer shares those sentiments or is capable of the same passion."

"So, you think that the articles J.H. had sent to the London papers were simply stirring words intended to rouse anger against the powers-that-be and compassion for the soldiers who were nothing more than cannon fodder?"

"I don't know. And neither did Victor. He said there was no doubt Jacob Harrow was a talented writer, but..."

"But what?"

"Victor always said that a writer's style was as unique as their handwriting, and he thought that Harrow's style had changed somewhat once he came back from the front."

"Surely that's not unusual, given that he was now writing from the comfort of his own home and about topics that weren't as incendiary."

"I honestly don't know, Sebastian. Had I known the man in Crimea, I might be able to offer some insight, but we had never met. At least not to my recollection. There's also another possibility," Gemma added.

"Which is?"

"The articles written by J.H. received a considerable amount of attention and praise. Their honesty and depth of feeling elicited a response not only in the common man but also in the loved ones of all those young men who were mown down in the prime of their lives because of their superiors' gross incompetence and mind-boggling arrogance. The articles ignited outrage and a demand for accountability, which were largely ignored. It's entirely possible that the Jacob Harrow, who was now writing for the *Daily Telegraph*, was no longer the idealistic youth who'd taken the Queen's shilling to defend the Empire against her enemies."

"So, you think he might have allowed the attention to go to his head?"

"I don't think it was so much notoriety as cynicism. Maybe the war had changed him. It changed all of us." Gemma tilted her head to the side and asked the question Sebastian had known would occur to her sooner or later. "Is there proof that Jacob Harrow wrote those articles?"

"According to Mr. Lawrence, the editor-in-chief at the *Daily Telegraph*, Harrow presented him with copies of all the articles he'd written in Crimea when he applied for the position. The articles appeared to be a first draft, with the author's notes and comments scribbled in the margins."

"Did anyone compare the handwriting to the letters that were received by the papers?" Gemma asked.

"I don't know, but Mr. Lawrence is no fool, Gemma. He would have realized soon enough if he had been duped, or the real J.H. would have come forward."

"Yes, I suppose that's true," Gemma said once she had glanced at the clock. "I really must be going, but it was a pleasure to see you."

"May I call on you again?" Sebastian asked.

"I'd rather you didn't come to the boarding house."

"Where can I see you, then?"

"My shift at the infirmary is from eight in the morning until five in the afternoon. You can meet me by the main entrance to the Foundling Hospital if you need to speak to me."

"And if I don't need to speak to you but simply want to spend time in your company?" he asked with a smile.

"I'm off this Sunday."

Sebastian nodded. "Then perhaps we can meet? How about by that bookshop you like in the Strand? Shall we say eleven?"

Gemma smiled shyly. "I'll look forward to it, but please let me know in the meantime how you're getting on with the case."

"Of course," Sebastian replied.

He paid the bill and walked Gemma back to the boarding house. The streets were nearly deserted, the majority of businesses closed down for the night, and colorful curtains drawn across windows to keep out both the cold and the curious stares. A streetlamp cast a pool of pale light onto the street before the boarding house, but it was nowhere bright enough to warn an unsuspecting pedestrian of impending danger, and Sebastian was secretly glad that Gemma's shift ended early enough that the streets were still crowded, and that Mrs. Bass insisted on a curfew. He needed to know Gemma was safe, especially when he was in no position to protect her.

"Give my love to Gustav," Gemma said with a smile when they stopped before the door.

"He misses you."

"I doubt it. Cats are notoriously independent. They love anyone who feeds them."

"I think he has a soft spot for you, though," Sebastian said.

Gemma had taken care of Gustav while Sebastian had been recovering from his injury and couldn't bend down to pet the cat or fill his bowl. She had offered to nurse Sebastian as well, but neither his pride nor his draconian landlady Mrs. Poole would allow her to visit him in his room, so they'd met in the parlor under Mrs. Poole's jealous eye and spoken of the books Gemma had brought him and of current events. Constant pain in his fractured clavicle coupled with a desperate need for opium had been their own sort of hell, but, for the first time in years, Sebastian had friends who worried about him and had visited him almost daily to make certain he was on the mend.

Colin Ramsey had overseen his physical recovery, and Gemma had lifted his flagging spirits.

"Perhaps you will have solved the case by the time we see each other on Sunday," Gemma said.

"Perhaps," Sebastian replied, but he had a feeling that this case would prove trickier than anyone had anticipated.

A curtain twitched in the ground-floor window of the boarding house and the movement caught Gemma's eye and obviously reminded her that when it came to a woman's reputation someone was always watching.

"Goodnight, Sebastian," she said and hurriedly walked away.

# SEVEN

Gemma shut the door behind her and leaned against it, ordering herself not to weep. She had promised herself she would make the best of the situation when she'd moved into this dreary lodging house. After all, what choice did she have? She couldn't afford to remain at the house she'd shared with Victor, and, even if she could have, the landlord would not have leased the premises to an unmarried woman. Gemma had never felt quite as alone as she had the past few weeks, not even in the days after Victor's death, when she had been preoccupied with finding his killer and making arrangements for the funeral.

She'd thought getting justice for Victor would help her make peace with his passing, but the acceptance she'd hoped for had not come, at least not yet. Instead, she felt untethered, a woman alone in the world who no longer belonged to anyone. On days when she was feeling more reasonable, she admonished herself and loathed the self-pity she had allowed herself to indulge in. She still had friends she could call on and knew with unwavering certainty that, should she need help, Sebastian Bell would drop everything and come to her aid. But she didn't need aid. She needed companionship, and love.

It was pathetically melodramatic, but she felt as orphaned as the children in her care, and, although she longed to pour her love into her charges, she realized it wasn't fair to teach them to expect the sort of affection and support they weren't likely to get from the other employees. The children had to grow a thick skin if they hoped to survive in a world where no one much cared if they lived or died. Some were angry and defiant, and others simply desperate for someone to notice them and show them a bit of affection. It was heartbreaking to think that most of them had never known love.

The babies were fostered with families living in the country and only returned to the Foundling Hospital when they were five. Although some of them had been well looked after, they still lost the only parents they had ever known when they were taken back to London and thrust into a hierarchy where the older children bullied the younger ones and those weaker by nature had no choice but to fight for survival. Life was so cruel, and so unfair, and, no matter how old one was when one found oneself alone, one felt just as small and insignificant as a child in an institution designed to break them down rather than build them up.

Gemma did her best for every child that came to her, but there was one little girl who tugged at her heart so much she treated her a little more tenderly. Lucy had just turned five and had come to the Foundling Hospital around the same time as Gemma. Lucy was small for her age and, according to Matron, had been sickly from birth. She'd lived with four separate families, all of whom had given her back when she proved too much of a drain on their time and resources. Lucy had silky fair hair, doe-like brown eyes, and skin so pale it was nearly translucent. She was the size of a child half her age and could barely eat a few bites before starting to feel ill and vomiting.

Having monitored her for days, Gemma had concluded that there was nothing physically wrong with the child. She was simply so frightened and unsure of herself that she made herself ill with worry. Lucy managed to eat and hold down her food when Gemma fed her separately from the others and talked to her while the child ate, telling her a story to distract her. The method was a success, but now Lucy was so attached to Gemma that she claimed to be ill just so she could spend an hour in the infirmary.

Gemma tried to comfort the child and help her adjust, but the little girl's desperation broke Gemma's heart and made her doubly aware of her own helplessness and vulnerability. She was lucky to have found a position and had to be careful not to lose it. Women who'd answered the call of duty and had sailed out to Crimea with Florence Nightingale had once been treated as heroes, but now that the war was over they were slandered and snubbed. Nurses who'd saved thousands of lives and sacrificed their own safety and comfort were said to be women of loose morals who'd used the war as an opportunity to satisfy their carnal desires.

Even their nursing skills were denigrated. Doctors felt threatened and undermined by women who had field experience, had assisted at multiple surgeries, and had made split-second decisions when treating patients. The male doctors wanted silent automatons who would take out bedpans, change soiled bandages, and obey without question, even when the nurse knew the doctor to be wrong and could suggest a more effective method of treatment. The best option was to look after private patients; but those positions came with their own setbacks.

Gemma's previous employer, Mr. Gadd, had treated her with kindness and respect and had offered her a live-in position after Victor died, but he'd made his romantic designs on her clear as soon as she returned to work after burying her brother. Gemma couldn't afford to compromise herself, nor did she wish to marry for the sake of shedding her spinster status. She longed for love, and she'd rather be alone than shackled to a man who saw her as nothing more than a glorified servant, there to look after his needs and tend to his ailing mother. Gemma enjoyed her work at the Foundling Hospital and so she had to do everything in her power to keep the position, since being dismissed would render her unemployable.

Peeling herself away from the door, Gemma set down her reticule, untied her bonnet, and hung her cape. It was almost time to go down to supper but, although she was hungry, she wished she could remain in her room and simply go to bed. She was so tired, and so sick of making polite conversation with people who barely looked at each other and had nothing in common save their loneliness and financial constraints. She had originally hoped to rent a room in Lydia Morton's lodging house, but all the rooms were occupied. It would have been nice to have a friend nearby though, someone who had also been in Crimea and understood what Gemma was feeling. Lydia had not been one of Gemma's closest companions at Scutari, but she was one of the few who'd kept up with her since coming back and who was also on her own.

Lydia bitterly envied the women who had been able to return to their families and resume the lives they'd once led, some of them now married and with homes and families of their own. In Lydia's eyes, their hard-won independence wasn't nearly as fine a thing as having a husband and a home, no matter how modest, and she wished keenly to find a man to marry. Gemma had those same thoughts from time to time but realized it was best to keep her feelings to herself if she hoped to protect her privacy and avoid unsolicited advice or prying questions from her housemates.

Seeing Sebastian was like spying a ray of sunshine after a week of rain, and, although she was happy he'd asked to see her again, Gemma also felt immense pride at being asked for her help. She might not be directly involved in the investigation, but there were still things she could do, like call on Lydia. She might have known Jacob Harrow in Crimea. Gemma tried to recall if Jacob and Lydia had spoken to each other at Victor's funeral, but she had been so distraught she'd barely noticed anything once the funeral service began. Recalling the funeral was like tearing off a stuck-on bandage, but Gemma refused to give in to self-pity. She patted her hair into place, pulled out a chair, and sat down at the tiny desk. Taking out a clean sheet of paper, she dipped her pen in ink and began to write.

She knew something of Jacob Harrow from Victor, albeit very little, and she had been in Crimea at the same time. Sebastian Bell could claim neither. Gemma was sure she could come up with several more ideas, if she cast her mind over that time and tried to recall anything she had heard about the famed journalist since returning to England.

By the time she headed down to supper, Gemma had jotted down several points and felt considerably more in control of her emotions.

# EIGHT

When Sebastian returned to his own lodgings he quickly ate his supper, a thin consommé followed by an equally thin fish stew. He then went up to his room and set out a bowl of fish bits for Gustav, the treat provided by Mrs. Poole, who still hoped that Sebastian would take a romantic interest in her and come to her room under cover of night. Gustav was curled in a chair and initially refused to acknowledge Sebastian's presence, but as soon as Sebastian set down the bowl the cat jumped down and began to eat greedily.

Gustav had developed quite an attitude of late, but Sebastian had weightier things on his mind than his sulking cat. He made a fire, poured himself a carefully measured tot of brandy —he permitted himself one drink a night—sank into his favorite chair, and scanned the article in the evening edition of the *Daily Telegraph*. Jacob Harrow's murder was front and center, the article bylined by one of the journalists Sebastian had interviewed that afternoon and no doubt written at Marshall Lawrence's behest. Disgusted by the callous and unnecessarily graphic description of Harrow's death, Sebastian tossed the paper aside, his thoughts turning to Gemma.

She wasn't the sort of woman to complain or court pity, but he'd seen the desolation in her eyes, and his heart went out to her. He understood loneliness and grief, but as a man he had more options than a woman who was on her own and nearing thirty. Unmarried women were surplus to requirements unless they had an elderly parent or relative who needed caring for, or an unmarried brother who needed someone to keep his house.

Gemma seemed to like her new job, but working with children could be more emotionally taxing than caring for wounded men. Children pulled on one's heartstrings, and Gemma's emotions were clearly engaged. Sebastian hoped her new situation wouldn't compound the isolation and grief she'd suffered after her brother's death. He would call on her again at the earliest opportunity.

If he knew Gemma Tate, and by now he had a fairly good idea how her mind worked, she'd have thought of something important to share with him pertaining to Jacob Harrow's murder and had probably drawn up a list of possible lines of inquiry, which would be well thought out and diverge completely from anything Sebastian had come up with himself. Gemma had been a great asset in the past, and he saw no reason not to seek her help in the future, especially if it gave him an excuse to see her.

Sebastian needed to consider his next course of action. Superintendent Lovell would expect an update on the case, and journalists from various papers would be camped out before the entrance to Scotland Yard. Now that they'd heard about the gruesome manner of Harrow's death, they'd be circling like vultures, charged with picking over the bones of the case for the delight of the public. Their interest was purely mercenary, but at times it was also damaging. Cruel caricatures meant to ridicule the police and paint the detectives as slow-witted and incompetent often appeared alongside the articles. They amused the public, sold newspapers, and infuriated the

commissioner, who was made to look a fool in front of the
Home Secretary and took out his frustration on Lovell. But
Lovell's helpless fury wasn't Sebastian's concern. During his
years with the service, he'd grown a thick skin when it came to
reporters and would not allow their taunts to distract him from
solving this case.

Resisting the urge to top up his drink, Sebastian stared into
the flames as he considered what he knew and how he could
best use the information to unpick the knot that was this case.
He'd need to track down Reginald Pickering and Ellis Baylor,
but first he planned to examine the contents of Jacob Harrow's
study. With Emma Harrow hopefully out of the way, the maidservant would be on her own and would have no choice but to
let Sebastian in. She might also know something of what
Harrow had got up to. Judith seemed the sort who'd listen at
keyholes and read her employer's correspondence, if only to
satisfy her curiosity and shift the balance of power within the
household. The leverage might be only in her mind, but whatever she had learned of her employer could paint a more
comprehensive picture of Jacob Harrow's private life.

Satisfied with his plan for tomorrow, Sebastian reached for
the book he had been reading and settled in more comfortably.
He needed to clear his mind if he hoped to sleep tonight, since,
tomorrow, the investigation would begin in earnest.

# NINE
## WEDNESDAY, DECEMBER 15

It was still dark when Gemma left the boarding house. She'd already had her breakfast and had almost two hours before her shift began, but Lydia's day at the hospital started early, and if Gemma hurried she just might catch her. It was bone-chillingly cold, and the sky was just beginning to lighten in the east, but the streets were already crowded with passersby. Only the wealthy had the luxury of staying abed until midmorning and then waking to a warm house and enjoying a hot breakfast. The working people of London set off early, having eaten whatever they had to hand and huddled into their well-worn coats and threadbare shawls. By the time the sun was up, they would have opened their shops and stalls, arrived at the workshops, laundries, and kitchens, and begun their workday, which wouldn't end until the sun went down again.

Gemma hastened in the direction of Lydia's boarding house and was rewarded with a glimpse of her friend as she stepped outside and hurried down the street, her head bowed, her shoulders hunched, and her arms crossed over her cape to keep it from blowing open in the wind. Lydia was an attractive woman, but this morning she looked tired, her skin pale in the feeble light of the winter dawn, and her lips pressed into a firm line.

"Lydia," Gemma called, and Lydia started, her head jerking up in surprise.

"Gemma. Goodness, you startled me. What are you doing here?"

"I was hoping to speak to you before you started your shift," Gemma explained, and fell into step with Lydia, who'd barely slowed down.

"Sorry, I'm in a rush," Lydia said. "Is everything all right?"

"Have you seen the papers?" Gemma asked.

"You mean the story about Jacob Harrow?"

"Yes. He was at Victor's funeral."

"Yes, I remember," Lydia said. She was staring straight ahead and shivering, her arms wrapping tighter around her waist. "It's awfully cold this morning," she said when she realized Gemma was looking at her. "I'd sell my soul for a mug of tea."

"Didn't you have breakfast?"

"The landlady doesn't serve breakfast until seven-thirty. She leaves me buttered bread and a cup of milk on the days I have an early shift, but on a day like today the milk is near frozen."

"Lydia, did you know Jacob Harrow in Crimea?" Gemma asked, the subject of breakfast exhausted. She felt a little guilty about the bowl of hot porridge and two cups of tea she had enjoyed, but was sure Lydia would find a hot drink before she started her work on the ward.

Lydia shook her head and looked away, fixing her gaze on a passing carriage.

"Are you certain? Inspector Bell said Jacob Harrow was shot and was treated at Scutari."

"Inspector Bell?" Lydia echoed, her expression hardening as she turned to stare at Gemma.

"Yes, why?"

"Gemma, heed my advice," Lydia said as they approached the entrance to the London Hospital. "Keep away from that man."

"Why?"

"Because he's trouble, and he will do nothing but put you in danger. That's what men like him do. They leave behind a trail of destruction."

"Why would you say that? You don't even know him," Gemma protested.

"No, I don't, but I've known plenty of men like him. They take what they need without any regard for the people they exploit to further their own interests." Lydia turned and pinned Gemma with an angry stare. "He's using you, Gemma, so don't go hanging your hopes on him. He'll forget all about you as soon as he moves on to another case and has no need of your expertise."

Without another word, Lydia yanked open the door and disappeared inside, leaving Gemma to ponder her words. She had never seen Lydia like this, not even in Crimea when they had all felt frightened, exhausted, and hopeless, and sometimes vented their frustration on those closest to them. As she walked away, Gemma considered that Lydia's outburst might have nothing to do with Gemma and everything to do with some doctor or patient who'd singled her out for attention and had planted a seed of hope for the future. She didn't think Lydia was susceptible to sweet words and false promises—they'd heard plenty of those at Scutari—but a lonely woman couldn't help but let her guard down from time to time, and perhaps this time Lydia had allowed herself to fall in love.

Gemma sighed heavily as she directed her steps towards the Foundling Hospital. Her heart went out to Lydia, but she was also disappointed. She had wanted to help Sebastian and, if she were honest, had hoped she would prove instrumental in solving the case. But Lydia knew nothing of Jacob Harrow, so, unless Sebastian was willing to entertain some of Gemma's other suggestions, her part in this case was over before it had begun.

# TEN

Having eaten a hasty breakfast, Sebastian set off for Ashburn Gardens. It was damp and bitterly cold, a billowing haze hovering above the rooftops as a forest of chimneys belched smoke into the frosty air. Sebastian preferred the winter. The summer months were unbearable with their stench of rotting vegetables, rancid meat, and steaming piles of horseshit left to bake in the streets. Last summer's miasma had been so noxious that the entire season had been dubbed the Great Stink due to the piles of human and industrial waste that had washed up on the banks of the Thames and had been left to rot due to lower water levels that had prevented the tide from washing them away. The suffocating foulness had finally brought much-needed attention to the lack of a city-wide sewage system and the health benefits it would provide, but Sebastian did not expect a resolution to be agreed upon anytime soon. The wheels of progress tended to turn with excruciating slowness, particularly when large sums of money needed to be spent.

Despite the coal smoke, the winter air was fresher, the tang of the Thames barely noticeable rather than overpowering. Of course, a person could only enjoy these pleasures if they had a roof over their head and a fire to warm them when they came indoors, but Sebastian was striding down the streets of Kensington instead of one of the seedier areas of London, and he was grateful not to see half-frozen children hovering in doorways or the bodies of those who'd died overnight being loaded into wagons that would transport them to the city's numerous dead houses.

Judith looked frightened when she opened the door, the bravado of yesterday a distant memory.

"Mrs. Harrow is not here," she said, and began to shut the door in Sebastian's face.

"I need to look in the study." Sebastian splayed his hand on the door to keep it open.

Judith shook her head. "She'll sack me without a character if she finds out I let you in."

"Then don't let her find out. I need to speak to you anyhow."

Judith blanched at his words. "I didn't do nothing wrong."

"I didn't say you did. Now, let me in."

Judith looked conflicted, but his air of authority and refusal to take no for an answer finally persuaded her. She stepped aside to let him in and shut the door as soon as he was inside. Taking a step back, she bumped into a console table and nearly toppled an ornamental vase, but barely seemed to notice. Her gaze was fixed on Sebastian, her breathing shallow, her eyes round as saucers.

"I'm not going to hurt you," Sebastian said, belatedly realizing that it was him she seemed to be afraid of and not the questions he intended to put to her.

"You said you'd lock me up in the cells."

"I need to ask you a few questions about Ellis Baylor and take a look in the study. And then I'll leave you in peace," Sebastian promised. "Any chance of a cup of tea? It's freezing out there."

That seemed to calm Judith a bit. A companionable chat over tea wasn't as threatening as him questioning her outright when they were alone in the house.

"All right. Come into the kitchen. I don't think we should use the dining room."

Sebastian followed her into the kitchen in the cellar. It was clean and bright, and pleasantly warm, with a massive cast-iron range and a dozen copper pots hanging on hooks. The kettle was already on the hob, steam hissing from the spout. Judith reached for tin mugs, then changed her mind and set out two china cups with saucers, a jug of milk, and a silver sugar bowl with matching tongs. Sebastian noted this minor act of defiance and hoped that she'd be willing to talk truthfully about her employers. Once Judith had made the tea, she poured out for them both, added milk and sugar, then finally met Sebastian's gaze.

"So, what is it you want to know about Ellis Baylor, Inspector Bell?"

"First, tell me about Mr. Harrow. What was he like?"

Judith shrugged. "All right, I s'pose."

"Was he kind to you?"

"He hardly noticed me unless I did something wrong. I broke a cup once, and he took it out of my wages. No bleeding cup costs as much as he withheld," she added bitterly.

"Was he a good husband, do you think?" Sebastian asked.

"He seemed to dote on Mrs. Harrow, but what do I know? Not like I've ever been married or had a sweetheart."

"Did they ever laugh together?"

The question obviously took Judith by surprise. "Laugh?"

"Yes. Laughter is a fairly good indication of a couple's ease with each other."

Sebastian and Louisa had laughed all the time, sometimes at something that was actually funny and sometimes at nothing at all. They had been young and happy and found joy in everyday things and each other. Sebastian sometimes wondered if that would have changed had they been given the chance to grow old together, but, since he'd never know, it was probably best not to dwell.

"Can't say as I've ever heard them laugh, but they did smile at each other from time to time."

"Did they talk much?"

"Like over dinner?"

"Or breakfast."

"Mr. Harrow always read the papers with his breakfast, but they did converse at dinner. Or he talked and Mrs. Harrow listened. He was a great one for talking."

"What did he talk about?"

"This and that. I didn't really listen. I just wanted to get dinner over with so I could clear up and go to bed."

"Did Mr. Harrow seem worried or upset these last few days?"

"Not that I saw."

Judith had relaxed somewhat and seemed to be enjoying the conversation. Sebastian didn't think too many people asked for her opinion and that she was relishing the attention, as well as drinking from a china cup. She held her cup carefully and took delicate sips.

"Now tell me about Ellis Baylor. What was he like?"

"He was a pig," Judith stated flatly. "I always made sure to lock my door at night or he'd push his way in."

"Did he have feelings for you, do you think?" Sebastian asked and was rewarded with a grimace of disgust.

"I once heard him say to the neighbor's footman that all women are beautiful in the dark, and even more desirable when they kept their mouth shut and their legs open."

"Sounds like a charming fellow. Why did Mr. Harrow dismiss him?"

"I think he stole something. It wouldn't be the first time."

"What did he steal?"

"He stole Mrs. Harrow's earbobs once. She had me look all over for them, but they were long gone, spent on gambling, I reckon. Ellis liked to roll the dice."

"Did Mr. Harrow threaten to have him arrested?"

"No, but he withheld his quarterly wages," Judith said.

"How do you know that?"

"Mr. Harrow said as much. Lucky for Ellis the earbobs were only paste, or Mr. Harrow would have thrown him to the wolves. Mr. Harrow also said that if I helped myself to anything I wasn't entitled to, I'd never see a farthing of the money he owed me."

"I don't suppose Mr. Harrow gave Mr. Baylor a character reference?"

"Lord, no. Why would he?"

"Do you know where Baylor went?"

"He said he'd had it with being in service and was going to join the navy. They don't require a character, and he'd get to see something of the world."

*And find his way to every quayside brothel*, Sebastian mused. Baylor sounded like an unsavory character, and Sebastian wondered why Jacob Harrow had hired him in the first place. Given Harrow's wartime experience and observant nature, he was sure to have had good instincts.

"How long was Ellis Baylor employed here?" he asked.

"Since Mr. Harrow came back from the war. I think they knew each other in Crimea."

"Did they, indeed?"

Judith shrugged. "At least that's what Ellis said. I never heard Mr. Harrow say as much."

"And what about the cook? What was she like?"

"Mrs. Warren was lovely." Judith teared up. "She was like a mother to me. I was sorry to see her go."

"Did she get on with Mr. and Mrs. Harrow?"

"As long as she cooked meals they liked, they got along just fine. And Ellis was always buttering her up, then asking to borrow money so he could blow it on the dice."

"Did Mrs. Warren lend him money?"

"She hid her money away, in case he decided to help himself, and told me to do the same."

"Do you have a key to the study?" Sebastian asked. He'd finished his tea and couldn't think of anything more he wanted to ask Judith.

Judith shook her head. "Mr. Harrow always carried the key on his person. And Mrs. Harrow took the key with her when she left."

"Did you never clean in there?"

"Every other week. Mr. Harrow would unlock the study and watch me from the doorway. It made me nervous, but at least it was quick. He only wanted me to sweep and dust."

Sebastian tried to remember if he'd seen a key among the possessions found on Jacob Harrow's body but was fairly sure there wasn't one. "Did anyone else come to call yesterday?"

"No. Just you."

"Did Mrs. Harrow leave the house at all before going to her parents'?"

"No. She asked me to pack a few things and left within the hour. She went directly to the house in Elm Tree Road. I heard her tell the cabbie."

"Show me the study."

Judith led Sebastian up the stairs and toward the back of the house and stopped before a closed door. Sebastian tried the knob, but unsurprisingly the door was locked. He had thought that might be the case, so he'd come prepared. He pulled a narrow metal case from his pocket and extracted a well-used tool. Judith watched in open-mouthed astonishment as he expertly picked the lock and pushed the door open.

"What the devil?" Sebastian muttered under his breath as he took in the disarray.

Judith peered into the study from behind him and inhaled sharply. "Oh dear God, we've been burgled."

Sebastian examined the room from the threshold before stepping inside. The heavy damask curtains were drawn, so the light was dim, but he could see that the papers that must have been on the desk were scattered on the floor and books were strewn across the carpet. Drawers had been turned inside out, and pages had been torn from a checkbook that lay open on the nearly bare desk. The room was so cold, Sebastian's breath escaped in great puffs of air, and Judith wrapped her arms about herself to keep warm. Sebastian entered the room and pulled aside the curtain to reveal an open window.

Swallowing back a growl of frustration, he examined the sash window and the ground beneath, but saw nothing helpful. It was too cold and dry for the ground to retain any footprints. The window wasn't damaged, and there was no dirt on the floor, so the intruder could have come from within. Judith's reaction to the ransacked room had seemed genuine, so the only person who could have staged a break-in was Emma Harrow. Sebastian saw no reason for her to go to such lengths to mask her desire to see what was inside her husband's study, so whoever had broken in had probably done so after Emma had left. And they appeared to have been searching for something.

Closing the window, Sebastian turned to Judith, who stood in the doorway, looking frightened and shivering with cold.

"Someone broke in while I was alone?" she asked in a small voice.

"Quite possibly. Did you hear anything?"

"No. I went up to my room after Mrs. Harrow left."

"Did you not have dinner?"

"I brought a tray upstairs. I didn't come down until this morning."

"Was anything out of the ordinary when you came downstairs?"

Judith shot Sebastian a look of stunned incredulity. "You mean besides my employer having been murdered and his wife having decamped to her parents' house, leaving me on my own? Not a thing," she said tartly. Sebastian recognized that her sarcasm was born of genuine fear and felt sympathy for the girl. If she had unwittingly walked in on whoever had broken in, the outcome could have been tragic.

"Can you tell if anything was taken?"

Judith looked around the room, but her gaze was blank, so Sebastian wasn't sure if anything registered. "No, I don't think so," she muttered at last.

"Are you sure?"

She seemed all set to answer in the affirmative when her gaze went to the mantel. "The dagger's gone."

"What dagger?"

"Mr. Harrow had a dagger right there," she said, pointing to an ornate metal stand that was now empty. Sebastian had taken it for some sort of decorative object but now realized it had been made to hold a knife.

"Can you describe it?"

"It was Ottoman and had a thin, curved blade," Judith said. "Mr. Harrow was very proud of it."

"When was the last time you saw it?"

"On Friday, when I cleaned in here."

"So you don't know if it was here yesterday?"

"No."

The description of the dagger fit with that of the murder weapon, but, if it had been taken only last night or early this morning, it couldn't have been used to stab Jacob Harrow in the heart or slice out his tongue on Monday night. Perhaps whoever ransacked the room had taken it as a souvenir of the crime, something to remind them of their daring.

"Get your things," Sebastian said gruffly. "You can't be here alone. It's not safe. Do you have any family you can stay with until this is over?"

Judith nodded but didn't budge.

"Well, go on, then," Sebastian prompted. That seemed to rouse her, and she hurried down the corridor, her footsteps loud on the tiled floor.

Once Judith had gone, Sebastian turned his attention to the desk. He picked up the checkbook and examined it more closely. There were several blank checks, the name Atrium Bank printed at the top. He'd never had reason to visit Atrium Bank but had walked past it when he was last in the City and knew it to be reputable. He riffled through the check stubs, but none of the payments Jacob Harrow had made looked suspicious. Setting the checkbook aside, he searched the rest of the drawers, but found nothing to interest him. It was the sort of detritus one generally found in people's desks—bills, old invitations, black-rimmed funeral cards, and adverts torn from newspapers.

Sebastian spent the next quarter of an hour examining every piece of paper, but didn't find any personal correspondence. Not so much as an old envelope. It was possible that someone had taken the letters, or more likely Jacob Harrow had thrown them away himself. Sebastian himself wasn't one for holding on to old correspondence, primarily because he didn't want anyone reading his mail. Perhaps Harrow had preferred to keep things private as well, even from his wife.

Likewise, there were no copies of articles he'd submitted to the paper or anything pertaining to a work of literary fiction. If Jacob Harrow had been working on a novel, his notes and anything he'd written to date were missing.

Casting a last look around the study, Sebastian noticed something protruding from beneath the edge of the curtain and bent down to investigate. He found a bankbook, or more accurately what was left of the bankbook. The cover bore the name of the bank, Atrium, Jacob Harrow's name, and an account number, but the pages inside had all been torn out. Sebastian checked the wastepaper basket and the hearth to see if perhaps whoever had torn out the pages might have tried to destroy them, but the ashes in the grate were cold and gray and bore no evidence of recently burned paper, and the wastepaper basket was empty. Still, this was telling. The intruder had made sure to obliterate any trace of Jacob Harrow's financial transactions. Sebastian took both the bankbook and checkbook. He would need them when he called at the bank.

Leaving the study tidier than he'd found it, he closed the door behind him and went in search of Judith, who was waiting by the door, a small satchel at her feet. She had already put on her coat and bonnet, and looked anxious to leave.

"Before we go," Sebastian said, "I want you to look at the remaining rooms to make sure nothing was taken. Can you do that?"

Judith was understandably reluctant to remain in the house any longer than she had to, but she nodded, clearly understanding the necessity of what Sebastian had asked of her. As the person who cleaned the rooms, she was the only one who'd know if the intruder had searched the rest of the house and taken anything else. Judith and Sebastian toured the ground-floor rooms, then went upstairs to check the bedrooms.

"Nothing else was taken," Judith said, her voice filled with certainty. "Just the dagger. Please, can we go now?" she added desperately.

Once Judith had locked the door behind them, Sebastian asked, "Which way are you headed?"

"Cannon Street."

"I'll give you a ride," he said. He needed to call in at Scotland Yard before visiting the bank. They walked to the cabstand together, each lost in their own thoughts.

# ELEVEN

Sebastian greeted Sergeant Woodward and headed directly for Superintendent Lovell's office. He would have liked to stop for a chat with the duty sergeant and catch up on the latest news, but time was of the essence. Superintendent Lovell appeared to be composing a letter, but looked up and set aside the missive when Sebastian knocked on the doorjamb. He looked about as sunny as a thundercloud.

"Come in, Bell. I trust you saw the evening edition of the *Telegraph*?" Lovell asked once Sebastian had shut the door behind him and sat. Superintendent Lovell removed his spectacles and proceeded to clean them with his handkerchief, something he did when he was agitated or needed time to think. Given how early in the conversation the spectacles had come off, Sebastian braced himself for a reprimand.

"I have, sir."

Lovell replaced the spectacles on his nose and focused his gaze on Sebastian. "So has the commissioner." He didn't sound angry, just weary, and frustrated. "Those damn journalists," he said, shaking his head in dismay. "Why can't the papers let us conduct an investigation before jumping to conclusions and stirring up public unrest? Now half the population of London thinks that Harrow got what was coming to him, and the other half fears they'll get their tongues cut out if they venture out at night."

"This wasn't a random attack, so they have nothing to worry about," Sebastian said.

"I didn't think it was but, until we make an arrest, no one will believe us and will think there's a sadistic lunatic stalking the streets. And the papers will intentionally incite the public's fears, especially the *Daily Telegraph*. Marshall Lawrence will turn Harrow's murder into a personal crusade and use his connection to the victim to denigrate the police service and attack Sir David."

"What does Marshall Lawrence have against the commissioner?" Sebastian asked.

Lovell compressed his lips and exhaled loudly through the nose. The sound was reminiscent of a steam engine. "All I know is that Lawrence bears a grudge against Sir David."

"Personal or professional?"

Superintendent Lovell shook his head. "I don't know, but what I do know is that we don't have the luxury of time. If an arrest is not made quickly, heads will roll."

"Meaning my head," Sebastian said.

"Do you have any leads?" Lovell asked, his closed expression all the confirmation Sebastian needed. His head was disposable, and if the case wasn't solved quickly and to the commissioner's satisfaction Lovell would offer up Sebastian as a human sacrifice in order to safeguard his own position and reputation. There was a time when the superintendent might have risked Sir David's displeasure and protected Sebastian from repercussions arising from a stalled inquiry, but that time had passed. Lovell was happy enough to make use of Sebastian's talents, but no longer saw him as a valuable asset. Lovell was the sort of man who always backed the winning horse, and that horse was now John Ransome, rising star of the Metropolitan Police Service.

Swallowing back his bitterness, Sebastian said, "I have identified two possible suspects but, although both men may have had motive, I think there's something bigger at play here."

"Go on," Lovell invited, his gaze alert behind the freshly cleaned lenses.

"Captain Pickering, who brought a case of slander against Jacob Harrow, then shot himself when he lost, had a brother."

"But why would he murder Harrow now? It's been more than two years."

"Reginald Pickering was fifteen at the time of the trial. Now that he is older, he might want to avenge his brother, but there's nothing to tie him to the murder as yet."

Lovell nodded. "I see. Have you questioned him?"

"First I have to find him."

"Who's the second man?"

"Jacob Harrow dismissed his manservant, Ellis Baylor, last week. According to the Harrows' maidservant, Baylor was suspected of stealing and was sacked without a character. Harrow didn't turn him over to the police, but he did withhold his wages. Judith said that Baylor had plans to join the navy."

"Sounds to me like the scoundrel should be grateful, not angry. The loss of wages is nothing compared to years spent in prison," Lovell said.

"I agree. And even if the man held a grudge, I can't see him going to such lengths. He could have just as easily stabbed Harrow in some dark alley and have done with it. Why remove his tongue and hang him off a gate? It just doesn't compute, especially since he didn't take the money Harrow had on him or his valuables, which would have fetched a tidy sum."

"So, what do you intend to do?"

"I need to definitively rule out Baylor and speak to Reginald Pickering. And there's another angle I'd like to pursue."

"Which is?" Lovell asked warily.

"Someone broke into Jacob Harrow's study and made off with his bank records. According to the maidservant, they also took an ornamental Turkish dagger."

"What are you thinking?"

"Harrow might have been engaged in unsavory financial dealings, so I will start by calling at Harrow's bank," Sebastian said.

"Many a murder is motivated by greed, but I very much doubt it was the motive here," Lovell said. He leaned back in his chair, his shoulders slumping and his forehead creasing with anxiety. Lovell's advancing years were suddenly more notice-able, and Sebastian couldn't help but wonder how long it would be before the superintendent began to seriously consider retirement.

"I need a result, Bell," Lovell reiterated. "This is a high-profile case, and the Home Secretary is said to be taking a keen interest in the investigation."

His shoulders dropped a notch. "The police service is constantly under attack, Sebastian, and we're helpless without ammunition. If we fail to prove our worth year after year, the service could be disbanded, the men who've dedicated their lives to upholding the law scorned and dismissed without a farthing in compensation. I want an arrest by the end of the week."

"I understand, sir. I won't let you down. But it would speed matters considerably if someone could help with the legwork," Sebastian said.

"What do you require?"

"I need to track down Reginald Pickering and Ellis Baylor. If Baylor has joined the navy as he said he would do, there will be a record and possibly an address where he's billeted until he's assigned to a crew." Sebastian took a moment to consider how to best find Reginald Pickering. "Officers who served with

Hugh Pickering in Crimea might know something of his brother's whereabouts."

Lovell nodded. "Get Constable Meadows on to it. He's a clever lad and will get the job done."

"Thank you, sir."

"Let me know what you discover," Lovell said. "Today."

"Yes, sir."

Constable Meadows was an earnest young man who'd proved himself resourceful in the past and took pride both in his work and in his appearance. His uniform was always clean and pressed, his shoes polished, and his dark hair oiled and neatly parted in the center. He despised slovenliness and often rebuked Constable Bryant for his rumpled appearance. Constable Meadows was one of those policemen for whom the job was intuitive, and Sebastian agreed with Superintendent Lovell that he was capable of taking on more responsibility, unlike constables who could be trusted to follow orders but didn't have the wits or the initiative to figure things out for themselves.

Meadows' dark gaze was serious as he took down Sebastian's instructions.

"Start with the Navy Office and ask to speak to the Clerk of the Acts. He's in charge of all the day-to-day business of the navy. If he can't help you, he'll be sure to direct you to someone who can. I need to know if one Ellis Baylor has joined the navy in the past week, and, if he did, where he was on Monday and Tuesday. Get an address for him, if they have it."

Sebastian waited for Constable Meadows to finish writing, then continued. "Once you finish there, head over to Pall Mall and ask at the Army and Navy Club. If you can't find anyone who served with Captain Hugh Pickering, try the Guards Club. There's little point in trying the United Service Club since it's

for high-ranking officers. Do not seek out either man. Do you
have any questions, Constable?"

"No, Inspector. You can rely on me," Constable Meadows
said, his chest puffing out with pride. He was clearly excited
about this solo assignment and pleased to have been chosen.

"Good man," Sebastian said. "Jot everything down or you'll
forget. That's a lesson I learned the hard way when I first joined
the service."

"Yes, sir. I will, sir."

"I will speak to you later, then," Sebastian said, and was
about to head out into the frigid December afternoon when
Sergeant Woodward hailed him.

"Seb, this came in for you while you were in with Lovell."

He handed Sebastian a folded square of paper. It was a note
from Chief Warder Thayer, asking Sebastian to come by at his
earliest convenience. Sebastian was impatient to begin his
inquiries at the bank, but Mr. Thayer wouldn't have summoned
him unless he had a good reason. He would have to stop by the
Tower before making his way to the City.

# TWELVE

When Sebastian arrived at the Tower of London, he went directly to the chief warder's residence. If the request for an interview had come from the Constable of the Tower, Sebastian would still have to see Mr. Thayer first, since he couldn't simply call on the constable as if they were old friends. There was an established protocol that had to be followed to the letter. Mr. Thayer was at home, his demeanor far from welcoming when he let Sebastian in and invited him into the parlor. There was no sign of Mrs. Thayer and no promise of a cup of tea.

Mr. Thayer seemed hesitant to explain his request, so Sebastian unbuttoned his coat and took off his hat, accepted a seat, and waited patiently for the man to screw up the courage to tell him whatever it was he needed to say. This seemed like a personal matter, so a visit to the Constable of the Tower didn't seem imminent.

"I'm deeply ashamed, Inspector Bell," Mr. Thayer said at last, his gaze fixed on the bare branches of a tree beyond the parlor window.

Sebastian waited, and the chief warder sighed with resignation and sank into a chair, splaying his hands on his thighs. "It's my son, Harry."

"Is he all right?" Sebastian asked, recalling the shy boy he'd seen on his first visit.

"Harry won't be able to sit comfortably for a while, but otherwise he's well."

"What has he done to earn such a severe punishment?"

"I'll let him explain."

Mr. Thayer pushed to his feet and went to the door, opened it and bellowed for Harry. He practically shoved the boy inside when Harry came running, and left the room, shutting the door firmly behind him. It seemed Mr. Thayer intended for Sebastian to question Harry on his own.

Harry looked like he'd been crying. His eyes were puffy, and his nose was red and irritated, probably from continual wiping. He looked at the chair his father had vacated with longing, but opted to stand. When he faced Sebastian, it was with the air of someone preparing for their execution.

"What happened, Harry?" Sebastian asked softly, recalling how he used to feel as a boy after being punished. He had been ashamed and remorseful, but also defiant and furiously angry with his father. From the distance of twenty-five years, he could admit that the few times his father had taken a belt to him he had richly deserved it and had left his father little choice. He was certain that the chief warder felt as awful as his son, and was equally convinced that whatever Harry had done had warranted a harsh punishment.

Harry began to cry, silent tears sliding down pale, liberally freckled cheeks. "Are you going to arrest me?" he sobbed.

"Arrest you for what?"

"Stealing," Harry hiccuped.

"What did you steal?" Sebastian deliberately kept his tone devoid of accusation, expressing only mild curiosity instead.

Harry sniffled. "Tim—my best mate—he devised a scheme.

I'd lift valuables off visitors to the Tower and he'd fence them to this cove he knows in Spitalfields."

"And then you'd split the profits," Sebastian said.

Harry nodded miserably and Sebastian felt a pang of sympathy for Mr. Thayer. Harry had put his father in an impossible position. If the truth came out, Mr. Thayer might lose not only his position but his son too; but if the chief warder covered for his son, he would be setting a terrible example, breaking the law, and possibly allowing a killer to go free, since Sebastian was sure this confession had something to do with the night of Jacob Harrow's murder.

"Well, I probably should arrest you, and Tim, but if you can help me with my investigation I might be willing to overlook your more colorful activities. You saw something the night Jacob Harrow was killed, didn't you?"

Harry nodded but didn't speak. His narrow shoulders were hunched, and he was staring at his feet. Sebastian almost asked him to sit, then recalled his difficulty and allowed him to remain standing.

"What did you see, Harry?"

"I was on the battlement of St. Thomas's Tower, and I saw a man rowing a dinghy toward Traitors' Gate. The second cove was lying in the prow. At first, I thought he was looking up at the stars, but once they got closer..."

The tears came faster now, and Harry fumbled for his handkerchief and blew his nose loudly.

"The man was dead, wasn't he?" Sebastian asked.

Harry nodded. "He was covered in blood and his eyes were staring."

"Was that the first time you've seen a dead body?"

"No, but I'd never seen anyone that's been murdered."

"Did you read about the murder in the papers?" Sebastian asked softly.

Harry shook his head. "I heard my parents talking about it."

"Can you describe the man who was rowing?"

"I couldn't see his face clearly. He had his back to me, but then he turned once he reached the gate and tied up."

Sebastian held his breath, praying all the while that Harry had seen something useful.

"He was well dressed, like a gentleman. And fit."

"Was he young or old?" Sebastian asked.

"Old. Your age," Harry added.

"Right. So what did this old man look like?"

"He was clean-shaven, and I think his hair was light."

"Did you see his eyes?"

Harry shook his head again. "They were shadowed by the brim of his hat."

"What sort of hat was it?"

"A bowler."

"Was there blood on him?"

"Not that I could see."

"Not even on his hands?" Sebastian asked.

"He must have washed them in the Thames. I would have."

"Yes, that would have been the clever thing to do," Sebastian agreed. "Was there anything else you saw?"

"I saw the meat hook in the bottom of the boat. It glinted in the moonlight." Harry shuddered. "I had terrible nightmares about it and my thrashing woke my parents. They thought I was ill because I was sweating and my teeth were chattering," he explained.

"Was that when you decided to confide in your father?"

"No," Harry mumbled. Sebastian waited. There was clearly more to this story, but the boy had to tell it in his own time.

Harry sniffled and blew his nose again, the tip as red as if he'd dipped it in crimson paint. "I was there to meet Tim that night, but I was frightened by what I'd seen and snuck away as soon as I thought it was safe. After I went home, Tim returned to the gate."

"Why?" Sebastian demanded.

"He wanted to see what the bloke had done with the body."

"And to empty the dead man's pockets, I reckon," Sebastian surmised.

Harry nodded again, his head going up and down like a marionette's.

"What did Tim take?"

"The gate was locked, so Tim couldn't get to the watch or the purse, but he was able to push his hand through the bars and slide his fingers into the left pocket of the man's coat."

"What did he take?" Sebastian asked again.

"There was nothing of value, just a bauble, but I thought it might be important."

"Do you have it?"

Harry unfolded the fingers of his left hand and showed Sebastian the object he'd been clutching. It was a blue glass disk the size of a pocket watch, the glass still warm from Harry's hand when Sebastian plucked it off the boy's palm. The disk was decorated with three circles. A black dot at the center was surrounded by a pale blue and then a white band, and a thin leather thong had been inserted through a small hole had been drilled close to the edge.

"Tim said it was worthless," Harry said, clearly disappointed. "Is it?"

"I don't know," Sebastian replied, his attention still fixed on the object. The design felt foreign. The glass disk looked like either a decoration or an amulet of some kind. Jacob Harrow might have had it on him at the time of his death, or the killer could have put it there for reasons known only to himself.

"Thank you, Harry," Sebastian said and slipped the disk into the pocket of his waistcoat.

"Does this help?" Harry asked eagerly.

"It does," Sebastian assured him and pushed to his feet.

"What will happen to me and Tim?" Harry cried, clearly agitated now that he'd done what his father expected him to do.

"Do Tim's parents know what you two got up to?"

Harry nodded.

"More to the point, does Tim also have a sore arse?" Sebastian asked.

Harry nodded again. "Tim's father really put his arm into it."

"Then I think you have learned your lesson. But if you break the law again, you will have me to answer to. And I won't be quite so forgiving next time. Is that understood?"

"I will never put a foot wrong again, sir. Not ever!" Harry exclaimed.

"I'm glad to hear it. And find a better friend. This Tim sounds like someone who'll be seeing the inside of a cell before long."

"Yes, sir," Harry replied. "I will, sir."

Harry was willing to promise anything now that his ordeal was at an end, but Sebastian thought that perhaps he should have been tougher on the boy and made him spend a night in the cells. Just to drive the point home. But if he did that, then Mr. Thayer's reputation would suffer, and Sebastian thought the man deserved some consideration for offering up his son when he could have just as easily swept the whole episode under the carpet. The blue disk wasn't a vital piece of evidence and would probably not make much difference to the investigation in the long run. Though if it did, then Sebastian would be profoundly grateful.

Sebastian said goodbye to a vastly relieved Mr. Thayer and stepped outside, heading toward the exit at a brisk pace. He'd wasted enough time on Harry Thayer.

# THIRTEEN

Sebastian found a hansom and directed the driver to take him to Atrium Bank, which was located in Princes Street, just around the corner from the Bank of England. Atrium Bank wasn't as imposing as some of the larger London banks, but the building conveyed an air of solidity and impeccable respectability. Stolid-looking cashiers sat behind a tall, polished counter fitted with a bronze grille. Several customers were being assisted, while two more waited their turn. Sebastian didn't think a cashier would have the authority to help him, so he approached a more senior employee, whose desk was behind a wooden partition topped with a glass screen. He would be someone who opened new accounts, consulted on loans, and addressed over-drafts and other client issues that went beyond basic trans-actions.

"How can I help you today, sir?" the man asked, smiling at Sebastian in a friendly manner. He probably assumed that Sebastian was there to open an account. Sebastian produced his warrant card, clearly surprising the man, who looked around nervously as if searching for assistance.

"I would like to speak to the manager," Sebastian said.

"What is this in reference to, Inspector?" the man asked, dropping his voice to a near-whisper.

"I'm investigating the death of one of your clients."

"Good Lord," the man said, but he seemed relieved that the inquiry had nothing to do with him personally. "And you believe his demise is in some way connected to the bank?"

"I'm not at liberty to discuss the details," Sebastian replied. "Kindly inform the manager that I'd like to see him."

"Of course."

The man returned a few moments later and invited Sebastian to follow him. He led Sebastian down a corridor that contained a number of doors bearing discreet bronze plates. These would be the offices of the partners and the senior management.

"Inspector Bell," the clerk announced when he approached the last door on the left, and stood aside to let Sebastian enter.

A tall, thin man of about forty-five rose to greet him. His hair had almost completely receded at the front, leaving a long, shiny strip of scalp flanked by sparse brown curls. He had a short beard and wore a pair of gold-rimmed spectacles that magnified his pale eyes.

"Bernard Allardyce, Manager," he introduced himself.

"Inspector Bell, Scotland Yard," Sebastian said, and showed Mr. Allardyce his warrant card.

"How can I be of assistance, Inspector?" Mr. Allardyce asked once they were both seated.

"Your client, Jacob Harrow, died under suspicious circumstances. I'm investigating the case."

"And how does Atrium Bank come into this?" Mr. Allardyce asked carefully.

"Someone broke into Mr. Harrow's study and removed pages from his bankbook. They also looked through his checkbook. I can only assume that the information was of some significance."

"I'm afraid I can't help you. All client information is confidential."

Sebastian had anticipated just such a response and was prepared to do battle. "Mr. Allardyce, I need to see a record of Mr. Harrow's transactions since he opened an account with the bank. You can assist me now, or I can obtain a warrant signed by a judge. It will take longer, but the end result will be much the same, at least as far as I'm concerned."

Sebastian didn't bother to spell out what that would mean for the bank, but he could see that Mr. Allardyce took his meaning. A warrant meant a police presence, a besmirched reputation, and possibly even an account in the papers that would leave the public and the bank's clients in no doubt that the institution was somehow involved in a murder investigation.

Mr. Allardyce sighed irritably but didn't seem overly surprised by Sebastian's response. He was simply protecting himself should the board members question his judgment. Now that the reputation of the bank was threatened, he had little choice in the matter and therefore couldn't be held accountable.

"Inspector, I need your word of honor that no one will find out that you were able to access a client's personal record. Such a breach of confidentiality can have a devastating effect on the bank's reputation."

"I understand completely, and you have my word, Mr. Allardyce. I'm not here to undermine the reputation of your establishment. I simply need information."

"Give me a moment." The manager left the room and returned a few minutes later bearing a thin folder, which he handed to Sebastian with obvious reluctance.

Inside were three sheets of paper, marked 1856, 1857, and 1858, and about a dozen cashed checks.

"Is this it?" Sebastian asked, looking up from the file.

"Mr. Harrow opened an account with us in May 1856. This is a list of all the transactions since."

Sebastian started with the register for 1856 and worked his way down, then examined the transactions for 1857 and 1858 and leafed through the checks. There were checks made out to various merchants, several cash withdrawals, and a surprising number of deposits. Three monthly deposits of £10 each began in June 1856 and continued into the present. Another deposit of £3 was also made monthly and on the same day.

"Do you know anything about these monthly deposits?" Sebastian asked.

Mr. Allardyce held out his hand for the pages and looked at the entries more closely. "I don't personally monitor the banking activity of our clients, so I couldn't tell you just by looking at the register."

"Surely there must be a way to trace these deposits. They were made monthly, and all on the first two days of the month. I expect an institution known for its stellar reputation must keep copious records of each transaction."

The praise mollified Mr. Allardyce somewhat but not enough to alleviate his obvious annoyance. No banking establishment wanted to involve itself in a murder, even if their contribution was entirely lawful in nature. To assist the police was to declare an allegiance to the legal process, and, if a client conducted dealings they wished to hide, they might decide to take their business to an establishment known for their discretion and neutrality.

"We keep a monthly ledger where every transaction is recorded and detailed," the manager conceded.

"Splendid. I need to see the ledgers for the past three months," Sebastian said.

"I'm afraid that's impossible, Inspector, since you would be privy to the transactions made by other clients who had nothing to do with Mr. Harrow."

"What do you suggest, then, Mr. Allardyce?"

"I will pull the ledgers and copy the notations made for deposits into Mr. Harrow's account. Will that suit?"

"For a start."

"As you wish," Mr. Allardyce replied stonily, and left the room.

It took the manager a long while to return, but when he did he came up trumps. He settled across from Sebastian and pushed a sheet of paper toward him. On it was a list of £10 deposits into Jacob Harrow's account starting October 1, 1858. Two lots of them were from Godfrey Price and Harold Wise, who had paid by check. Mr. Allardyce had noted the bank from which the funds had been drawn. Both men banked with Drummonds of London. The £3 deposit was from James Harrow, whose bank was in Brentwood, Essex. The remaining £10 deposit was not annotated, the name of the payee left frustratingly blank.

"Who's the fourth person?" Sebastian asked.

"The fourth individual made a cash deposit directly into Mr. Harrow's account."

"Does this mean they were privy to his account number?"

"No. The name on the account was sufficient to process the transaction."

"This person made a deposit every month for over two years. Surely someone must know who they are. Did they not sign a deposit slip?"

Mr. Allardyce compressed his lips like a stubborn child, so Sebastian pushed harder. "Mr. Allardyce, give me the name and you won't be hearing from me again."

"Are you sure about that, Inspector Bell? For all I know, you will come back tomorrow with a new list of demands and a dozen constables."

"A man was murdered. Your client. I can't imagine that you wouldn't wish to help catch his killer."

"And are you certain that one of these people is connected to Mr. Harrow's demise?" Mr. Allardyce asked tartly.

"Four people made a monthly payment to Jacob Harrow. What does that look like to you, Mr. Allardyce?"

"Perhaps they owed him money."

"Do you really believe that?"

Mr. Allardyce sighed heavily. "No, I don't."

"Then give me the name of the fourth person."

"It's Constance Wallace, wife of General Henry Wallace."

"Do the Wallaces have an account with this bank?"

"They do not."

"So, Mrs. Wallace came in every month and deposited ten pounds into Jacob Harrow's account?"

"She did. And if you don't have any further questions, I'd like you to leave now, Inspector," the manager added.

"Thank you for your assistance, Mr. Allardyce. You were most helpful."

"My pleasure."

It clearly wasn't, but Sebastian had got what he'd come for, and that was what mattered. As he walked down the crowded street, he considered what he'd learned. Three men had made regular deposits to Jacob Harrow by check. This explained the monthly letters Emma Harrow had mentioned. The men had sent in their checks on the appointed day, and Jacob Harrow had deposited them into his account. Someone would send money regularly either because they were repaying a debt, or they were paying for something else entirely. Sebastian could believe that the £3 checks could be in repayment of a loan, but not the rest. Jacob Harrow would have to have lent large amounts of money to set up such a demanding pay schedule, money he didn't appear to have had.

Harrow had opened his account with Atrium Bank after the war in Crimea had ended, in March 1856, and he had returned to England. Where had he banked before that, and when had the payments actually begun? Ten pounds was a substantial amount. It was more than Sebastian earned in a month, and he received an inspector's wage. The constables made just over a guinea per week, so less than five pounds a month. A deposit of £33 per month explained the fashionable neighborhood, beautiful house, comfortable furnishings, and his ability to employ three servants when most working men could barely afford one. Many households relied on a charwoman who came in a few times a week, with the mistress of the house cooking all the meals. Emma Harrow had probably never so much as boiled an egg, much less produced three meals a day.

Sebastian wasn't sure if a journalist was paid weekly or per article, but he didn't imagine the wages were enough to support the kind of lifestyle Jacob Harrow had obviously enjoyed. This smacked of something entirely different, and Sebastian would gladly bet his last shilling that blackmail was involved.

Since James Harrow had paid the least, Sebastian decided he would speak to him last. He would begin with the two men who banked with Drummonds, then have a quiet chat with Mrs. Wallace. He was fairly sure her husband wasn't aware of the payments his wife made, and Mrs. Wallace would have some explaining to do if her secret came to light.

# FOURTEEN

Obtaining clients' addresses from Drummonds took some persuading on Sebastian's part but, once the manager saw the benefits of cooperating with the police, Sebastian was able to get what he'd come for. The Wallaces didn't bank with Drummonds, but on a hunch Sebastian stopped in at the Bank of England, and was able to discover that the general and his wife resided in Charles Street, Mayfair. He decided to call on Harold Wise first, since he didn't live too far away, and Sebastian was eager to get some answers.

The house was one of an identical row of the sort of modest homes that were usually occupied by middle-class families who either made their money in trade or through some form of skilled labor, such as medicine or law. The door was opened by an attractive young woman who was clearly not a maidservant. Her mauve gown appeared to be of good quality, but even to someone like Sebastian, who didn't know much about women's fashion, it looked a few years out of date. Her rich brown hair was pulled back into a simple knot.

The woman's expression instantly turned to one of annoyance. "Whatever you're selling, we're not interested," she said.

"I'm not selling anything. Are you Mrs. Wise?"

"*Miss* Wise," she replied warily.

Sebastian showed her his warrant card. "I need to speak to your brother."

"What is this about, Inspector?" she asked. She looked puzzled, and Sebastian suspected that he was about to upend her safe world.

"This is not a discussion to have on the doorstep, Miss Wise," he replied quietly.

A curtain in a window across the street was already twitching, and a middle-aged woman who was passing with a shopping basket slung over her arm slowed her step and nodded to Miss Wise in greeting, her greedy gaze raking over Sebastian, most likely in an effort to determine if he might be a suitor.

Miss Wise acknowledged the neighbor's greeting, then turned back to Sebastian. "Come in."

She invited him into the sitting room and offered him a seat. Sebastian unbuttoned his coat, loosened his muffler, and laid his hat on his thigh, all the while appraising the room. It was sparsely decorated, the furniture and carpet showing signs of prolonged use. The curtains were a bit faded, and the fire in the grate was meager for such a cold day. Miss Wise, who'd settled across from Sebastian and adjusted her skirts, seemed in no hurry to fetch her brother. She fixed him with an inquisitive stare.

"Did you know Jacob Harrow?" Sebastian asked.

"He's that journalist who wrote about the war in Crimea. Harold doesn't like me to read the papers, but I did read the article about that poor woman that was found dead in Highgate. Couldn't sleep for a week," she added with a shudder.

"Yes, I can imagine how distressing that was for you," Sebastian said. He waited for her to say something about Jacob Harrow's death, but Miss Wise remained silent, watching him with barely contained impatience.

"Jacob Harrow was murdered, Miss Wise. Did you not know?"

She looked stunned, her hand flying to her bosom and her mouth opening slightly as she absorbed the news. "I haven't been out, and we no longer have the papers delivered. But what does this have to do with Harold, Inspector Bell?"

"I believe Jacob Harrow and your brother knew each other. I thought Mr. Wise might help me fill in some blanks."

"Blanks?" Miss Wise echoed. "What on earth do you mean?"

"Miss Wise, I really do need to speak to your brother," Sebastian reiterated.

He was surprised the man hadn't come to see to whom his sister was speaking. If he was vigilant enough to monitor what she read, he'd certainly not care to leave her alone with a strange man. In fact, now that Sebastian thought about it, he realized that the house was awfully quiet for the time of day. It was as if the two of them were alone.

"Are you here on your own, Miss Wise?" Sebastian asked.

She shook her head. "Harold is upstairs. He's been ill and hasn't left his bed in days. We do have a maidservant, but it's her afternoon off."

It seemed important to her that he should know they could afford a servant.

"Then perhaps you can take me up to see your brother. I'll be brief," Sebastian promised. "It's important."

Miss Wise looked torn between sending Sebastian on his way and allowing him a few moments with her brother. She appeared to come to the correct conclusion that Sebastian would return if she refused, and decided to get the ordeal over with.

"All right, but please, don't tire him out," she said as she rose to her feet.

"I won't. Has he been ailing long?"

"Harold is consumptive. He needs rest and fresh air. I can see to the former, but there's nothing I can do about the latter, not in this stinking city," she added bitterly.

"I'm sorry," Sebastian said.

There was no cure for consumption, and Harold Wise would eventually succumb to the disease. Unless Miss Wise was lying on her brother's behalf and he was suffering from something considerably less fatal. However, if she was telling the truth, Sebastian dared not get too close. Consumption was highly infectious, and he wondered if Miss Wise had been advised to take precautions against becoming ill herself.

Sebastian stopped just inside the door, but Miss Wise went in, approaching the man in the four-poster bed. Now that Sebastian could see him, he thought she had probably been truthful. Harold Wise looked so insubstantial as to take up almost no space at all. He was terribly pale, and the handkerchief he clutched in his right hand was stained with blood. The room looked as worn as the man and smelled of death.

"Harry, this is Inspector Bell from Scotland Yard. He needs to speak to you. About Jacob Harrow," Miss Wise added, lowering her voice.

Harold Wise looked from his sister to Sebastian, his gaze uncomprehending. "How can I help you, Inspector?" he rasped.

Sebastian had hoped that Miss Wise would leave them to speak in private, but she remained by the bed, standing guard should her brother have need of her. Sebastian longed to tell her to move away to protect her health, but he supposed she knew the risks and chose to ignore them.

"Mr. Wise, Jacob Harrow is dead. He was murdered."

Harold Wise tried to smile, but it looked more like a grimace of pain. "How?"

"He was stabbed, then his body was mounted on Traitors' Gate."

Harold Wise chuckled, the laugh turning into a phlegmy

cough. "I suppose he finally got what was coming to him," he said once he could speak again.

"Why were you paying him?"

Miss Wise turned to her brother, once again clearly taken by surprise. It was obvious she had questions, but Harold shook his head, warning her to keep quiet. He sighed. "I'm not long for this world, Inspector, so I may as well tell you the truth. Ruth, would you mind making me a cup of tea?" he asked politely.

"You mean you'd like me to leave," Ruth snapped.

"I would like to speak to Inspector Bell privately, but I would also very much like some tea. Inspector, would you care for a cup?"

"Thank you, no."

Ruth Wise left the room and shut the door behind her. Sebastian remained where he was and hoped that was far enough to ward off contagion. He longed to open a window and let in some fresh air, but the cold and damp would not benefit the sick man.

"I don't want my sister to know the truth. She is the only person who still believes in me and will miss me when I'm gone," Harold Wise said.

"What did Harrow have on you, Mr. Wise? Or do you carry a military rank?"

"It was Lieutenant Wise before I resigned my commission. I was quartermaster for the 10th Royal Hussars. We were in Crimea," he said. He began to cough again, his thin body quaking with the force of his hacking. He reached for a glass of water on the bedside table, took a few sips, then settled back against the pillows.

"Please continue, Mr. Wise," Sebastian said. He desperately wanted to leave but couldn't go until he got what he'd come for.

"Jacob Harrow approached me in April 1856, a mere week after I returned from Crimea. He said he had proof that I had helped myself to supplies and sold them to line my own pockets. He said that if I didn't pay him for his silence, he would go public with the information."

"And were you stealing?" Sebastian asked.

Harold Wise smiled dolefully. "I didn't see it as stealing. Only as an allocation of supplies to those who had greater need of them."

"But you made a profit."

"I did, yes. If found out, I would have faced court-martial and death."

"Did you have any associates?" Sebastian asked.

Harold Wise shook his head. "I didn't. It was too risky to let anyone in on my operation."

"So how did Jacob Harrow find out?"

"I don't know, but he had enough to prove his case against me." Harold Wise began to cough again, and the fit lasted long enough to leave him breathless. He dabbed at his mouth, then tossed the bloodied handkerchief to the floor, and took a clean one from a stack by the bed.

"I'm glad Jacob Harrow is dead, Inspector, but I didn't kill him. I might have been a soldier, but to kill in battle is very different from killing someone in cold blood. I'm only glad Ruth will never have to deal with that vile man."

"Do you think he would have demanded that she continue to pay him?"

"Without doubt. He was that mercenary. Knowing Ruth will be safe from him will make my passing easier."

Sebastian nodded. There was no way this frail man could have murdered Jacob Harrow and mounted him on the gate. Unless he had friends who were willing to help or someone who'd do it for money, he wasn't the killer. And if Sebastian had to guess, he'd say that money was very tight and there wouldn't be much left for Ruth Wise once her brother passed. They were either living off a dwindling inheritance or burning through the profits Harold had made during the war.

Sebastian drew the blue disk out of his pocket and showed it to Wise. "Ever see this?"

Wise began to shake his head, but then another coughing fit overtook him, and he balled up his handkerchief and held it to his mouth.

"Thank you for your candor, Mr. Wise," Sebastian said, and left, glad to get away from the sickroom.

He met Ruth on the stairs, a tea tray in her hands. She looked up at Sebastian, visibly relieved that he was leaving.

"Miss Wise, has your brother had any visitors of late?"

Ruth looked angry. "No one comes to visit him, not since he became ill. It's like he's dead to them already."

"And does your brother correspond with anyone by post?"

"He asked me to post a letter to Jacob Harrow on the last day of November. Aside from that, there's no one."

"Thank you," Sebastian said. "I will see myself out."

As he stepped outside and breathed in the cold, smoky air, he wondered what would become of Ruth Wise. He doubted Harold Wise owned the house, and suspected that there was in fact no maidservant. Ruth Wise probably managed the house and nursed her brother all by herself. Sebastian hoped he had set something aside for her future. At least the Wises wouldn't have to make any more payments, but that was probably cold comfort for a woman who would soon be left entirely on her own. Sympathetic as Sebastian was to Ruth's plight, there was nothing he could do for her, so he put the Wises from his mind and walked away.

# FIFTEEN

Next stop was Mayfair. The stately buildings that lined the street spoke to safety and comfort, and, in most cases, generational wealth. General Wallace might not be titled, but his rank and distinguished military service assured him a place in society —which made his wife's payments to a lowly reporter all the more intriguing. Whatever Harrow had on her had to be damning or she would have had her husband deal with the man and end the blackmail before it had begun.

The crisply uniformed maid who answered the door looked at Sebastian with obvious surprise when he introduced himself and asked to speak to the lady of the house. He hoped Mrs. Wallace would be at home and available to see him, as it was prime time to both pay and receive social calls. Sebastian didn't get the impression that she currently had any visitors, since there were no carriages waiting at the curb and he doubted that ladies of Mrs. Wallace's acquaintance would arrive in a hansom or on foot, unless they lived nearby.

The maidservant seemed paralyzed by indecision. She could hardly turn away an inspector of the police, but to allow a policeman into the house, especially through the front door, might earn her not only a reprimand but some sort of punishment if General Wallace was a hard man. She wisely decided to allow Sebastian to wait in the foyer while she consulted her mistress instead of leaving him on the doorstep where he was sure to attract attention from the neighbors, who would quickly deduce that he wasn't a mere tradesman.

Sebastian thought that Mrs. Wallace's decision whether to speak to him would largely depend on whether her husband was at home. If he was, Sebastian would be asked to leave, since Mrs. Wallace could ill afford to reveal her dealings with Jacob Harrow. Fortunately, it seemed the general was out. Sebastian was escorted into a charming drawing room that was pleasantly warm and smelled of coffee and cake. The room was decorated entirely in chinoiserie, the pale green wallpaper printed with peony blossoms and exotic birds. Several ornamental urns with a similar motif stood on spindly tables, and a double-edged sword with oriental markings was displayed above the mantel. The only item in the room that didn't fit with the theme was a portrait that hung above the sideboard and bore a discreet name plate that identified the subject as General Wallace, the man's ruddy cheeks and woolly muttonchops in keeping with the colors of his red and white uniform. The general had to be close to fifty when the portrait was painted, and rather corpulent, his barrel chest decorated with medals.

Mrs. Constance Wallace was at least twenty years younger than her aging husband. She was slender and graceful and wore a gown of teal silk that accentuated her lustrous chestnut curls and blue-green eyes. The low table bore two cups, two plates, and three-quarters of an orange-peel cake left on a flowered platter. It seemed there had been a caller after all, who must have just left. The maidservant hastily collected the dirty crockery and removed the tray, leaving the door open behind her.

"Do sit down, Inspector," Mrs. Wallace said, and settled

herself on the pale pink settee, her skirts spread about her like the petals of some exotic flower. "What is this about?" she asked irritably.

Sebastian took a moment to answer, studying the woman in a way that was meant to make her uneasy. She didn't seem the sort to spill her secrets. She had too much to lose, and Sebastian would fare better if she were slightly unnerved.

"I'm investigating the murder of Jacob Harrow," he said at last. "I trust you're familiar with the name."

"Why on earth would I be?" Mrs. Wallace countered airily, but Sebastian had noticed a spark of panic in her eyes.

"It is my understanding that you were making monthly deposits into his account at Atrium Bank."

Mrs. Wallace's gaze flared with anger. "And how would you know that, Inspector?"

Sebastian had given his word not to compromise Mr. Allardyce or the establishment he worked for, so he resorted to a harmless lie. "Mr. Harrow kept a record of the payments at his home."

Mrs. Wallace's hands began to tremble, and she clasped them in her lap and bowed her head, as if in prayer.

"Mrs. Wallace, it is not my intention to endanger you in any way or create problems in your marriage. I simply need to understand what transpired between you and the victim."

Mrs. Wallace's head snapped up. "It is not your intention to cause problems?" she exclaimed. "Are you not here because I am a suspect? I expect an accusation of murder might cause something of a stir," she added bitterly.

"Why were you paying Jacob Harrow?" Sebastian asked again.

"Because he was blackmailing me."

"With what?"

"An affair that ended years ago."

"Was he blackmailing your lover as well?" Sebastian asked.

Mrs. Wallace looked away, her gaze drifting toward the window. "The man I loved was wounded in Crimea, during the charge of the Light Brigade. He died of his injuries." Her eyes filled with tears, and she looked down at her clasped hands to hide her distress.

"When did the blackmail start?" Sebastian asked once Mrs. Wallace appeared recovered enough to continue.

"May 1856."

"Did Jacob Harrow confront you directly?"

Constance Wallace scoffed. "We never met. He sent me a letter saying that, if I did not pay ten pounds into his account at Atrium Bank on the first of every month, he would tell my husband of the affair. He claimed to have proof."

"What manner of proof?" Sebastian asked.

"I honestly don't know."

"Would your lover have kept your letters or said something to one of his friends?"

Mrs. Wallace shook her head. "He would have taken our secret to the grave, if only to protect me."

"Yet, somehow, Harrow knew," Sebastian replied, wondering all the while if Constance's lover might have confided in someone despite his vow to keep the affair a secret. "Ten pounds is not a trifling amount. How did you hide the payments from your husband?" he asked.

"My husband gives me a generous allowance."

"Enough of an allowance to pay someone to murder your tormentor?"

Mrs. Wallace smiled dolefully. "I wish I had been brave enough to defy Harrow or find a way to stop him, but I paid, Inspector. I paid him month after month, desperate to protect my marriage and reputation. And most of all to shield my daughter. If the truth were made public, Georgiana's life would be destroyed." She drew a shuddering breath and looked directly at Sebastian, not a trace of remorse in her gaze. "I won't lie. I'm glad Jacob Harrow is gone. I only hope someone else won't pick up where he left off. If he had proof..."

"I don't believe there was any physical proof but, if someone contacts you with renewed demands for payment, I need to know. You can send a message to Scotland Yard, and I will do what I can."

"Thank you, Inspector Bell," Mrs. Wallace said. Her shoulders relaxed somewhat, and she permitted herself a smile. She was beautiful when she smiled, and for a moment Sebastian could imagine the passionate young woman who'd risked everything to snatch a few moments of happiness with the man she had loved. He wondered if Georgiana was her lover's daughter but saw no reason to ask. She was entitled to her secrets, and, as long as she hadn't hired someone to murder her tormentor, she would be safe.

"Where were you Monday night?" he asked.

"The general and I attended a supper given by Brigadier Lemming and his wife. We did not return home until close to three in the morning. Two dozen people saw us. Does my husband need to know of our conversation?" Mrs. Wallace asked, the tension returning.

"Not if you had nothing to do with Jacob Harrow's murder."

"The maidservant might tell him of your visit."

"Then I suggest you make certain she doesn't," Sebastian replied.

If Mrs. Wallace had been duplicitous enough to devise ways to meet her lover, she could invent a plausible excuse for Sebastian's visit. He bade her a good day and stepped out into the foyer, glad to see that the maidservant was nowhere near and had not been eavesdropping on the conversation. Walking to the nearest cabstand, he instructed the driver to take him to Southwark and settled in for a long ride.

As the hansom rolled over Westminster Bridge, Sebastian

gazed out over the tranquil river. The watery thoroughfare was dotted with countless vessels despite the bitter cold. An elegant frigate under full sail was headed out to sea, and, for just a moment, Sebastian wondered what it would be like to stand on deck and watch London grow smaller as he left all he knew behind and embarked on a new life. He'd put his plan to join the Pinkerton Detective Agency on hold, both because his position at Scotland Yard had seemed secure and because, for the first time since Louisa's death, he didn't feel as lonely or abandoned.

For a brief moment he considered writing to his brother, then changed his mind. Simian had no wish to hear from him. Even after all these years, he was still angry that Sebastian had left, even though Simian had inherited the family farm and had appropriated the money their father had so carefully put aside for their future. He hadn't even come to Louisa's funeral, nor had he written to express his condolences. The rift had been painful at first, but now all Sebastian felt was sadness. Simian was the only family he had left in the world. Perhaps he should be the bigger man and write to Simian anyway, Sebastian mused as the frigate passed beneath the bridge and emerged on the other side, gliding toward the open sea. Perhaps Simian would agree to a long overdue reconciliation.

As the carriage navigated the traffic on Westminster Bridge Road, Sebastian's thoughts turned back to the investigation, and he considered his upcoming interview with Godfrey Price. Both Harold Wise and Constance Wallace had admitted to the blackmail and had divulged the reason for their ensnarement. What was Godfrey Price guilty of, and was he better positioned to rid himself of his blackmailer?

Sebastian had come across all manner of lowlives in his line of work, but he held blackmailers in particular contempt. It took a unique brand of chicanery to ferret out people's deepest, darkest secrets, and deliberate, calculated cruelty to terrify the victims to the point where they paid without question, desperate to protect their good name and the lives they had built on lies.

How had Jacob Harrow come by the damning information, and how had he managed to keep his prey on the hook for so long? At this point, Sebastian would give his eyeteeth for a solid lead, but he'd been a copper long enough to know that clues didn't miraculously fall into one's lap. It took attention to detail and dogged policework to solve a case, and he would follow every lead, no matter how tenuous, until he found the elusive thread that would unravel the mystery.

# SIXTEEN

The Price residence was on Tooley Street in Bermondsey. The area was distinctly undesirable to anyone who harbored pretensions to gentility, the house bordered on shabby, and the woman who answered the door was no servant. She was heavily pregnant, and a small, dark-haired boy stood at her side, tugging on her hand in obvious fear of the strange man on the doorstep. Mrs. Price was short and, except for the rounded belly, slight, and had the look of someone who was perpetually run off her feet. Sebastian suspected that the Prices didn't employ a maid and that, like the Wises, this was not a family that could well afford to give away ten quid a month since men who labored day and night to save lives were compensated no better than barber-surgeons. Whatever transgression Jacob Harrow had held over Godfrey Price, he had clearly been bleeding the man dry.

"My husband is not in, Inspector," Mrs. Price said when Sebastian introduced himself. She didn't seem particularly alarmed to find a policeman at her door, just impatient to get back to whatever she had been doing.

"When do you expect him?"

"I really don't know. If your business is urgent, then you can find my husband at Guy's Hospital. That's where he spends most of his time," Mrs. Price said with obvious resignation. "It's that way." She gestured eastward with her hand.

"Thank you," Sebastian said, and left.

He could have stayed and questioned her first, but he wasn't sure how much Mrs. Price knew and didn't want to distress her in her condition. Nor did he wish to terrify the already frightened child. If he needed to speak to Mrs. Price, he would double back once he had a clearer understanding of the situation.

It wasn't a long walk to the hospital, and the building soon came into view. The hospital was enormous, with a main entrance worthy of a palace, wrought-iron gates, and several wings built around a cobblestone courtyard. Three additional wings behind the main building formed a square courtyard at the center that was bisected by a fourth wing. Whoever had built the hospital had spared no expense, and the building was decorated with columns, statues, a portico that wouldn't have looked out of place on a Grecian temple, and a roof crowded with chimneys and gables. Several conveyances were parked near the main entrance, the coachmen waiting patiently for fares, and a number of people came and went on foot, some looking relieved to be leaving, others noticeably afraid or in shock.

Mr. Price, when Sebastian finally tracked him down to the Surgeon's House, was a tall, slim, dark-haired man with a pencil moustache and a weary gaze. He had removed his smock before coming to speak to Sebastian, but there was dried blood on his shirt cuffs and beneath his fingernails, and Sebastian wondered how many patients he had operated on since coming to work that morning. An aura of fatigue emanated from him in waves, and he looked hungrily at the buttered bread and steaming mug of tea a nurse carried past them on a tray.

"Is there somewhere we can speak privately?" Sebastian asked. The corridor wasn't a place to question a man about possible blackmail, and he thought the surgeon might respond more readily if he was comfortably seated.

Godfrey Price led Sebastian past a patient ward where dozens of beds stood arranged in neat rows for easy access, and uniformed nurses traversed the space as they went about their duties. There was an eerie silence on the ward when Sebastian passed the open door, as if all the patients were already dead. He followed Price to an empty room. It had to be an examination room, since there was an elevated table, a linen screen behind which the patient could undress, and a chair and small desk for the doctor. Godfrey Price sat heavily in the only chair, leaving Sebastian to lean against the examining table.

"What's this about, Inspector?"

"Jacob Harrow was murdered, Mr. Price."

"I know. I've seen the papers. Terrible business. But what does his death have to do with me?"

"I believe he was blackmailing you."

Godfrey Price's astonishment didn't seem quite genuine. "And what makes you think that?" he exclaimed.

"You mailed him a check for ten pounds that he deposited on the first of every month. I'd say that's irrefutable evidence. Why were you paying him?"

"You're correct, Inspector," Godfrey said with a heavy sigh of resignation. "He was blackmailing me. A few more months and he would have completely bankrupted me."

"What did he have on you, Mr. Price?"

Godfrey Price sighed. "I must have your word that what I tell you will remain confidential."

"I can't give you my word until I know what it is you're going to tell me," Sebastian pointed out. "But it is not my intention to fit an innocent man for the crime. If you had nothing to do with Harrow's murder, then you have nothing to fear."

Godfrey Price shot him a look of pure skepticism. "There are those in your profession who wouldn't think twice about sending an innocent man to the gallows as long as they were credited with getting a satisfactory result."

"I'm not one of those men, and I don't know anyone who'd want to see an innocent man hang. We follow the evidence, Mr. Price, and we present our case to a court of law. So I ask again. What did Jacob Harrow have on you?"

The surgeon sighed heavily. "I didn't kill him, which is not to say I hadn't thought about it. But I'm sworn to preserve life, not take it, and that's what I've done since I qualified as a surgeon."

"So, what was so shocking that you had to pay out money your family desperately needs to keep it quiet?"

"When I was in Crimea, I became involved with one of the nurses. We were very discreet, but somehow Harrow found out. In itself, the affair wasn't all that shocking. I certainly wasn't the only one to seek a bit of sanity in an insane situation, but I might be the only one who made it legal."

"You married her?"

Godfrey Price nodded. "We were married in Scutari, but we didn't tell anyone. We'd decided to keep it to ourselves until after the war was over."

"And what happened?"

"Before leaving for Crimea, I'd become engaged to a woman I'd known my whole life. Our families were close, and Joanna and I had always planned to marry. It wasn't until I met Agnes Frye that I realized what I had with Joanna was not love but certainty and a comfortable friendship. I planned to break things off with Joanna when I returned—I didn't want to do it by post—but by the time I came back the relationship with Agnes had soured. I discovered that I wasn't the only man she had been carrying on with, but I was the only one foolish enough to commit myself to her."

Sebastian nodded. "So, you married Joanna when you returned and never told her that you were married already."

Godfrey nodded. "That about sums it up."

"Where's your lawful wife now?"

"I have no idea. I haven't seen her or heard anything about her whereabouts since leaving Crimea."

"How did Jacob Harrow know of your marriage? Did Agnes tell him? And was she in on the blackmail? I imagine she would have welcomed a few quid every month."

"I don't think Agnes was the one who told him. I know how this sounds, Inspector, but Agnes is not a malicious person by nature."

"Then how would you describe her?" Sebastian asked. Perhaps Godfrey Price wasn't best placed to comment on someone's character.

"Unconventional, and a tad gullible. Her trusting nature often led her into potentially dangerous situations."

"Blackmail is as dangerous as it gets," Sebastian said. "Are you certain she wasn't involved?"

"I have no reason to think she was. But she may have unwittingly betrayed us."

"To Harrow?"

Godfrey Price shook his head wearily. "I don't know that Agnes ever knew Jacob Harrow, but she was close with another nurse. I suspect she confided in her."

"And you think this nurse was the one to tell Harrow?"

"It's the only possibility that makes sense."

"Why tell Harrow? She could have extorted you on her own."

"I don't think it was on her own initiative, but once presented with the idea she likely saw the advantages of such an arrangement. I'm certain Jacob Harrow did not give her an equal share. Perhaps just enough to keep her from walking away, but, as long as he was paying her, she would always be willing to testify that Agnes and I were indeed married. The two of them had the power to end my marriage to Joanna and destroy my surgical career. I would be untouchable if anyone found out."

"Do you think this woman will try to keep the blackmail going now that her accomplice is dead?" Sebastian asked.

"I sincerely hope not."

Sebastian flipped open his notebook and fixed Godfrey Price with an expectant look. "Her name?"

"Lydia. Lydia Morton."

Sebastian experienced a jolt of recognition. Lydia Morton was Gemma's friend. He had met her at Victor Tate's funeral, and now that he thought back he remembered her as being attractive. She had a sensual kind of charm, and she had struck him as the sort of woman who understood the power of her beauty, unlike Gemma, who was utterly oblivious to her allure.

"Lydia Morton?" Sebastian repeated, just to be sure.

"Yes. She's here in London. An acquaintance from Scutari has seen her. I hope you intend to question her, Inspector."

"Certainly I do, but right now I'm questioning you," Sebastian replied.

He couldn't quite believe the man could be so foolish as to marry two women and hope to get away with it, but people did mad things in times of war, and, as much as Sebastian wanted to judge Godfrey Price, he didn't seem the vindictive sort. Only reckless and easily manipulated.

"Where were you on Monday evening, Mr. Price?"

"I was here."

"Until what time?"

"I slept at the hospital. The matron and several nurses can vouch for me. I had performed an amputation late in the afternoon. The patient, a child of ten, had a gangrenous foot. It might have been saved had the parents brought him in sooner, but the infection had spread, and he would have died without the surgery."

"So, why did you have to stay the night?" Sebastian asked.

"A few hours after the surgery, Willie—that's the patient—developed a high fever, and the site of the amputation became swollen and inflamed. The matron sent a message to my home, asking me to return to the hospital. I monitored Willie throughout the night."

"Do you do that for all your patients, Mr. Price?"

Sebastian didn't have much personal experience of surgeons, but Colin Ramsey always complained about the butchery some surgeons resorted to and the unnecessary pain and suffering they inflicted on their patients, out of either ignorance or sheer indifference. They treated their patients like sides of beef, he would say, hacking at them until some of them died of shock, while others succumbed to postoperative infection and passed a few days later. A few survived, but perhaps, Ramsey thought, it wasn't due to the skill of the surgeon but the patient's strong constitution and even stronger will to live.

"Inspector Bell, hundreds of men died either on my operating table or on the ward post-surgery while I was in Crimea. That sort of loss leaves one either hardened beyond recognition or completely destroyed. Many surgeons of my acquaintance attributed the deaths to God's will, but I know that a good number of those who died could have been saved had the conditions been more sanitary and the surgical intervention timely. These days, I focus on one patient at a time, and I do everything in my power to help them. No ten-year-old should die because I had failed to do my very best to keep him alive."

"And is he alive?" Sebastian asked, hoping the child was on the road to recovery.

"Willie will be a cripple for the rest of his life, but he will have a life. Hopefully a long one."

"What time did you leave the hospital on Tuesday morning?"

"Around eight. I returned home, breakfasted, and had a few hours' kip before coming back to work."

"I will need to check your alibi, Mr. Price."

Godfrey Price nodded. "Of course. The matron is currently on the surgical ward."

"Is this yours, Mr. Price?" Sebastian asked as he pulled out the blue disk he'd taken from Harry Thayer and showed it to the surgeon.

Price looked confused. "No. What does it have to do with the case?"

"It was found on Jacob Harrow's body."

The surgeon shrugged. "Could be a Christmas ornament. Perhaps Harrow had purchased it that day."

The blue bauble was like no Christmas ornament Sebastian had ever seen, but he supposed it was possible. He returned the disk in his pocket and said, "I'd like to speak to the matron now."

"Please, follow me. I will introduce you," Godfrey Price said and strode from the room.

As they drew closer to the surgical ward, the air in the corridor became close, and Sebastian could smell blood and pus beneath the ever-present stench of carbolic. Someone was moaning softly, and a child in a cot near the door screamed in pain and called for his mother. Through the open door, Sebastian could see several nurses. They moved between the beds, their aprons covered with all manner of muck and their expressions blank in the face of the patients' suffering. They checked the dressings, adjusted pillows and blankets, and offered words of comfort to those who seemed in need of sympathy. The child stopped crying and stuffed a thumb in his mouth, looking at Sebastian from beneath tear-sodden lashes.

"If you'll just wait here," Godfrey Price said. "You're not allowed on the ward."

Sebastian had no wish to go any further. He waited in the corridor for Matron to come out to speak to him, but he kept his eye on the surgeon to make certain he didn't coerce the woman into lying for him. The conversation was brief, and the matron, who looked stern and efficient, glided toward the door.

By the time Sebastian left the hospital half an hour later, he had questioned the matron and two nurses who had been on duty Monday night. All three women swore blind that Godfrey Price had never left the hospital. Although Sebastian believed they had all seen him at some point on Monday night, he also realized that, if the surgeon had left the hospital for a few hours during the night, he could have crossed the river, killed Jacob Harrow, disposed of his body, and come back. The hospital was huge and, if Price had told the matron or the nurses he'd gone to another wing or had stepped out to check on his pregnant wife, they wouldn't think anything of it and would feel obligated to cover for him.

Godfrey Price had a compelling motive and could have created an opportunity, and for that reason Sebastian wasn't ready to dismiss him as a suspect. He saw no reason to take him into custody, since for the moment Price thought he was safe, but Sebastian had to speak to Lydia Morton sooner rather than later. The surgeon had no proof that Lydia was involved—his theory was based entirely on speculation—but he could be right. There were no payments made to Lydia from Jacob Harrow's account, but that meant nothing since he could have simply paid her in person.

Or maybe there had been no accomplice at all, only people who lacked discretion. If Agnes Frye had told Lydia about the marriage, Lydia could just as easily have told someone else, and they, in turn, could have passed it on until the news reached someone who saw a way to make use of the information. Sebastian would have to ask Gemma about Lydia, but he didn't think Gemma would be friendly with someone whose character was in doubt. Still, Lydia Morton was now on his list and, until he could rule her out, there she would remain. And he'd also inquire about Agnes Frye. Perhaps Gemma knew her too.

Sebastian pulled out his watch and checked the time. He'd call on Gemma at the Foundling Hospital, find out where Lydia Morton was employed, then return to Scotland Yard to check in with Constable Meadows and update Superintendent Lovell on his progress. And somewhere along the way, he'd have to grab something to eat. He was starving.

# SEVENTEEN

Sebastian met Gemma by the entrance to the Foundling Hospital just as she was leaving. Her obvious pleasure at seeing him again so soon wasn't lost on him, but he had no time to waste on pleasantries, not if he hoped to catch Superintendent Lovell still at his desk. Sebastian quickly filled Gemma in on what he had learned from Godfrey Price and, although she looked utterly scandalized and had her own questions, he couldn't take the time to answer them.

"I only have a few minutes," Sebastian explained as he offered Gemma his arm and drew her away from the entrance. He had no wish for their conversation to be overheard.

"What do you need to know?" Gemma asked, and Sebastian was relieved that she didn't seem offended by his brusqueness.

"Did you know Godfrey Price in Crimea?"

"Yes, I did. I assisted him many times. He's a competent surgeon and cares deeply about his patients."

"What about Agnes Frye?"

"I knew Agnes. I can't believe the two of them are married,"

Gemma exclaimed, lowering her voice mid-sentence as an elderly woman shot her a look of reproach as she passed.

"Where can I find Agnes? I need to speak to her," Sebastian said.

"I don't know. Agnes and I were never really friends," Gemma said.

Sebastian suspected she was just being tactful. "Not your sort?" he teased with a knowing smile.

"It's not that," Gemma said. "Living and working with someone nearly around the clock and in abominable conditions will sometimes foster intimacy, but, once the situation changes, sometimes there isn't much left to talk about. I never expected to remain in contact with Agnes once we arrived in England, and we had little to do with each other on the voyage back."

"You never suspected Agnes of having affairs?"

"I don't know how she found the time," Gemma replied.

"It doesn't take long," Sebastian said, and Gemma gave him a stern look that said, *You weren't there. You have no right to judge.* "Godfrey Price described Agnes Frye as gullible. Was she?"

"She was a bit naïve," Gemma said. "Idealistic. I think she probably gave her trust too easily."

"She could have placed her trust in Jacob Harrow. Do you think she might have been involved in blackmailing Godfrey Price?"

"I honestly couldn't say, Sebastian. What I have just learned of her proves that I didn't know her at all. She could have been taken in, or maybe her innocence was feigned and she was just looking for the perfect mark."

"And what about Lydia Morton, what sort of person is she?" Sebastian asked. He'd have to find a way to track down Agnes Frye on his own.

"Why do you ask?"

"She may have been involved," Sebastian admitted with some reluctance.

Gemma looked surprised, but didn't question his reasons for suspecting Lydia, possibly because she had recalled that he was under a time constraint and it would take too long to explain.

"Lydia is the sort who invites confidences but never reveals much about her own life. Do you think she could be in danger?" Gemma asked instead.

"She might be. How did she seem when you saw her this morning?"

Gemma sighed and averted her gaze. "Peevish. She advised me to stay well clear of you and your investigation."

"She must care about you," Sebastian replied.

He chose not to add that Lydia might have something to hide and probably feared that Gemma's involvement would invite undue scrutiny. Gemma would figure that out on her own now that she suspected that Lydia might know more than she let on. Sebastian had been surprised and then worried when he'd heard that Gemma had gone to see Lydia. It had been a kind thing to do and he was grateful that she wanted to help him, but, if Lydia was involved, now Gemma would be known to the killer and might be in danger.

"Godfrey Price is not capable of murder," Gemma stated with unwavering certainty.

"Everyone is capable of murder under the right circumstances," Sebastian replied. "Godfrey Price had a solid motive and, if he was the one to murder Jacob Harrow, anyone else who knows his secret could be in danger."

Gemma gave Sebastian a stubborn look. "Jacob Harrow was a despicable man but, if Godfrey married his current wife under false pretenses, then he has no one to blame but himself. He can hardly go murdering everyone who knows, especially now that he's known to you."

"I don't disagree, but if he was comfortable with the deception he might be just as comfortable with murder."

"Hardly the same thing," Gemma scoffed.

"Desperate people do desperate things. That's something that never changes."

"I suppose not." Gemma looked up at Sebastian, her expression stern. "Lydia is a competent nurse, and she needs the income, Sebastian."

"It's not my intention to make trouble for her. I only want to speak to her."

"I would hate to see her lose her place."

"If she's done nothing wrong, then she won't," Sebastian promised. "And one more thing."

He pulled the disk Harry had given him out of his pocket and showed it to Gemma. The object glowed blue in the light cast by the streetlamp, the black center staring like a malevolent eyeball. "This was in Jacob Harrow's pocket. Have you ever seen its like?"

"Yes, I have. In Scutari. It's an evil eye charm. A *nazar*," Gemma said softly. She reached out and ran a gloved finger along the outer edge of the disk.

"*Nazar?*" Sebastian repeated.

"That's what it's called in Turkish. The locals wear it for protection against evil, or mount it on walls or doorways. I saw the charms sold in the street."

"Godfrey Price didn't seem to know what it was."

"He rarely left the building, and I expect he had more pressing concerns on his mind when he did," Gemma replied.

"Did the English buy these charms?" Sebastian asked.

"Not that I noticed," Gemma said. "Do you think Jacob Harrow carried it with him for protection?"

"If he did, it had failed him utterly," Sebastian said. "It's also possible that the charm belongs to the killer, and he left it in Harrow's pocket. A calling card of sorts."

"Another connection to Scutari," Gemma observed.

"So it would seem. And now, I really must go."

Gemma nodded gravely. "Please, keep me informed."

"I will. And Gemma—" She gave him a look of such cherubic innocence that he had to assume she knew precisely what he was about to say. "Do not involve yourself in the investigation. Do you hear me?"

"I do."

"Do I have your word? We're dealing with dangerous people," he said, hoping he had impressed on her just how perilous her meddling could be.

"You have my word," Gemma replied solemnly.

"I will hold you to that."

"I know," Gemma said, a smile tugging at the corner of her mouth.

Sebastian would have loved to stay a little longer, but his personal desires would have to wait until this case was resolved to his satisfaction.

## EIGHTEEN

Gemma had almost reached the boarding house when she turned on her heel and walked the other way. She'd promised Sebastian that she wouldn't involve herself in the investigation, and she meant to keep that promise, but she had thought of something that could help and wouldn't be able to rest until she tested her theory. Besides, the errand she was about to undertake would not put her in any danger. It was simply an information-gathering expedition, and she wouldn't mention it to Sebastian unless she learned something that might be of use.

It took her twenty minutes to get to Clerkenwell, and then she hurried to Bowling Green Lane and spent another ten minutes looking for the visitors' entrance to Clerkenwell Prison. The prison was massive and held hundreds of prisoners, most of them awaiting trial at the Middlesex Sessions House, practically next door. When Gemma entered through the narrow door and presented herself to the guard on duty, he looked at her as if she had lost her mind.

"Visiting hours are over," the man said, his gaze roaming over Gemma's body in a way that made her distinctly uncomfortable. "But exceptions can be made," he added, now openly leering at her.

"I'm not here to visit a prisoner," Gemma said. "I need to speak to Miss Frisk. Is she still here?"

"No, she's not here," the man replied, his irritation mounting. "She's off home."

"Do you know where she lives?"

"And why would I tell you?"

"Please, sir, it's important that I speak to her. Miss Frisk and I know each other from Crimea. We were both nurses."

The man's eyebrows lifted a fraction, but Gemma thought she saw a glimmer of respect in his dark eyes. "You must have seen some awful things," he said, his tone softening. "My younger brother was wounded in Crimea. Had his leg shot clean off. He said if it wasn't for the dedication of the nurses, he never would have left that hospital alive or made it home."

"What was your brother's name?" Gemma asked.

"Peter Leghorn. Did you know him?"

Gemma could have lied and said that she had nursed Peter Leghorn, but she didn't believe in getting what she wanted by way of deceit. "No, I didn't know him, but I'm glad he survived."

"Me too," Mr. Leghorn said. He glanced toward the corridor to see if anyone was coming, then leaned closer and lowered his voice. "Miss Frisk rents a room at Mrs. Butler's lodging house in Clerkenwell Close. I reckon you'll find her at home."

"Thank you," Gemma said, and hurried out into the frigid darkness.

She didn't feel safe walking alone at night, but anything was better than being inside the prison. Even though she'd only seen the entryway, the dingy room had made her feel oppressed, and she could almost feel the desperation of those who'd passed through it, knowing they weren't going to leave unless their innocence was proven and they were released, or they were carried out in a pine box and buried in a pauper's grave. She hoped she'd never have reason to visit the prison again.

Gemma wasn't sure how Mary Frisk might feel about seeing her again. She and Mary had not stayed in touch once they'd returned to England and, if not for Lydia, Gemma would have had no idea where to find the woman. Lydia had managed to keep tabs on everyone, and although she didn't actively seek out their company, she still knew where they were all employed and how life was treating them now that they were back.

Mary Frisk had not been popular with the other nurses at Scutari. Even though the women had looked out for each other, as with any group of people there were divisions and vicious gossip. Small coteries had formed, with Agnes and Mary clinging to their own friends while Gemma had been closer with a different set of women. Lydia had easily moved between the two. That was one of her talents, and Gemma had always admired her for it. Although she was now aware of a quiet disloyal voice beginning to wonder how well she knew Lydia after all, and if she had been wise to trust her.

When she found Mrs. Butler's boarding house, Gemma knocked on the door and waited to be admitted. She suddenly felt very tired, and her feet were numb with cold. She might also miss supper if she didn't return to her own boarding house in time, since the landlady wasn't likely to keep anything back for her.

A woman of about sixty, presumably Mrs. Butler, opened the door and looked Gemma over, likely taking in her mourning attire and obvious fatigue.

"I don't have any rooms to let, lovey," she said, offering a sympathetic smile. "You can try Mrs. Reddick's two streets over."

"I'm not looking for a room. I would like to speak to Miss Frisk. Is she in?"

"She is." Mrs. Butler seemed a kind soul. She didn't leave Gemma to wait in the cold. "Come in and warm yourself in the parlor. I'll let Mary know you're here. What is your name?"

"Gemma Tate. Miss Frisk and I were nurses in Crimea together."

"I thought you had the look of a nurse about you," Mrs. Butler said.

"What look is that?" Gemma inquired.

"You all look jaded, lovey."

Gemma stood before the hearth and warmed her hands while Mrs. Butler went to fetch Mary Frisk. She hoped Mary wouldn't ask her to leave.

When Mary came into the parlor, Gemma was surprised by how much she'd changed. She had to be around forty-five now, but she could have been mistaken for a woman of sixty. Mary's hair was streaked with gray, lines of worry were etched into her face, and her shoulders were stooped, as if she carried a heavy burden.

"Gemma, it's lovely to see you," Mary said cautiously. "What brings you here?"

"Hello, Mary," Gemma said, and felt awful for coming to see Mary only because she needed help. "How have you been?"

The two women settled in worn chairs and faced each other, each taking stock of the other.

"Surviving," Mary Frisk said. "I was lucky to find work at the prison. It's a miserable place that sucks the life out of you, but it's steady work, and the wage is decent. It's difficult to find work when you get older," she explained. "Doctors prefer to be surrounded by pretty young girls that look up to them. No one wants the likes of me."

Gemma nodded in understanding. Pretty young nurses were frequently harassed by the doctors, who didn't think the women were worthy of respect. Some doctors belittled them and ordered them about as if they were skivvies; others went so far as to grope and even demand sexual favors from nurses who were too scared to complain for fear of losing their livelihood.

Mary smiled bitterly, revealing two missing teeth. "I might be old, but I'm not safe," she said. "There are guards who don't care what you look like. They'll take what they can get."

"Is there no one you can speak to?" Gemma asked, horrified by the treatment Mary had to endure just to keep a roof over her head.

"No one cares. They'll just find someone else. I see mostly to the guards," she said. "No one bothers to treat the prisoners. If they get hurt, they're left to bleed, and if they're sick they often sleep in their own vomit."

Gemma's hand flew to her mouth. "That's awful," she cried. "Do the governors of the prison know how the prisoners are treated?"

"Of course they do. Take my advice, Gemma. Don't ever break the law. Once you find yourself in a place like that, you'll pray for the good Lord to take you, because every day is worse than hell." Mary squinted at Gemma, and she thought that the woman probably needed spectacles. "I can only assume Lydia told you where I work. Is she all right?"

"Lydia is well. I saw her this morning."

"Has something happened?" Mary asked. Gemma still hadn't explained the reason for her visit, and Mary was becoming visibly anxious.

"Everything is all right, Mary. It's only that I urgently need to find Agnes. Do you know where she might be?"

"Agnes? Agnes Frye?"

"Yes. Are you in contact with her?"

"Did Lydia not tell you?"

"Tell me what?"

Mary shook her head. "Agnes is dead."

"How? When?" Gemma cried.

Mary sighed. "Agnes was always a bit daft, if you ask me,

but she'd really gone and done it when she followed her captain to Ireland."

"What captain?" Gemma asked.

"All I know is that he was in the 4th Royal Irish, and they had met in Crimea. Agnes did say that he was unhappily married, but being Catholic he was unable to obtain a divorce from his wife."

Mary spoke about adultery very casually, and Gemma wondered if she sympathized with Agnes's situation or if she simply didn't care. On further reflection, she decided Mary wasn't the sort to judge, not when she herself had been judged every day since returning from Crimea and probably found wanting, especially since she had no male relative to look after her and was forced to fend for herself.

"What happened?" Gemma asked.

"Agnes lived with him for a time, but then the good captain reconciled with his wife and left Agnes high and dry. She would have come back, but she was near her time and had to wait until her child was born. Died in childbirth, the poor lamb, the child with her."

"God rest her soul," Gemma said, and blinked away tears. Agnes must have been frightened and alone at the end, with no one there to look after her or offer words of comfort. "How do you know what happened?"

"Agnes asked her landlady to write to me should anything happen to her. I reckon she wanted someone to know, or it'd be as if she'd never even lived."

"What of her family?"

Mary shrugged. "I don't know that she had any."

"And the captain?"

"He saw them decently buried, but I expect he was glad to be rid of them both. Gone back to his old life, like nothing happened. It's good to be a man, ain't it?" Mary asked angrily. "Do what you want, hurt whomever you please, and still enjoy the blessings you were born with." She peered at Gemma in the light of the dying fire. "Why'd you need to find Agnes, anyway?"

Gemma rose to her feet. "It no longer matters. Thank you for telling me what happened."

Mary smiled mirthlessly. "I take it I won't be seeing you again?"

"Perhaps our paths will cross someday," Gemma replied noncommittally.

She felt desperately sorry for Mary and hoped life wouldn't be too unkind to her, but she understood the reality of the other woman's situation all too well. There wasn't much Mary could hope for, not at her age. The prospect of growing old and alone with no money to fall back on was not only terrifying but all too real. Gemma fled the boarding house and hurried home. She was back well before supper, but she was no longer hungry. Just scared, and sad.

# NINETEEN

Whitechapel reminded Sebastian of an ant heap, one that someone had kicked to see what would happen. He could recall doing that himself when he was a boy, and the result had been much the same. The streets were congested with wagons pulled by tired nags that refused to move, people who seemed to move in all directions at once, vendors with wheelbarrows and trays slung over their shoulders, and ragged-looking children who darted about, their grimy fingers quick to pick the pocket of anyone who wasn't careful with their purse. Two women, one of them nursing a busted lip and a black eye, were arguing loudly on a street corner, and a group of rowdy men, who were already in their cups despite the early hour, were barreling down the street and clearly looking for a fight. The streets were pungent with the reek of rotting vegetables, manure, and the yeasty sourness of spilled ale that wafted from the opening and closing doors of seedy taverns.

Sebastian lowered his head as he walked past the men, so as not to invite any aggression if he happened to look at them the wrong way. Despite his oath to uphold the law, he wasn't about to get in their way or try to keep the screaming women from pummeling each other. He had other business to attend to, and the killer he sought was infinitely more dangerous than a few rowdy drunks. Jacob Harrow's victims were like lambs led to the slaughter, paying month after month and praying that their secrets would remain safe. One victim had had enough, and, on Monday night, the hunter had become the hunted.

Even though Sebastian had identified several possible suspects, he had no physical evidence that linked any of them to the crime since the killer had been clever enough to cover his tracks. Some might say that the payments were proof enough, but the victims had been paying for years and might have continued to do so if Jacob Harrow hadn't been murdered. What Sebastian needed was evidence that would stand up in a court of law, not theories that could be easily disproved by a clever lawyer. If Lydia Morton was involved, she could fill in the blanks and help Sebastian narrow down the possibilities, but Lydia was a long shot, a woman who might or might not be a bridge between Sebastian and the killer.

As he strode down the street, Sebastian tried to block out the cacophony all around him and listen to his gut instinct, but it was frustratingly silent. The most likely suspect was Godfrey Price, but Sebastian didn't have enough evidence against him to make an arrest. The fact that he'd lied to his life partner, had stood up in church and sworn before God that there was no impediment to his marriage, wasn't enough to accuse him of murder. Sebastian would wait and see what Lydia Morton had to say before making a decision regarding Price. For the moment, he didn't think the surgeon was going anywhere. He had too much to lose.

The London Hospital wasn't as sprawling as Guy's, but it was still sizable for an institution located in such a densely populated part of London. It sat squat, solid, and surprisingly silent on the corner of Whitechapel Road. Sebastian approached the door and pulled the handle, but the door was locked, the windows dark.

"It's closed, mate," a man who appeared around the side of the building said. "They lock the doors at six."

"It's a hospital. How can it be closed?" Sebastian asked, dismayed that he was too late and wouldn't get the chance to speak to Lydia Morton this evening.

The man shrugged. "If they don't lock the doors, people will keep coming all night."

"What about the patients on the wards?"

"They get their supper, then it's lights out."

"And the nurses?" Sebastian asked.

"There are only a few nurses on the night shift, and one doctor."

"And how do you know this?"

"I'm one of the porters. Just heading home." He peered at Sebastian in the darkness. "You don't look too bad. I reckon whatever ails you can wait till tomorrow."

Sebastian sighed and turned away from the door. The man was right. It was after six, and Lovell had probably gone home as well. It had been a long, tiring day, and it was time Sebastian went home himself. He'd question Lydia Morton tomorrow.

# TWENTY
## THURSDAY, DECEMBER 16

Sebastian set off for the hospital directly after breakfast. When he arrived, he was relieved to see a steady stream of visitors, be they patients or family members and friends who'd brought them in. As soon as he entered the reception area, he was assaulted by the now-familiar smells of carbolic and illness. A stern-looking nurse sat behind a high counter, a thick register open before her, while a line of patients waited to speak to her. When Sebastian walked straight to the front, the nurse refused to listen and told him to get in line. Everyone had to wait their turn. No exceptions. It was another forty minutes before Sebastian finally reached the front of the line. The nurse looked at him and frowned.

"You don't look ill. Sign in and have a seat. It'll be a long wait to see a doctor."

"I'm not here to see a doctor," Sebastian said. He showed the nurse his warrant card. "I need to speak to one of the nurses. Lydia Morton."

"Lydia Morton?" the woman asked, as if she'd never heard the name.

"Yes. She does work here, does she not?"

"She does, but I haven't seen her today."

"Can I speak to the matron?" Sebastian asked.

The nurse nodded. "That would be Matron Healy. She's on the ward. I'll have someone ask her to come down. You can't go up," the nurse added, having noted Sebastian's obvious impatience.

"Why not? It'll be quicker than waiting for someone to get her."

"Because those are the rules," the nurse replied patiently. "Do you want to speak to Matron Healy or not, Inspector?"

"I do."

"Then take a seat and wait until she comes down."

There were two benches, every available space on them occupied by individuals who needed to be seen. One man suffered a coughing fit and then spat a gob of phlegm into the corner of the room. A girl of about fifteen sat rocking back and forth, moaning with pain, her arms wrapped around her stomach. A boy of about seven had thick, greenish snot leaking from his nose and dripping into his mouth, and his eyes were crusted with what looked like pus. The boy's mother wiped his mouth with a rag that was stiff with dried secretions. A laborer carefully cradled his arm, which was probably broken and obviously causing him great pain since he was pale as death, his forehead covered with perspiration.

A seat opened up, and Sebastian gestured to an elderly woman who'd come in after him. He didn't know what was ailing her, but she was swaying on her feet and clearly needed to sit down. Sebastian stood off to the side, close to the door, where a gust of fresh air blew in every time someone went in or out and dispelled the overpowering miasma. The nurse behind the counter beckoned over one of the porters, pointed to Sebastian, then sent the porter off to fetch Matron Healy.

It took more than a quarter of an hour for the woman to finally come down. She looked tired despite the early hour, her pinafore was stained, and strands of hair had come loose from her neat bun. She glanced around the waiting area, spotted Sebastian, and gestured for him to follow her. They didn't go far, only into an adjacent corridor where they could speak without an audience.

"I'm Matron Healy. How can I help you, Inspector?"

"I was hoping to have a word with Lydia Morton."

"Miss Morton didn't come to work today," the matron replied crisply, looking annoyed.

"Is it her day off?"

"Her day off is on Sunday. If she's ill, she should have sent word. One more unexcused absence and she will lose her place."

"Has she been unwell?" Sebastian asked.

"She looked perfectly fine to me the last time I saw her. I expect she had some personal business to attend to." A spark of anger flared in the matron's dark gaze. "These nurses who've come back from Crimea think they know it all. They challenge the doctors and look down on the rest of us, as if all we're fit to do is take out nightsoil and make tea for the doctors. I've been doing this my whole life," Matron Healy went on. "And I won't have the likes of her undermining me at every turn."

"No, I don't expect you will," Sebastian said. He wondered if Lydia knew how close she was to losing her job. "Is Miss Morton a competent nurse?"

"She knows what she's about. I'll give her that," Matron Healy said grudgingly. "And she has a way with the patients. They open up to her."

"Would you know where Miss Morton lives?"

Matron Healy nodded. "She rents a room at Mrs. Bede's boarding house, 123 Brick Lane."

"Thank you, Matron."

"If you speak to her, you tell her that if she's not here sharpish tomorrow she shouldn't bother to come back."

"I will."

Sebastian was eager to get outside. The air was far from fresh, especially since a pile of steaming horseshit had just been deposited by a passing nag, but it was less malodorous than the air at the hospital, and the cold was pleasantly bracing. He walked briskly toward Brick Lane, all the while wondering why Lydia Morton hadn't shown up for work or sent a message. The lodging house wasn't far from the hospital, and there was usually someone willing to take a message if the person was too ill to leave the house. Might Lydia have read the papers and decided to lie low? Had anyone else been blackmailed by Jacob Harrow? And was it possible that Lydia was a victim rather than a possible accomplice?

Sebastian located the correct address and used the tarnished brass knocker to announce his presence. As he waited for someone to come to the door, he reflected that the boarding house looked grim and inhospitable. The grimy windows glinted dully in the afternoon light, and the step was cracked in several places, as was the soot-stained brickwork. There were shingles missing from the roof, and the smell of boiled cabbage wafted through the crack beneath the door. No smoke curled from the chimney pots above; the landlady apparently economized on coal while the lodgers were out.

A rail-thin, dark-haired woman in her forties answered the door. Her hair was scraped back from her face, and her puffy eyes drooped at the corners as if she hadn't slept in days. She wore a shabby gray gown, and her hands were red and chapped, presumably from endless housework. Sebastian couldn't smell any fumes on her breath, but the puffiness in her face and the spiderweb of broken capillaries in her nose and cheeks spoke to a fondness for strong drink, and he was sure that, if he looked, he'd find a bottle of gin in her room.

"No men allowed," the woman said, her voice lacking inflection.

"I'm Inspector Bell of Scotland Yard. Are you the landlady?"

"That I am. Mathilda Bede."

"I need to speak to one of your lodgers, Mrs. Bede."

"Which one? Most of them are out just now."

"Miss Morton. She didn't come in to work today, so presumably she's at home."

Mrs. Bede nodded. "She's in 'er room. I reckon she's ill. Didn't come down for breakfast neither, and she were retching last night, so ye'd better watch yerself, Inspector. Could be catching."

"Thank you for the warning," Sebastian said.

He wouldn't be at all surprised if Lydia had caught some ailment at the hospital. There was always sickness going about, more so in the winter months when it was so easy to catch a chill or come down with a fever.

The landlady stepped aside to allow Sebastian to enter, then showed him to a small parlor that faced the street. The room was clean but a bit shabby, with worn settees, faded wallpaper, and bare floorboards. If Lydia Morton was engaged in blackmail, she was doing a fine job of keeping her clandestine income secret. The place was drab, and Sebastian suddenly had a new appreciation for Mrs. Poole's establishment, which although not exactly luxurious was at least cozy and well maintained.

Mrs. Bede left Sebastian and went to inform Lydia that she had a visitor, while Sebastian made himself comfortable in one of the chairs. His stomach reminded him that he hadn't eaten since breakfast, which had consisted of nothing but toast and marmalade. After he spoke to Lydia Morton, he'd grab something to eat. He'd seen a street vendor selling soup that she ladled from a large, covered pot. Sebastian thought it might be pea soup, which he liked; but he didn't think that'd be enough to tide him over till supper. A hot pie, then, he decided, and his mouth watered at the prospect.

He turned toward the door when he heard footsteps in the corridor, but it was the landlady.

"Lydia's not answering the door. Locked it from the inside. Likely sleeping it off, whatever she's got."

"Do you have a key?" Sebastian asked as he pushed to his feet.

"I 'ad a spare, but I lost it. What d'ye need a key for?" Mrs. Bede asked, her eyes narrowing in suspicion.

Ordinarily, Sebastian would simply come back later, but this time his instinct tolled like a church bell, telling him that Lydia Morton wasn't answering because she wasn't able to get to the door. He didn't have his lock pick on him, so he would have to break in; but he couldn't put his shoulder to the door without causing his healing clavicle irreparable harm. He'd need someone to help him.

"I'll be back shortly," he told Mrs. Bede. "In the meantime, try to find that key."

Back in the street, Sebastian headed toward the Whitechapel police station to request assistance. He was nearly at the corner when he spotted a familiar figure, dressed in a blue constable's uniform and tall top hat, striding purposefully down the opposite side of the street.

"Constable Haze," Sebastian called out, and waved to get the young man's attention.

Daniel Haze turned and peered in Sebastian's direction, clearly surprised to be hailed by name. Having recognized Sebastian, he waited for an opening in the traffic, then hurried across the street. Haze smiled, his brown gaze warm behind the fogged-up lenses of his spectacles and his cheeks ruddy with cold. "Inspector Bell. I'm glad to see you up and about. I heard you were badly injured during your last investigation."

"Thank you, Constable. I'm quite recovered, but I am in need of urgent assistance."

"How can I help?" Constable Haze asked. His eyes radiated sincerity and an eagerness to be helpful, and Sebastian thanked his lucky stars that he'd run into him.

"I need you to break down a door."

If Haze was surprised, he didn't show it. "Lead the way."

"How's Mrs. Haze?" Sebastian asked as he guided the constable to Mrs. Bede's boarding house. Last time Sebastian had seen Daniel Haze, the young man had confided that he was to become a father in the spring.

Daniel Haze beamed. "Sarah is well. Thank you for asking. She would like to go home to Essex for Christmas. She says it's not Christmas unless she can decorate a tree with the baubles her father bought her when she was a girl and attend the Christmas service at St. Catherine's. That's where she was christened and where we were married," he explained.

"I hope you mean to take her," Sebastian said, and felt his heart squeeze with sadness. Since Louisa's death, he'd spent every holiday alone and hadn't bothered to go to church. What he wouldn't give to spend the day with his family; but the only way he could do that was if he spent Christmas in a graveyard.

"I do. I'm looking forward to going home for a few days," Constable Haze said. "I haven't seen my mother in months, and Sarah misses her parents as well. They'd welcome a chance to spoil her."

"I might be going to Essex myself," Sebastian said. "I need to interview someone in Brentwood."

"That's not far from Birch Hill, where I grew up," Haze said. "Have you ever heard of it?"

"I'm afraid not, but I'm sure it's a fine place," Sebastian replied.

"It is, but not much call for a policeman in a village that small. And there's already a parish constable."

They had reached the boarding house, and Sebastian knocked on the door once more. Mrs. Bede let them in and did not prevent them from going upstairs. Instead, she led the way and pointed to Lydia Morton's door. Sebastian knocked, then called out Lydia's name several times. There was no answer, and the silence beyond had a hollow quality, as if the room was empty of human presence. Sebastian turned to Mrs. Bede, who was anxiously hovering by the stairs.

"Are you certain Miss Morton hasn't left? Perhaps you were busy in the kitchen or stepped out to the necessary. It doesn't sound as if anyone is inside."

Mrs. Bede shook her head. "I 'eard 'er moving about last night, and I didn't see 'er leave today. I'd 'ave noticed. Besides, she'd 'ave wanted 'er breakfast before she went out."

"All right, then," Sebastian said, and gestured to Constable Haze.

"Be careful, Constable," Mrs. Bede cried. "I can ill afford to replace the door." She was twisting her hands in agitation, and Sebastian hoped he wasn't making an error of judgment. He thought Lydia Morton could probably have slid past the landlady if she didn't wish to be seen. Perhaps she'd fled London, having heard the news about Jacob Harrow, or maybe there was something else entirely on her agenda.

Daniel Haze stood back, then rammed his shoulder into the door. The flimsy lock didn't stand a chance; the door burst open, leaving both the door and the doorjamb intact, to the landlady's great relief. Inside, all was quiet and still. Even if Lydia had been sleeping, the sound of the crashing door would have woken her, unless she was too ill to stand or call out. The living space consisted of a tiny sitting room and a bedroom, much like Sebastian's own lodgings at Mrs. Poole's. The sitting room was tidy, and frigid. The ashes in the grate were cold and smelled acrid. If there had been a fire lit last night, it had long since burned out.

Sebastian approached the bedroom door and knocked loudly. "Miss Morton? Are you in there?" he called. There was no answer, so he tried the doorknob. It turned easily, and he pushed the door open. The room beyond was dark, the curtains drawn against the bright light of the winter afternoon. Sebastian had expected to find the room empty, but Lydia Morton was in bed, her fair hair spread on the pillow. She would have looked like she was sleeping if her chin weren't covered in blood, her skin bluish in the light from the open door.

"Lord preserve us," Mrs. Bede moaned when she took in the body. "What's she gone and done to 'erself?"

"Perhaps it's best if you wait outside, Mrs. Bede," Sebastian said before moving further into the room. He was glad Constable Haze was there to assist him.

"All right," Mrs. Bede conceded. "I'll just be in the kitchen should ye need me."

"Thank you," Sebastian said. "Please don't say anything if anyone returns."

Mrs. Bede shook her head. "I won't. It's too awful, this," she muttered.

Sebastian waited until she had left, then opened the curtains to let in more light and approached the bed. Lydia looked peaceful, her eyes closed, her lashes fanned across her cheeks. Her face was turned upward, as if she had been looking at someone when she died, and if not for the blood Sebastian might have thought she'd died in her sleep. He carefully pulled down the counterpane and took in Lydia's body. She lay on her back, her arms at her sides, and wore a plain, high-necked nightdress that showed signs of wear. Her throat was bruised above the neckline, and there were fingermarks just below her ears. Whoever had strangled her had used only one hand to choke the breath from her body.

Sebastian didn't see any obvious wounds or lacerations below the neck, so he turned his attention to Lydia's face. He used his thumb to pull down the chin and peered inside her mouth. The tongue was missing, the appendage cleanly severed at the base. Sebastian was distracted from his examination by the sound of gagging, and turned around to find Daniel Haze retching into the chamber pot.

"It's in the glass," Constable Haze choked out after he had set down the pot and wiped his mouth with the back of his hand.

Sebastian followed Haze's gaze, and then he saw it. A severed tongue was floating in a glass of water that stood on the bedside table. The water had turned pink from the tiny amount of blood that must have oozed out in the intervening hours. The glass seemed to magnify the organ and made it appear grotesquely distorted and too large to fit into the mouth of the woman who no longer had need of it.

"Are you all right, Constable?"

Daniel Haze nodded. "I'm sorry, Inspector. I'm afraid I was taken unawares."

"Happens to the best of us," Sebastian assured him.

He felt a bit queasy himself, but thought Colin Ramsey would want to examine the severed tongue. He looked around for something to use, then spotted an embroidered velvet reticule hanging from the back of a chair. Inside was a clean handkerchief, a small coin purse that still held a few bob, a tortoiseshell comb, and a thin, black address book.

Did Lydia carry the book with her because she thought she might need to leave in a hurry and would require the address of a friend she could seek refuge with, or because she worried about keeping the information safe? And if she did want to keep the book from falling into the wrong hands, was it because she was worried for her friends or terrified that she'd be tracked down by whoever was in pursuit? It was impossible to know now that the woman was dead, but it might help him to have a record of the individuals she'd kept in contact with.

Sebastian opened the book and flipped through the pages. His heart grew cold when he realized that several sheets had been torn out. The missing names began at the letter L and went through T. The next page in the address book was devoted to surnames beginning with the letter U. Someone was now in possession of Gemma's name and address, and, if Lydia had been a diligent recordkeeper, she would have updated the information when Gemma moved into the boarding house in Birkenhead Street. Even if she hadn't, though, Gemma would be easy enough to find. She had left a forwarding address with her former landlord, should she receive any post or in case someone came looking for her.

Sebastian shoved the book into his pocket and helped himself to the handkerchief. He spilled out the liquid into the chamber pot and used the handkerchief to wrap the tongue, which he left near the glass until he was finished with the reticule. He had hoped there might be a secret pocket or perhaps a slit in the lining that could conceal a letter or anything else that might tell him what Lydia Morton had been up to, but he found nothing.

Placing the tongue in the reticule, he left it on the chair and strode toward the window. He'd noted that it was firmly shut when he'd opened the curtains, but now he needed to take a closer look. Unless the killer had got in through the front door, the only other way into the room would be through the casement window. Lydia's room faced the back of the house, and the window was about twenty feet off the ground, but a drainage pipe ran alongside the corner of the building, which was close to the window. Sebastian opened the window and leaned out. He held on to the windowpane to retain his balance, and used his right hand to grab hold of the pipe and pull hard. The pipe held fast, a testament to some builder's craftsmanship.

It was sturdy enough to support an adult and would make it relatively easy for someone intent on breaking in to scramble up, push open the window, and climb in, then shimmy back down. The person would have to be agile, but even a novice housebreaker could manage it if they were intelligent enough to conceive of the plan and assess the pipe before beginning to climb.

Sebastian peered at the ground below but saw no footprints or any other noticeable disturbance. For the second time that week, he wished it had rained so he would have something tangible to work with. He could hardly identify the intruder by their footprints, but it would help to know if it was a man, a woman, or a child, and if there was just one person or several. The earth was too dry to tell him anything.

"Is there anything I can do to help?" Constable Haze asked.

Sebastian shut the window and turned to Haze. His normal color had returned, and he was looking around with renewed interest, probably hoping to spot a clue Sebastian had missed.

"Constable Haze, I need you to find me a wagon."

"To take the body to the city mortuary?" Daniel Haze asked, already moving toward the door.

"I'm taking her to my own surgeon. Tell the driver he's to go to Blackfriars. And while I wait, I am going to search Miss Morton's belongings and see if I can find anything that can help me identify her killer."

"Do you think she was murdered by the same person that killed Jacob Harrow?" Constable Haze asked, his gaze sliding toward the reticule.

"I believe she was, Daniel. I believe she was."

Sebastian pulled out his pocket watch and checked the time. He'd deliver the body to Colin, then go to see Gemma. It was only right that he told her about Lydia in person and alerted her to possible danger. The thought of Gemma galvanized him into action. The only way to keep her safe was to solve this confounding case before the killer set his sights on the woman who had been Lydia's friend and confidante.

# TWENTY-ONE

As soon as Constable Haze left, Mrs. Bede burst in, looking distinctly wild-eyed. "I want 'er out of 'ere, Inspector. All me lodgers will leave if they find out she were murdered on the premises. It's dangerous enough for a woman out on 'er own, but to be murdered in yer own bed, why that's enough to chill yer blood, that is."

"I will have the body removed as quickly and as quietly as I can, Mrs. Bede," Sebastian promised. "In the meantime, I need to ask you a few questions. Why don't we speak in the other room," he suggested when he saw Mrs. Bede's gaze darting toward Lydia's supine form.

Mrs. Bede nodded and followed Sebastian into Lydia's sitting room, where she sank into a chair. Sebastian took the only other chair, pulled out his notebook, and faced the frightened woman. "Who owns the building, Mrs. Bede?"

"Mr. Ellington."

"Does Mr. Ellington come here often?"

Mrs. Bede shook her head. "Been a few months now since I seen 'im."

"So how does he collect the rents?" Sebastian asked.

"'E sends 'is son. The boy's thirteen," Mrs. Bede added.

"When was the last time the rents were collected?"

"December first."

"So neither Ellington has been here since?"

"No. I 'xpect the boy will come in the new year."

"Do the Ellingtons keep a key to the front door and the tenant rooms?"

"Mr. Ellington 'as a key to the front door, but the lodgers' keys are kept 'ere," Mrs. Bede replied.

"Do the Ellingtons use their own key to enter the building?"

"No, never. Silas, that's their boy, 'e always knocks."

Sebastian made note of this, then continued. "How many lodgers do you have, Mrs. Bede?"

"Six, including Miss Morton, that were. I don't rightly know what I'll tell the others," she lamented, shaking her head. "Can 'ardly tell 'em she up and left."

"The others will have to be told," Sebastian said.

"Why?" Mrs. Bede wailed.

"Because I need to speak to them."

"Must ye, Inspector? They'll be too frightened to shut their eyes at night."

"I'm sorry, but I must. They may have seen or heard something."

"Like what?" Mrs. Bede asked.

"Whoever killed Lydia Morton might have come in through the door," Sebastian said.

"No. They couldn't 'ave!" Mrs. Bede cried. "The door's kept locked, and I'm the only one as answers it when someone comes calling." It took her a moment to catch on, but then she exclaimed, "No. It couldn't be one of me lodgers. They're not capable of doing such violence."

"May I have the names of your lodgers, Mrs. Bede?"

The landlady nodded but wouldn't meet Sebastian's eye. Her hands were shaking in her lap, and she looked like she was going to be ill. And who wouldn't be terrified? A young woman had been murdered while she slept, her tongue severed and left floating in a glass. Sebastian wished he could reassure Mrs. Bede that she was safe and that the killing had nothing to do with her or her boarding house, but he couldn't. Not until he knew more.

It was possible that the killer had come in through the window and had targeted Lydia Morton because of her association with Jacob Harrow. If she had been in on Harrow's extortion racket, she'd needed to be silenced in order to put an end to their scheme once and for all. But even if that were true, it was also plausible that the killer was within. She might have done the killing herself, or let someone in at the appointed hour, either because they were acquainted or because she had been threatened and feared for her life. She might also have been handsomely paid to open the door and turn a blind eye.

And there was also a third possibility. Lydia Morton's death might have no connection to Jacob Harrow at all, and the killer might have decided to sever the tongue and leave it where it was sure to be found in order to mislead the police and cover their own tracks. The clever misdirection would immediately connect the two crimes in the minds of not only the police but also the public, who were sure to come to their own conclusions based on suggestions from the newspapers, which would make much of the similarities and try the case in the court of public opinion. At this stage Sebastian had no idea if the two deaths were linked, but he couldn't ignore the fact that the victims had known each other, and they had both been very obviously silenced. Jacob Harrow and Lydia Morton had also known Gemma, which was very worrying.

"Mrs. Bede, the names," Sebastian asked again. "Time is of the essence." That seemed to shake the landlady out of her malaise.

"Hester Grint, Eva Taylor, Annie Leyton, Barbara Wicklow, and Penny Lake," Mrs. Bede recited dutifully.

"And was Lydia Morton on good terms with the rest of the women?"

Mrs. Bede shrugged. "She were cordial."

"Was she close with anyone?"

"Only Barbara Wicklow. They was friendly-like."

"When would be the best time to find everyone at home?"

"I serve supper at seven. They're all 'ere by then. Can I go now?" Mrs. Bede asked. She looked a decade older than when Sebastian had arrived, and he thought she might cry, but he couldn't let her leave just yet.

"I just need to ask you a few more questions. It will help me catch whoever did this," he explained.

Mrs. Bede nodded reluctantly. "Go on, then."

"Did Miss Morton seem frightened or upset recently?"

"Not that I saw."

"Did you happen to notice if someone was watching the house?" Sebastian asked.

"No, but then I weren't looking, was I? How could I know this would 'appen to poor Lydia? I'm not clairvoyant, Inspector."

Mrs. Bede's fear and shock were beginning to turn into anger and dismay, which meant that her goodwill toward him was rapidly coming to an end. A rant against the police service was sure to follow since it was human nature to seek someone to pin the blame on. Mrs. Bede could hardly blame Lydia, although there were those who blamed the victim, and the killer had yet to be identified. But Sebastian was there, before her, and he represented the police's failure to keep her and her premises safe from a faceless enemy.

"Did Lydia have any gentlemen callers?" Sebastian asked.

"No, but that don't mean she weren't seeing someone, does it?"

"No, it doesn't."

"This would never 'ave 'appened if ye 'ad more men on the streets. Just cause we 'ere in Whitechapel are poor don't mean we don't matter. I wager no one comes through the windows in bleeding Belgravia or Mayfair, do they? No, it's us that's 'elpless as little lambs. And it's us that suffer 'cause the police is there only to protect the wealthy," Mrs. Bede ranted.

"Mrs. Bede, I will do everything I can to find the killer and bring them to justice, but I can't do that without your help. You have the power to see them hang."

"Do I?" Mrs. Bede asked, her confusion obvious.

"I lodge in a boarding house myself, and I know that a capable landlady sees everything and knows what goes on. I can see you are a clever and observant woman. Surely you must have noticed something. It could be your testimony that helps me to unmask the killer."

Mrs. Bede sat up straighter and looked Sebastian in the eye. "Ye reckon, Inspector?"

"I do," Sebastian said, nodding gravely. "I'm lost without you."

Mrs. Bede squared her shoulders like a soldier going into battle. "I'll tell ye all I know."

"Good. Now, tell me about Lydia."

"She kept 'erself to 'erself. Most of them do."

"Why's that?" Sebastian asked.

"This is not the sort of place women want as a permanent 'ome, now is it? They still 'ave 'opes of making a better life for theirselves. Once they start settling in and making friends, they feel like they'll never leave."

Sebastian nodded. He could understand that. The thought of living in Mrs. Poole's boarding house for the rest of his life was more soul-crushing than he cared to admit, and he couldn't help but wonder if his German neighbor, from whom he had inherited his cat, Gustav, had died of loneliness and if he would have minded if he knew that he'd be buried in London and not in his native Bavaria. Sebastian thought Herr Schweiger would be glad to know that Gustav had found a new home with Sebastian and was well cared for.

"Did Miss Morton have any family?" Sebastian asked. He hoped someone would claim the body and make sure the victim was decently buried. If Lydia had no one, she would end up serving as a teaching tool for Colin Ramsey and then end her brief and unfortunate journey in a pauper's grave.

Mrs. Bede shrugged. "I don't know. She may 'ave, but she never mentioned naught to me."

"When was the last time you saw her?"

"Last night, 'bout eight."

"How did she seem these past few days?" Sebastian asked.

"Don't know. All right, I s'pose. She'd been looking tired."

"For how long?"

"A few weeks. I reckon she were under the weather. I 'aven't been feeling me best meself. This cold and damp gets right in yer bones. Mr. Ellington, 'e's not generous with coal."

Sebastian nodded. The house was cold and damp, but it made little sense to heat the rooms while the lodgers were at work. As long as Mrs. Bede remained in the kitchen, next to the range, she'd be warm enough throughout the day.

"Did Lydia receive any post?" Sebastian was running out of questions to ask the landlady, but he had yet to learn anything that might move his investigation along.

"She received a letter from time to time."

"Who from?" Sebastian asked.

"I don't snoop on me lodgers, Inspector. Never looked at the name. Not me business."

Sebastian fixed Mrs. Bede with a cold stare. "I find it hard to believe you never noticed the name. Who were the letters from, Mrs. Bede?"

The landlady sighed, realizing he wasn't going to let it go. "J. Harrow."

"Was there a return address?"

"No. Just 'is name."

So, the letters could have been either from Jacob or James Harrow; but, given what Sebastian knew, it was more likely they were from Jacob. "I need to search these rooms."

"Go on, then," Mrs. Bede said with obvious resignation, but made no move to leave.

"I'd prefer to do it in private."

"She owed me money for extra coal, she did."

"That's nothing to do with me," Sebastian replied.

"Well, I can't let ye take 'er till the debt's been paid."

"You've changed your tune."

Sebastian was certain that Lydia did not owe Mrs. Bede money, but this was the landlady's only chance to profit from the tragedy and she wasn't about to give up, not when there was money to be made that would never wind up in Mr. Ellington's pocket. "Would you prefer that I leave her here until she starts to leak? What will your lodgers say then?"

Mrs. Bede looked horrified, but Sebastian wasn't about to back down. He would make sure to take Lydia's coin purse with him and contribute whatever money she had to her burial.

"No, ye take 'er, Inspector. I'm sure Mr. Ellington will understand," Mrs. Bede finally conceded.

"I'm sure he will," Sebastian agreed.

Mrs. Bede turned on her heel and walked out, shutting the door carefully behind her. She was probably grateful there was still a door to shut.

Alone at last, Sebastian returned to the bedroom and turned his attention to the victim. She had either been in bed or getting ready for bed when the intruder entered her room. He or she must have taken Lydia by surprise—or perhaps she had already been asleep, making the killer's task easier; by the time she had begun to suffocate and woke, it would have been too late to do anything to save herself. Otherwise, the other lodgers might have heard her scream as she tried to fight off her assailant.

Sebastian took Lydia by the chin and turned her face toward him. Given the amount of blood on her chin and neck, he thought that perhaps the killer had severed her tongue immediately before her death, while the blood was still pumping, then dropped the appendage into the glass. Perhaps Lydia had been unconscious, or maybe she had been unable to cry out. He'd have to ask Colin which had come first, strangulation or the removal of the tongue.

Letting go of Lydia's face, Sebastian pulled down the counterpane and looked more closely at the body and the state of the bed. Lydia Morton was tall for a woman and looked healthy and strong. Whoever had overpowered her had to be tall and strong as well, and straddling her would give them an additional advantage. Sebastian searched for indentations in the mattress where the killer might have planted their knees, but saw nothing to support his theory. But something else caught his eye. He ran his hand over Lydia's nightdress, pressing the loose fabric closer to her body. Lydia had a small, rounded belly that was taut, either with rigor or with pregnancy. At this stage, possibly both.

Sebastian rested his palm at the center of the bump, and a memory, so sharp it nearly brought tears to his eyes, swam before him. He recalled placing his hand on Louisa's belly and feeling their child move within, Louisa smiling joyfully before putting her hand over his. How happy they'd been, and how innocent of what was to come. Sebastian pushed the painful memory away and forced himself to concentrate on the woman before him. If Lydia Morton was with child, then somewhere out there was a man who had put it there.

If Jacob Harrow had been Lydia's only correspondent, it was quite possible that he was the father, which gave Emma

Harrow a powerful motive to kill them both. She wouldn't have done it herself; there was no way she could have overpowered either victim—but, if Jacob Harrow had given her a generous allowance, she could have easily found someone to do the deed and then staged the break-in in the study.

"Oh, what a tangled web we weave," Sebastian muttered as he covered the body and turned away from the bed.

# TWENTY-TWO

There wasn't much in the way of personal possessions in the sitting room. Sebastian checked everywhere, including inside the chimney breast and beneath the furniture. Living in a lodging house, Lydia might not have wanted to leave personal items on display, but there were always convenient hiding places if one had a mind to conceal something. Likewise, he found nothing of interest in the bedroom. There was Lydia's nurse uniform, two gowns, one serviceable and well-worn and the other made of deep-blue silk and probably worn only on very special occasions. There was a pair of sensible brown shoes and another pair of black lace-up boots. A navy-blue woolen cloak and a matching bonnet hung on a peg by the door.

Sebastian rifled through Lydia's undergarments, collars, and plain cotton stockings, but found nothing of interest. If she had kept a journal or had saved her correspondence, it wasn't there. He walked the length and breadth of both rooms, examining every floorboard to see if perhaps there was a hiding place beneath the floor, but there was no obvious change in sound that would indicate a hollow space. Perhaps Lydia hadn't kept anything of a personal nature, or perhaps the killer had taken the items with them. There was no way to know for certain.

Sebastian groaned with frustration. He needed something to go on, but all he had was a body. Not even a bloodied knife or muddy footprints. Whoever had done this was mindful and clever, which, to Sebastian, did not point to a hired thug but to someone who was careful to protect their identity while deriving the greatest amount of pleasure from their kill.

"The wagon is downstairs, Inspector," Constable Haze said as he entered Lydia's rooms. "You'll need to pay the driver," he added apologetically.

"Thank you, Constable. If you would just help me bring the body outside."

"Of course." The constable's gaze went to Sebastian's shoulder. "I can get her down, Inspector. You shouldn't be doing any heavy lifting, what with the injury and all."

"Have you ever lifted a dead body, Daniel?" Sebastian asked.

Daniel Haze shook his head.

"They're heavier than you might expect. You won't be able to get her down the stairs and through the door on your own."

"Then why don't you wait with the wagon and send the driver up? He's a burly fellow. He'll help me get the job done."

As much as Sebastian wanted to protest, he had to admit that Daniel Haze had a point. Lifting Lydia Morton's body would probably set his recovery back by several weeks, and his shoulder was already aching dully after two days of walking for hours and being jolted in cabs. Sebastian suppressed a smile when he thought of what Gemma would say. *Stop playing the hero* was a phrase that sprang to mind. "Thank you, Constable. I'll take your suggestion," he said.

He wrapped the body in the blanket and carefully tucked in the ends, then picked up Lydia's reticule and went downstairs to speak to the driver. The man, who was nearly as wide as he was tall, wasn't happy with Sebastian's request, but a half-crown sorted him out and he headed inside, leaving Sebastian to mind the wagon.

Once the body was safely stowed in the wagon bed, Sebastian climbed onto the bench next to the driver and directed him to Colin Ramsey's house in Blackfriars. The driver didn't seem to care that he was transporting a body but appeared mortally offended to be sharing a bench with a copper and made his feelings known. Words like *useless swine, bluebottle,* and *clodhopper* were muttered under his breath, but Sebastian ignored him. He was lost in his own thoughts, his mind on the case and all the loose threads that had revealed themselves in the past few days, and how they might relate to each other.

When they arrived at their destination, Sebastian left the driver to wait while he explained the situation to Colin and asked him to open the cellar door. The unexpected arrival of human remains no longer shocked Colin, but the identity of the victim seemed to surprise him. He disappeared inside, leaving Mabel to shut the door, then exited via the cellar and approached the wagon. Colin grabbed Lydia Morton's body by the legs while the driver hefted the shoulders, and together they got the body down to the cellar and onto the dissecting table. Sebastian followed them to the cellar, eager to have a word with Colin.

"I need you to wait for me," Sebastian said to the driver before the man headed back out into the street.

"What d'ye think, I'm a bleeding cab?" the man retorted.

"I'll pay you."

"To do what? I've already carried yer corpse."

"I need a ride," Sebastian said. "Just give me a moment."

"Fine. But I ain't waiting long."

"Two minutes," Sebastian said, and turned to Colin, who was already unwrapping the body.

"Can you autopsy her today?"

"I'm sorry, but I have a prior engagement. I'm giving a talk at the Royal College of Surgeons," Colin said proudly. "I'll perform the postmortem first thing tomorrow. Come by around ten?"

Sebastian handed him the reticule. "Her tongue's inside," he said.

"Of course it is," Colin muttered.

"There's also a coin purse. The money is to pay for her funeral if no one comes forward to claim the body."

"I'll see it done," Colin promised.

"Till tomorrow, then."

Colin didn't reply. He wasn't ready to begin the post-mortem, but he was clearly intrigued and eager to take a peek. Sebastian left Colin to it and exited the cellar, shutting the door behind him. He half expected to find the wagon gone, but it was still there, the driver's shoulders hunched and his gaze fixed on something in the distance.

"Take me to Scotland Yard," Sebastian said once he'd climbed onto the bench.

"They have hansoms for that," the driver grumbled.

"You want the money or not?"

Sebastian could find a hansom, but it would take time, and he had to speak to Constable Meadows, brief Superintendent Lovell, find something to eat, and then return to Mrs. Bede's to deal with the lodgers.

# TWENTY-THREE

The duty room was chaos, with several constables attempting to subdue two men who were trying to kill each other and spouting the sort of obscenities Sebastian hadn't heard in a long while. Sergeant Woodward was watching the melee with amusement from behind the counter, while Constable Hammond, trying to get cuffs on one of the men, had just taken a punch to the gut and was doubled over in pain. Constable Bryant retaliated by punching the man in the face. He had a wicked right hook, and the man was thrown against the wall on impact, his head colliding with the plasterwork with an audible crack. Constable Hammond was quick to twist the man's arms behind his back and get the cuffs on before he could regain his equilibrium and go for the constable, while the second miscreant, infuriated by what he probably perceived as police brutality, charged the two constables.

"Should we help them out?" Sebastian asked Sergeant Woodward.

"Nah, they have it all under control."

"Where's Meadows?"

Sergeant Woodward jutted his chin toward the break room,

then returned to his post, ready to book the two men before they were brought down to the cells, while Sebastian went in search of the constable.

Constable Meadows sat slumped in a chair. He was sporting a black eye and a busted lip, and had his head tilted upward. He held a handkerchief to staunch the bleeding from his nose.

"Are you all right, Constable?" Sebastian asked. "Did that just happen?"

Constable Meadows didn't get a chance to respond.

"Meadows here stopped a lady from being robbed in Oxford Street," Inspector Ransome announced as he came into the room. "And when I say lady, I mean lady. Duchess of something or other. Meadows singlehandedly chased off a gang of pickpockets, but not before he took a few punches to the face. I doubt that will make the papers," Ransome added bitterly. "She did give him a few bob as a reward, though. Didn't she, Constable?"

"I didn't do it for the money," Constable Meadows mumbled. "I saw she was in trouble and went to help."

"Good thing you had your truncheon, or they might have killed you," Inspector Ransome said, his expression growing serious. "They should arm us, they should," he said. "What good is a truncheon against knives and guns?"

"Will never happen," Constable Meadows said through his swollen lip. "They won't want shootouts in the street, or knife fights. Imagine the carnage."

"Well, sometimes it takes violence to stop violence," Ransome said. "You mark my words. This will only get worse as these gangs grow more reckless." He lifted the kettle experimentally, found it to be nearly empty, and left the room in a huff.

"Get yourself home, Constable. Your missus will look after you," Sergeant Woodward said as he poked his head in the door.

"I need to speak to Inspector Bell."

"Well, make it quick, and I'll take you home," Sergeant Woodward said, then left them to talk in private.

"Were you able to learn anything?" Sebastian asked.

Constable Meadows took the handkerchief away from his face, examined it, and stuffed it into his pocket. His nose was no longer bleeding, but his face was smeared with blood, so Sebastian took his own handkerchief, wet it with the last of the water from the kettle, and began to clean the younger man's face.

"You don't have to do that," Constable Meadows protested, clearly embarrassed, but Sebastian waved his objections away.

"It's no trouble. Go on, tell me."

"Well, I went to the Navy Office, like you said. Took a long time, but they finally found someone who was able to give me an answer. Ellis Baylor did join up and was assigned to the crew of HMS *Valiant*. Seems there were a number of deaths on the voyage back to England and she was short a few deckhands. The *Valiant* sailed for Cochin on December the thirteenth with Baylor aboard."

"So Baylor couldn't have done it," Sebastian said, almost to himself.

"No, he couldn't have," Constable Meadows agreed.

"And Reginald Pickering?"

"Well, then I took myself to Pall Mall. Took an age there too," Constable Meadows said, shaking his head. "They wouldn't let me inside. A policeman on the premises doesn't look good, does it, but I was finally escorted to a private parlor and told to mind myself, as if I were a thief. I was graciously permitted to speak to four officers who'd served with Captain Pickering. Three knew nothing of the brother, but the last one said he thinks Reginald Pickering has been working at a gymnasium in Aldgate. McCrory's, it's called."

"Well done, Constable," Sebastian said. "Your help is invaluable."

Constable Meadows brightened. "Really? You think this Reginald Pickering will help you crack the case?"

"I won't know until I speak to him. Is Superintendent Lovell here?"

"No, left when it all kicked off," Constable Meadows said, and jutted his chin toward the duty room. He looked thoughtful for a moment. "You know, I always thought I'd like to be a detective, but now I'm not so sure."

"Why's that?" Sebastian asked.

"Well, it's exhausting, innit? And there's not much of a payout."

"You got that right," Sebastian agreed. "But sometimes, when you see justice done, you think that's payout enough."

"I s'pose," Constable Meadows replied. "I'd best get on home. I can barely see out of my right eye."

"Need help?"

"Nah. I'm all right."

Constable Meadows pushed to his feet and ambled from the room. Sebastian returned his soiled handkerchief to his pocket, then followed him outside, where he nearly collided with Constable Bryant.

"Bryant, with me," Sebastian said, quickly realizing he could use the constable's help. Constable Bryant was young and inexperienced, but he'd proven himself to be observant and resourceful and Sebastian was certain he was up to the task.

"Where are we off to, guv?" the constable asked excitedly as he trotted after Sebastian.

"You're going to interview possible witnesses."

"What about you?"

"I have some personal business to attend to."

"What am I meant to ask them?" Constable Bryant asked, his ginger brows furrowing with anxiety.

"I'll fill you in on the way. Don't worry, Constable, you'll do just fine."

"Yes, sir," Constable Bryant cried. His eagerness was sweetly endearing.

Once outside, Sebastian found a hansom and instructed the cabbie to take them to Whitechapel.

# TWENTY-FOUR

By the time the two men arrived at the boarding house, the lodgers had all returned from work. The women sat in the parlor, white-faced and silent, their fear palpable, while Mrs. Bede hovered in the corridor, keeping a watchful eye.

"I'm Inspector Bell of Scotland Yard, and this is Constable Bryant," Sebastian explained to the assembled lodgers. "We're investigating the death of Lydia Morton and would very much appreciate your help."

Sebastian was in no doubt that the women already knew from Mrs. Bede that Lydia had been murdered, but thought it best not to say so outright. If they were frightened out of their wits they might not share what they knew, for fear of attracting the killer's attention to their cooperation with the police.

"Constable Bryant will speak to each of you in turn. Please tell him everything you know, even if you think it might not be relevant. No detail is too small," Sebastian added. The women nodded silently, their gazes firmly fixed on Sebastian. "Constable, you may begin. Write everything down," he reminded the young man.

"Yes, sir."

Sebastian left Constable Bryant to it, instructed Mrs. Bede to bolt the door, and set off for Gemma's boarding house. When the landlady—he couldn't recall her name—opened the door to him, he held up his warrant card and pushed his way in, completely ignoring the woman's outraged expression and squawk of protest.

"I need to speak to Miss Tate. Privately," he added.

"You can't be here," the woman screeched.

"I have to deliver distressing news and I'll be damned if I do it out in the street or in a public place. Fetch Miss Tate and bring her some sherry."

"I don't have any sherry," the landlady spat out.

"Then whatever you have on hand. Whisky or brandy will do."

"Spirits are not included with the rent," the landlady replied acidly.

Sebastian fished in his pocket and handed over all the change he had. "And bring the bottle," he said in a tone that brooked no argument.

"Uncouth pig," the landlady muttered under her breath.

"What was that?" Sebastian called after her.

"I said, be back in a tick." She darted up the stairs before Sebastian could reply, so he made himself comfortable in the parlor and waited for Gemma to join him.

When she entered the parlor Gemma looked frightened, and her eyes sought Sebastian's in silent inquiry. He was just about to speak when the landlady entered with a bottle of brandy and a glass and set them down on an occasional table with unnecessary force. She glared at Sebastian, then retreated, but left the door wide open in case he should decide to give in to his manly urges and attempt to ravish Gemma right there in the parlor. Sebastian found grim satisfaction in the thought that, if he was to try, Gemma would probably crack his skull with the bottle and then promptly offer him medical assistance.

Following the direction of Sebastian's gaze, Gemma partially closed the door, then advanced into the room and sank onto the well-worn settee. She folded her hands in her lap and looked up at Sebastian, who pulled up a chair and sat as close to her as propriety would allow.

"What's happened?" Gemma asked softly.

There was little point in delaying the inevitable. "Lydia was murdered last night," Sebastian said softly.

"No!" Gemma cried, her face turning bone-white and her eyes widening with shock. "Oh, I can't bear it," she moaned helplessly as she wrapped her arms around herself and began to sway back and forth, tears spilling down her cheeks and dripping onto the bodice of her gown. Sebastian handed her his handkerchief and she accepted it wordlessly, pressing the lawn square to her eyes, then wiping her streaming nose. In the face of such brutal news, her usual fortitude deserted her and she looked completely shattered.

"Why must everyone die?" she whimpered, her shoulders quaking with sobs.

It wasn't so long ago that Sebastian had asked himself the same question. First he'd lost his parents, then Louisa and their baby boy. When he was at his lowest all he wanted was for someone to hold him so he wouldn't fall apart, but he was a man, and no one had dared approach him and offer such intimate comfort. Propriety be damned: Sebastian sprang to his feet and pulled Gemma into his arms, holding her tight as she wept. Gemma felt slight in his arms, the top of her head coming to just below his chin and her heaving bosom pressing against his chest. She smelled of lavender soap and something faintly flowery, and Sebastian wished he could hold her forever, but knew he should let her go. The landlady pushed open the door and fixed him with a malevolent stare, then slid her gaze to Gemma in silent warning.

Sebastian held Gemma away from himself and she sank

back onto the settee, her shoulders hunching as if under a great weight, the damp handkerchief balled in her trembling fingers. He poured a large brandy and held it out to her, leaving her no choice but to accept his offering. Gemma took a sip, then another, then set the glass on the low table before her. Without thinking, Sebastian reached out, picked up the glass, and took a healthy swallow before returning it to the table.

The landlady was still in the doorway, standing with her arms crossed and her mouth compressed into a thin line of disapproval. Sebastian had to admire her dedication to protecting her lodgers' interests. She was right, of course. His reaction to Gemma's distress was not only inappropriate but completely unprofessional, so there was no denying that he and Gemma had a personal relationship that had no place in her boarding house.

"If you're quite finished, Inspector," she said.

Gemma turned her tearstained face to the landlady. "Please, give us a moment, Mrs. Bass."

Mrs. Bass snorted like a horse and moved away from the door, but no doubt remained within earshot, not only because she felt responsible for Gemma but because she wanted to hear what was being said.

"How?" Gemma whispered. "How did Lydia die?"

"She was strangled."

Gemma fixed Sebastian with an anguished stare. "Did she suffer, Sebastian?"

He nodded. It seemed wrong to lie to her. "I think it was the same killer as Jacob Harrow, Gemma."

Gemma began to tremble again, and Sebastian was quick to hand her the brandy. She didn't protest and drained the glass, so he immediately poured some more, but although Gemma accepted the glass she made no move to drink the contents this time. She sat still, her gaze fixed on the cold hearth, and Sebastian sat with her, offering the only comfort that was in his gift.

Gemma had seen all manner of brutal death, but this wasn't a stranger she'd nursed for a few days and then lost to their injuries. This was a woman she'd known well and had been close to at a time when the bonds of friendship meant the difference between sanity and certain madness. She needed time, and he would give her as much time as he was able before the landlady showed him the door.

"Why do you think it was the same killer?" Gemma choked out at last.

"He left Lydia's severed tongue by her bed."

Gemma's hand flew to her mouth, and she looked like she was going to be ill.

"Are you all right?" Sebastian exclaimed. "Was I wrong to tell you?"

Gemma shook her head and dabbed at her eyes again. "No. I'm glad you did. It was just a shock. Was it...?" She couldn't finish the sentence, but he understood what she was asking.

"Based on the amount of blood, I think it was removed before she died."

"Good God!" Gemma cried. "It's barbaric."

Sebastian looked away, afraid Gemma would see the suffering in his eyes and realize that his thoughts had turned to Louisa and the baby she had been carrying. Louisa's belly was slit while she was still alive, and he had always prayed that the child within hadn't felt any pain; but, having seen the carnage, he thought that both his wife and son had died in unimaginable agony.

"We have to find this monster," Gemma exclaimed, her grief solidifying into incandescent anger and a sense of purpose. "We have to see justice done."

"Gemma, I need to find him. You need to keep well away from this case," Sebastian replied sternly.

"Well, I won't," Gemma snapped. "Lydia was my friend, and if you shut me out I will conduct my own investigation."

"You will do no such thing," Sebastian countered, and cut his eyes at the open door. Mrs. Bass would feel no compunction about throwing Gemma out if she thought her conduct unbecoming.

Gemma nodded in understanding, but the stubborn set of her chin told its own story.

"Gemma, I will keep you informed. I promise. But you must be careful," Sebastian said. He didn't want to alarm her, but he needed to impress on her that she might be in danger. "Have you noticed anyone hanging about, watching you?"

"No. Why?"

"Because you were close to Lydia, and you knew Jacob Harrow."

Sebastian saw understanding dawn and was sorry he'd had to frighten her, but he had no choice. "Lock your door and window at night," he said. "And come straight back after work. I don't want you out there alone after dark."

Gemma nodded. The brandy was taking effect and she seemed calmer, and more composed.

"I think it's time you were on your way, Inspector," Mrs. Bass said as she walked into the room. "Miss Tate, I will thank you to return to your room."

Sebastian would have liked nothing better than to give the meddlesome woman a piece of his mind, but he kept silent. He didn't want to make things difficult for Gemma. She needed time to grieve and was the sort of person who'd prefer to sort through her feelings in private.

He picked up the bottle of brandy and handed it to Gemma. "Take that with you. It's paid for."

"Thank you," Gemma replied. "Goodnight, Inspector, and thank you for delivering the news in person."

Mrs. Bass scoffed, but Sebastian ignored her. "Goodnight, Miss Tate. Remember what I told you."

Gemma nodded and walked out of the room, taking the brandy and the glass with her.

When Sebastian returned to Mrs. Bede's he found Constable Bryant outside, gazing up at the night sky, his breath coming in gauzy puffs as he stepped from foot to foot to keep warm.

"What have you learned, Constable?" Sebastian asked without preamble.

Bryant shot Sebastian an apologetic look. "Not a whole lot, guv. The women talked nineteen to the dozen, mostly about how frightened they were, but hardly said anything worth repeating about Miss Morton. The lodgers all kept themselves to themselves and barely knew her."

"Surely someone must have noticed something," Sebastian protested, exasperated.

Constable Bryant took out his notebook and flipped it open, tilting the page toward the streetlamp so that he could read what he'd written.

"Annie Leyton saw Miss Morton with a tall, dark-haired, well-dressed man about a fortnight ago. They appeared to be arguing. She couldn't tell me anything more about the man's appearance. She also thought she heard the springs of Miss Morton's bed creaking last night."

"What time?"

"She couldn't say. There's no clock in her room. Could be the creaking Annie Leyton heard was Lydia and her man," Constable Bryant suggested.

"Which raises the question, was Lydia murdered by her lover? If she was, then it had to be someone other than Jacob Harrow, since he was already dead," Sebastian replied.

"Plenty of men are tall, dark-haired, and well dressed, sir," Constable Bryant pointed out. "The man Annie saw with Miss Morton could have been anyone."

"And the creaking could have been the result of a struggle. Anyone else see anything?" Sebastian asked.

"Barbara Wicklow said she saw a boy. Twice," Constable Bryant continued. "A guttersnipe of around ten years. He were out back, by the privy, looking up at the windows."

"Did she ask him what he was doing there?"

"She did. The boy said his stomach pained him something awful and he were just looking for a bit of privacy."

"Did she describe the child?" Sebastian asked. This was like pulling teeth, and just as painful.

Constable Bryant shook his head. "Scrawny and dirty. That were all she noticed. I don't suppose that's very helpful, guv."

"No, it isn't. Half the children in London are scrawny and dirty."

"That's what I told her," Constable Bryant said.

"What else, Constable? Women are observant creatures. Someone must have noticed something worth mentioning," Sebastian pressed.

"They did, but it were more speculation than fact."

"Tell me anyway," Sebastian invited.

"Hester Grint said Miss Morton were no better than she should be, but I think that were just female vanity talking. She's not very comely, Miss Grint." Constable Bryant took a deep breath and continued, his head bent over the page because the light was so poor. "Eva Taylor expressed the opinion that the nurses that went out to Crimea are women of loose morals, who were hoping for an opportunity to indulge their unnatural urges. She were certain Miss Morton had a fancy man since she'd clearly got a taste for carnal pleasure while living in such heathen place."

Sebastian felt angry on behalf of all the decent, caring women, like Gemma, who'd risked their safety and their very lives to answer the call of duty and go out to Crimea to nurse the wounded; but he also realized that Eva Taylor could be right about Lydia Morton. Who knew what Lydia had got up to in Crimea, and what she'd been up to since she'd returned home? Until he learned the results of the postmortem, he could hardly rebuke Eva Taylor for jumping to unwarranted judgments. He'd come to similar conclusions himself.

"Is that all?"

"Penny Lake thought Lydia Morton was with child."

"Why did she think that?" Sebastian snapped. This could be important to the investigation, and Bryant had left it till the very end.

Bryant shrugged. "She heard Miss Morton retching one morning and was prepared to stake her life on the assumption that she were carrying on with one of the doctors at the hospital and were hoping to trap him into marriage."

"Where did Miss Lake think the assignations took place? It wouldn't have been here, not under Mrs. Bede's piercing gaze," Sebastian said, jerking his head toward the boarding house.

"She thought they made use of the broom cupboards and the like. I'm afraid that's all I got, guv."

"Well done, Constable."

"Thank you, sir."

"Go on home." Constable Bryant lived near Highgate Cemetery, so it would take him a long while to get back.

"Goodnight, Inspector Bell."

"Goodnight," Sebastian muttered, his thoughts firmly fixed on Lydia Morton and her all-too-brief life as he exited the building.

Too tired to walk home, he found a cab and climbed in. He leaned against the cracked leather of the well-worn seat and looked out at the quiet, dark streets, the only light coming from uncurtained windows and the wavering glow of the streetlamps. Christmas was a week away, a time when some folk looked forward to the festivities and others dreaded the cold, lonely, and often hungry day and wanted nothing more than to get through it. Complicated as this case was proving to be, Sebastian was grateful to have something other than memories and regrets to occupy his mind, but he was too worn out after a day on the go to try to piece together what he had learned.

As the swaying motion of the hansom lulled him into a relaxed state, he shut his eyes and dozed off, waking only when the cabbie called to him that they'd arrived.

# TWENTY-FIVE

## FRIDAY, DECEMBER 17

Friday morning found Sebastian at Scotland Yard. The duty room was quiet, with just Sergeant Woodward reading yesterday's edition of the *Illustrated Police News* and sipping at a mug of tea.

"All right, Sebastian?" he called out when Sebastian walked in.

Sebastian nodded wearily.

"I wager you wish someone else got this case," Sergeant Woodward said. "Nasty business."

"Murder usually is."

"Not all murder is created equal," Woodward tossed back.

He held up the paper so Sebastian could see a sickeningly detailed illustration of Jacob Harrow hanging off Traitors' Gate, his chin and shirtfront covered with blood, the meat hook considerably larger than the original so that the readers could easily imagine the scene and relish the horror.

"I'll take a stabbing or a bashed skull any day," Woodward went on. "It's these high and mighty intellectuals that bother me. They try to disguise the basest of human instincts behind symbolism and righteous indignation."

"I see you're feeling particularly philosophical today," Sebastian joked. "Don't you worry, Albert. You'll get your heart's desire before the day is out." He decided not to mention Lydia's murder, not before he'd made his report to the superintendent.

"I hope so. Can't stand being bored," Woodward complained.

"Is Lovell in?"

"In his office."

Sergeant Woodward returned his attention to the paper, and Sebastian headed to Superintendent Lovell's office. Lovell looked tired, his shoulders slumped, the smudges beneath his eyes a testament to a restless night. He steepled his fingers on the desk, his gaze radiating annoyance.

"You're two days late, Bell. We need to wrap this case today," Lovell said. Sebastian was in no doubt that he'd got an earful from the commissioner last night.

"There's been a development, sir. Lydia Morton, a nurse connected to the Harrow case, was strangled on Wednesday night. Her tongue was severed and left in a glass by her bed."

Lovell's eyebrows sailed upward, and his expression instantly transformed to one of astonishment, and then relief. At least now he'd have an explanation for his department's lack of success in apprehending Jacob Harrow's killer. This was the sort of development he could work with, presuming a charge of double murder was imminent.

"Why didn't you tell me?" Lovell exclaimed.

"By the time I got back yesterday, you had already gone."

"Do you expect me to wait around all night?" Lovell snapped.

"No, sir."

"What do you mean to do?"

"We need to bring in Godfrey Price," Sebastian said. "He

suspected Lydia Morton of working with Jacob Harrow and feared she'd pick up where Harrow left off."

"But do you have evidence to charge him?"

"At the moment, it's all circumstantial," Sebastian said.

"Talk me through it," Lovell requested.

"Jacob Harrow knew that Godfrey Price wasn't legally married to his current wife and was blackmailing him over the information. Godfrey believed that Lydia Morton knew too, which meant he thought they had the power to destroy not only his family but also his surgical career. His skill as a surgeon might account for the severed tongues. Price has an alibi for the night Harrow was murdered, but he could have slipped out. I have yet to verify his movements on the night Lydia Morton was killed."

"Do you think he's our man?"

"I'm still not entirely convinced."

"Why?" Lovell countered. "Surely you must have a theory by now."

"The killer is someone who wants to bring attention to the crime and get their deeds into the newspapers. He is confident that we will never connect him to the murders and so is free to enjoy the results of his handiwork. Godfrey Price doesn't strike me as someone who wants recognition. He has too much to lose."

"But he's impulsive, as his two marriages indicate, and capable of deception," Lovell pointed out.

"He is, but in this instance his objective would be to rid himself of people who were bleeding him dry, not to court public scrutiny."

"So, you think the murderer is an attention seeker?"

"Perhaps more than that," Sebastian mused. "An avenging angel of sorts."

"Avenging angel?" Lovell scoffed.

"I think this is someone who wanted not simply to kill but to humiliate and perhaps even warn someone else. You cross me, this is what will happen."

"So if not Price, then who? Have you another suspect?"

Sebastian leaned back in his chair, his gaze on Lovell. He hated to admit that he was no closer to solving the case but felt he owed Lovell an explanation rather than a stalling tactic.

"Jacob Harrow was blackmailing three people that we know of, and the sums he demanded from his victims were substantial. It's possible that there were others who paid him in person or by some other means. Of the victims known to us, Harold Wise, who was pilfering supplies from the army, is too ill to lift a spoon, much less tackle a man of Harrow's size. The family is in dire financial straits, so I highly doubt he had the funds to hire someone to do it for him. Mrs. Wallace was blackmailed with the threat of exposing an extramarital affair. She admitted that her husband gives her a generous allowance, but I can't see that she would be interested in such a public display. A quiet death would be much more the thing."

"Yes, I agree," Lovell said.

"Harrow's cousin was also paying him monthly, but it was a much smaller sum, probably a repayment of a loan. I have yet to speak to him. He lives in Essex."

"Tell me more about Lydia Morton," Lovell invited him. "What was her role in all this?"

"Lydia Morton knew Jacob Harrow in Crimea. Given that she was murdered two days after Harrow and had her tongue cut out, I have to assume that the two murders are connected. If Jacob Harrow was silenced, then it stands to reason that Lydia Morton was privy to the victims' secrets as well and had the power to blackmail them anew. If the point was to free themselves, then she had to die," Sebastian explained. "However, Lydia had a lover, and I'm almost certain that she was expecting a child." He took a deep breath and added, "It's also quite possible that whoever killed Lydia Morton took advantage of Jacob Harrow's murder to cover up their own crime."

"Do we know anything about this lover?" Lovell asked.

"It's possible that Lydia Morton was Jacob Harrow's mistress, which would give Emma Harrow a motive for murder. She is not physically capable of committing such an atrocity herself, but she might have found someone who was willing to do the deed. The Harrows were not short of funds, and she will be well provided for in her widowhood, if Harrow's bank balance is anything to go on."

"Christ almighty!" Lovell exclaimed. "The more you learn, the less you seem to know, Bell."

"There's another potential suspect as well. Reginald Pickering. Brother of Captain Hugh Pickering, who sued Harrow for slander and committed suicide after he lost the case."

"You've found him, then?"

"He is said to work at a gymnasium in Aldgate. I will head over there as soon as I get the postmortem results on Lydia Morton."

"The corpse will wait, the killer will not. If Pickering gets wind of your interest, he might flee London until things quiet down. Get to Aldgate and speak to this Pickering fellow. You need to either rule him in or rule him out before you proceed."

"And Price?"

"I will have him picked up and brought in for questioning in connection with Lydia Morton's murder." Lovell leaned back and studied Sebastian through the lenses of his gold-rimmed spectacles. He still looked tired, but there was a faint glimmer of relief in his gaze. Godfrey Price's arrest would buy him time with the commissioner and give the papers a story to embroider over the next few days, giving Sebastian the time he needed to pursue his investigation.

# TWENTY-SIX

Aldgate was heaving with carriage traffic, pedestrians, and street vendors, so Sebastian paid the cabbie as soon as the hansom came to a standstill and walked the rest of the way. It took close to a half-hour, but he finally found the gymnasium, which was located on the ground floor of a three-story redbrick building in Aldgate High Street. It bore a discreet sign above a black-painted door, and the windows were blacked out, presumably because the owners didn't care for onlookers to peer inside. The door was unlocked, so Sebastian walked in, curious to see what a gymnasium looked like since he'd never been inside one.

The interior had been gutted to create a large space that was divided into several sections. Two men, both in their twenties and stripped down to their waists, were engaged in a bareknuckle fight in a roped-off ring. A few people looked on, but this appeared to be a practice fight, most likely in preparation for more formal combat where bets would be placed, and admission might be charged. The men outside the ring called out and offered conflicting advice, but the fighters were intent on each other, cognizant that even a moment's distraction could cost them the match or result in injury. One man's eye was already swollen. The other had a bloodied nose, but he was clearly the better fighter. He was weaving and ducking, no doubt determined to tire his partner before delivering a decisive blow. Sebastian thought this was probably a good way to relieve one's aggression, but saw no appeal in the idea of getting pummeled until he was knocked down.

The rest of the gymnasium was empty, since it was still very early in the day, but there were foils and sabers hanging on a rack mounted on the wall, and several odd contraptions that looked more like torture devices than tools for fostering physical strength and improved health. There were a few climbing ropes and a bench with weights and belts that looked like it had been borrowed from an asylum for the insane. All the equipment was situated along the walls, presumably to leave enough space for the crowds that would gather for the fights.

The man with the swollen eye was finally brought down, and the victor left the ring and found a towel to wipe his bleeding nose. On closer inspection, he was younger than Sebastian had first thought, and had a full head of sandy hair and pale eyes. He fixed Sebastian with a shrewd gaze.

"Did you need a tour, mister?" he asked. "We're taking new members."

Sebastian showed the young man his warrant card. "Inspector Bell of Scotland Yard. I'm looking for Reginald Pickering."

"You found him," the young man replied cheerily. "Whatever it is, I didn't do it." He held up his hands as if surrendering to the police.

"A word in private, Mr. Pickering?"

"As you like," Reginald Pickering replied. "Let me just get dressed. It gets cold when you're not moving about."

"You all right, Reg?" one of the men called when his gaze fell on Sebastian's warrant card.

"Right as rain, Will," Reginald called back. "Come, let's talk in the office, Inspector."

Reginald led Sebastian to a small office located at the back of the main space. It was furnished with a desk, three cane chairs, and a stove that glowed warmly in the sullen December light filtering through a grimy window set high in the wall. Reginald reached for a kettle, shook it to see if there was water inside, and set it on the stove.

"I could murder a cup of tea. Can I offer you one, Inspector?"

"Thank you, no," Sebastian replied, and settled in one of the guest chairs.

Reginald used the towel to wipe the sweat off his body, pulled on his shirt, and tucked it into his trousers before putting on his waistcoat.

"Much better now," he said with a happy smile, and settled behind the desk. The kettle would take a while to boil, and he looked ready to get started.

"I'm sure you're aware that Jacob Harrow was murdered a few days ago," Sebastian began.

"Yes, but what's it to do with me?"

"Your brother shot himself after the court failed to uphold his complaint against Harrow," Sebastian reminded him.

Reginald's face clouded with the memory of that time, but he shook his head. "My brother was a puffed-up buffoon who doesn't deserve my pity." He smiled sadly. "I know I shouldn't speak ill of the dead, but I not only lost a brother that day but what was left of my family. Hugh chose his so-called honor over his duty to me and wasted the precious gift that is life on some trivial poppycock that would be forgotten within the week."

There was pain in Reginal's eyes, but also anger at a brother who'd abandoned him. Where other boys might have given in to self-pity, Reginald had clearly chosen to distance himself from

Hugh's act of cowardice and become the sort of man he could be proud of.

"So, you felt no desire to avenge him?" Sebastian asked.

"If you think I stabbed that man through the heart, cut out his tongue, and hanged him on Traitors' Gate, you are mad, Inspector. I value my life and my liberty and would never risk losing either over something that had nothing to do with me."

Sebastian took the blue disk out of his pocket and held it up between two fingers. "Ever see one of these?"

"No. What is it?" Reginald's reaction seemed genuine.

"An evil eye charm," Sebastian replied.

Reginald shrugged. "I don't believe in such things. I think we make our own luck. Don't you?

Sebastian replaced the bead in his pocket and asked, "Did you know Lydia Morton?" He watched Reginald closely for a spark of recognition at the name, but Reginald looked at him blankly.

"Never heard the name."

"She was seen with a man fitting your description. Fair-haired, clean-shaven, handsome."

"Surely there are many men who fit the bill." Reginald laughed. "You being one. Not that I'm telling you you're handsome."

Sebastian suppressed a smile. He had noticed Reginald's resemblance to himself. The boy could be his younger brother, or cousin, but Sebastian was sure they weren't related.

"Have you worked here long?" he asked.

"I don't work here. I own the place."

"So why is it called McCrory's?"

"Angus McCrory was the fellow that opened the gymnasium about ten years back. He gave me a job and a place to live two years ago when I had nowhere to go, and was kind to me. Kinder than my own father ever was. Or my brother. When he died, he left the gymnasium to me, and I kept his name above the door as a tribute."

"Did he not have children of his own?"

"His only son died in Crimea. Another casualty of a pointless and brutal war."

"You must have been pleased to inherit a thriving concern."

"I was surprised, and humbled. Angus was a good man, and he owed me nothing. He has a brother in Scotland. By rights, he should have left the business to him, but I don't know if the man even knows his brother is gone. They weren't on good terms. Kind of like me and Hugh."

"Where were you on Monday night?"

Reginald laughed merrily. "I was right here, refereeing a match between two well-known fighters. At least fifty people saw me."

"And after?"

"And after, we went down the street to the Armory Inn and had us a party. I staggered home around three, drunk as a newt, and slept until nearly noon the next day. The barkeep at the Armory can vouch for me, as can every man here now. They were all with me."

Sebastian couldn't help but admire the lad. Despite the losses he'd suffered, he was not only confident and self-assured, he seemed genuinely content with his lot—a rare thing.

"I will be checking your alibi," Sebastian said.

"Be my guest."

Sebastian stood and turned toward the door. Reginald Pickering had a motive and was strong and agile enough to have carried out both murders, and he could have easily made certain he had an alibi for both nights; but years of experience told Sebastian that Pickering wasn't his man. There was much one could tell from speaking to someone and watching their reactions and body language. Unless Reginald Pickering was a consummate actor, he had been completely genuine; and, if what he'd said about the gymnasium was true, he certainly had no reason to risk his life at this juncture to avenge a brother who had died more than two years ago and by his own hand.

Nor did Reginald appear to have a motive to murder Lydia Morton. She was nearly ten years his senior and, as far as Sebastian could see, could have done him little harm. Sebastian would still do his due diligence, question the men outside and speak to the barkeep at the Armory, but he didn't expect to hear anything different.

Once finished in Aldgate, he wolfed down an eel pie and took himself off to Blackfriars to see Colin Ramsey.

# TWENTY-SEVEN

Having cleaned and bandaged a deep cut for Tommy, who was always getting into scrapes, Gemma sent him on his way and sank into a hardback chair, folding her hands in her lap. This was the first break she'd had since starting her shift that morning, and she felt weary and heartsick, tears never far away. News of Lydia's death was already in the *Telegraph*, and Gemma strongly suspected that her landlady had rushed to the newspaper office before the lodgers had returned home and sold her story and the editor had made certain it made the front page of the morning edition. The article had hinted that there might have been a romantic connection to Jacob Harrow, which was even more disgraceful since the man was one of their own and surely deserved a bit of respect. Gemma was in no doubt that next week's edition of the *Illustrated Police News* would paint an even more sordid picture and insinuate that Lydia had deserved what happened to her.

Gemma sighed and looked out at the overcast sky, watching a lone bird that flew past the window, its plump body like a smudge of charcoal on a dirty wall. It put her in mind of Lydia's spirit, and she wondered where Lydia had gone. Having spent several years in a war zone and witnessed the senseless carnage and pointless deaths of thousands, Gemma no longer believed in heaven and hell, at least not as they were described by the clergy. Heaven and hell were right here, on earth, and she'd known both. Perhaps the soul did go somewhere after death, or maybe there was just nothingness beyond, an eternity of non-being. In Lydia's case, Gemma thought that might be the more desirable option.

Perhaps it was disloyal to think such things about a woman who'd been so cruelly dispatched, but Gemma wasn't fool enough to believe that Lydia hadn't in some way brought about her own end. Lydia had had her good qualities. She'd been a competent nurse, a fiercely independent and intelligent woman, and she had been there when someone needed a friend. Lydia had been the sort of person who showed up, whether it was for a celebration or a funeral. She had been the only one of Gemma's Crimea friends to come to Victor's funeral and offer her support. Most of the other women had drifted away as soon as they returned to England, the devotion they had felt toward one another dissipating like morning dew.

Many of the women had been like Gemma, daughters of good families who fervently believed in their cause and thought they could help the brave soldiers who fought for the glory of England. They had quickly been disabused of their beliefs and had instead done their utmost for wounded and dying men while keeping away the despair that threatened to overwhelm them if they gave it any quarter. They had clung to each other the way a drowning man holds on to a bit of flotsam, their sanity hanging by a thread; but once they returned home they wanted no reminders of the nightmare they had lived through.

Lydia hadn't been like those women. She had grown up in an orphanage and learned to fend for herself from an early age. She'd had no illusions either about the war machine that had sent thousands to die for a cause that had little bearing on the lives of Englishmen or the moral superiority of those who'd volunteered to be there. Lydia had understood the wickedness of men, and women, and, where most would simply tut-tut with disapproval or pretend not to see what was happening, Lydia had been one to call a spade a spade. It seemed that she had used that spade to dig her own grave.

Gemma had never asked what Lydia was up to—she'd had no wish to know—but now that Lydia was dead, she felt honor-bound to help Sebastian apprehend her killer, despite his warning. Gemma was no detective, and her experience in investigating homicides was negligible, but she was certain she could be instrumental in moving the case forward. And she also wanted Lydia to know, if her spirit was out there somewhere, that someone had cared enough to avenge her passing and apprehend the killer.

Gemma was convinced there had to be a Crimea connection, and, although she was sure Sebastian would figure it all out eventually, he couldn't possibly decipher the relationships between the individuals involved without her insight. She wouldn't place herself in any danger; she was no fool, but she would call on several old friends of Lydia's after her shift and ask a few discreet questions. It was the least she could do. And she would start with Barbara Wicklow. Lydia had never told Gemma how she knew Barbara, but she had mentioned that Barbara had helped her to secure a position at the London Hospital and had informed Lydia as soon as a room became available at the boarding house where she lodged. Barbara might have no idea what Lydia had been involved in, but she could at least tell Gemma about Lydia's final hours, since she would have seen her at supper and had probably conversed with Lydia before she had retired.

And Gemma would pay a condolence call on Jacob Harrow's wife. Sebastian had mentioned that she had gone to stay with her parents in Elm Tree Road. Gemma checked the time on the pocket watch. Victor had given her on their last birthday and replaced it in her reticule. The older children would be going out to the British Museum after luncheon, a special Christmas treat organized by the governors of the hospital. Gemma's presence was not required, and there were no critically ill children currently in the infirmary. She could nip out for an hour and be back before anyone noticed she had gone. Suddenly impatient, she wished time would pass more quickly. She wouldn't admit it out loud, but the thought of investigating gave her something of a rush.

# TWENTY-EIGHT

Sebastian arrived in Blackfriars just before noon. Mabel let him in but then excused herself to check on something in the kitchen, so he stopped into the drawing room to say hello to Mrs. Ramsey. She occupied her usual chair, her hands folded in her lap, her gaze on something beyond the window or perhaps on nothing at all. In the pale light of the winter afternoon, her face had a gray cast, and her eyelids were almost translucent as they drooped over her staring eyes. When Sebastian bid her a good day, Mrs. Ramsey gaped at him, her brows knitting as if she were trying to recall if they had met before.

Sebastian's own mother had died when he was eighteen, and, as much as he still grieved for her, he was suddenly glad she had been spared this merciless deterioration of the mind that stripped away not only the painful memories but also all the happy, cherished moments that a person accumulated during their lifetime. Mrs. Ramsey was a shell of her former self and would only get worse, an emotional burden Colin would have to bear until she finally drifted away, as insubstantial in body as she was in mind.

"Good day to you, young man," Mrs. Ramsey said haltingly. "Are you one of Colin's friends from school? He's just back for the Christmas holidays."

"Is Colin here?" Sebastian asked when the other man failed to appear.

"I think he's out with his father. They do enjoy spending time together. Sometimes I'm a bit jealous of their bond, but it's as it should be. A son should look up to his father." She smiled dreamily, as if she expected her men to walk in at any moment and tell her of their adventures over luncheon.

"Mr. Colin is here, Mrs. Ramsey," Mabel said as she walked into the room. "He's in the cellar. Working as usual. Why don't we go for a nice walk before luncheon? You haven't been out in days, and the fresh air will do you good."

Mrs. Ramsey nodded absentmindedly, and Mabel smiled wistfully at Sebastian. "Mr. Ramsey is expecting you, Inspector. You know the way."

"Thank you, Mabel," Sebastian said, and made his way down to the cellar.

Colin looked up from his work, his hand suspended in midair, a needle between his elegant fingers.

"Sorry I'm late," Sebastian said. "I had to go to Aldgate. The living take priority over the dead."

"I'm actually just closing her up," Colin replied. "Mother was unwell this morning, so I was late getting started."

"Tell me," Sebastian said as he looked at the woman on the table.

He'd attended a number of postmortems since becoming a detective, mostly for victims of murder, but he never got used to examining the dead, with their bodies sewn together like Frankenstein's monster. Only a few days ago, Lydia Morton had been gloriously alive, going about her business and never imagining that she was about to meet with such a gruesome end.

Sebastian always did his best to maintain professional detachment, but he still felt sorry for the woman, and, judging by the look on Colin's face, so did he.

Colin tied off the thread and stood back, his gaze now on Sebastian. "The victim was in good health before her death. She is adequately nourished, her skin is supple, and her hair lustrous. She had slight scoliosis, but the curvature in her spine wasn't severe enough to impact her daily life or to be readily noticeable."

"What's the cause of death, Colin?" Sebastian asked. Colin had a tendency to go on, but Sebastian wasn't interested in conditions that had no relevance to the victim's death.

"Death by asphyxiation, but there are several other injuries."

Sebastian waited for Colin to continue.

"The injuries paint a rather comprehensive picture of her final moments, and they must have been awful," he said with a heavy sigh. "I always say that a quick and easy death is a reward in itself." Colin must have realized how that had come out, and was quick to apologize. "I'm sorry, Sebastian. I didn't mean—"

"It's all right, Colin. You don't have to walk on eggshells around me. Louisa is gone, and nothing can ever hurt her again. Please continue."

"I think the victim was asleep when the killer entered her bedroom. He or she straddled Lydia and wrapped their hand around her neck. She woke and began to struggle. There are several torn nails and scratches on her neck, just here, but I'm sure you saw them when you examined the body at the scene."

Sebastian nodded. "She tried to loosen her assailant's grip on her neck and scratched herself in the process."

"Precisely," Colin agreed. "The victim has several broken ribs, ninth and tenth on both sides. I believe this is the result of the killer's knees pressing on her ribcage during the struggle. Likewise, there's bruising to the hips from when the killer straddled her. Once incapacitated, Lydia was unable to call for help."

"And the tongue?"

"Severed at the base while she was still alive. I expect her final moments were horrific."

Sebastian nodded. He wouldn't wish such an end on anyone. "So, the killer was sending the same message as with Jacob Harrow," he said, not wishing to dwell on what Lydia must have felt as she lay dying.

"Are you any clearer on what that message is?" Colin asked.

"Jacob Harrow was a blackmailer, and Lydia might have been his accomplice. If they traded in people's secrets, then cutting out their tongues symbolizes their eternal silence."

"Yes, I expect it does." Colin looked down at Lydia and ran his hand over her hair, a tender gesture meant as an expression of sympathy. "There's something else."

"She was pregnant," Sebastian said. "About four months?"

Colin nodded at Sebastian as if he were a gifted pupil. "Yes, she was, but that's not what I was about to say." He turned toward a table he used to hold containers and instruments and picked up an enamel bowl. "She had six gold nuggets in her stomach."

"What?" Sebastian exclaimed and peered into the bowl. Six golden balls, cleaned of whatever gore had been in the victim's belly, rolled around the bottom, the dull light glinting off their bright surface. "So she must have known."

"Known what?" Colin asked.

"That whoever killed Harrow would come for her, only she didn't think they would kill her."

Colin nodded. "She must have thought they were after the gold and swallowed it to keep it safe."

"I expect this was her nest egg, meant to support her and her child for years to come." Sebastian cocked his head and looked at Colin. "Are you sure she was asleep when her attacker arrived?"

"You think that the killer demanded she hand over the gold and killed her when she refused?"

"It's possible."

"Yes, I suppose it is, but don't you think someone would have heard the struggle? The longer she remained alive, the greater the chance she would call for help."

"Perhaps not," Sebastian replied. "Lydia was courageous and self-assured. She might have thought that she could talk her way out of the situation, and the last thing she'd want to do was draw attention to the fact that she was in possession of the gold."

"How do you think she came by it?" Colin asked.

"My best guess would be that she had converted her savings into gold because she didn't want to leave the money lying around and didn't trust the banks. She must have had a safe hiding place in her room, but after Jacob Harrow was murdered she became nervous and decided to swallow the gold nuggets to keep them safe."

"I expect she would have kept swallowing and passing them until she felt it was safe to stop. Not very pleasant, but effective," Colin observed.

"I don't think the killer was after the gold," Sebastian mused. "For one, he or she wouldn't have killed her so quickly if they were there to steal her savings. They would have tried to discover where the stash was hidden. And that's if they even knew about the gold. For another, they would have probably ransacked the room, but it didn't appear as if it had been searched."

"So you think it was always their intention to murder?" Colin asked.

"I do. I don't believe this case is about the money, at least not Lydia's money. This is about reclaiming power, and, with

Jacob Harrow and Lydia Morton dead, the killer will now feel secure, unless someone else was involved. I wish there was a way to tell who fathered her child."

Colin chuckled. "If only science were capable of such sorcery. You're asking for the moon, my friend. Does it really matter?"

"It would be helpful to know who else was part of this equation and if the pregnancy had anything to do with the motive."

"I thought you said this case was about reclaiming power."

"Lydia might have been blackmailing the child's father," Sebastian said. "If only the postmortem could tell us what she was involved in."

"The dead are very good at keeping their secrets," Colin replied, and cast a questioning gaze at Sebastian. "Can I keep her?"

Sebastian shrugged. "I suppose." He took one of the gold nuggets and handed it to Colin. "Use this to have her decently buried once you're done, and order a stone."

"What are you going to do with the rest?"

"For now, it's evidence. Once the case is closed, I don't know. Perhaps she had family we don't know about, but no one has come forward yet."

"What will you do next?" Colin asked.

Sebastian consulted his pocket watch. Godfrey Price might already be on his way to Scotland Yard, but there was also the possibility that he had been in the operating theater when the constables arrived and wouldn't be ready to be interviewed for a while yet. If Sebastian understood anything of the man, it was that he wouldn't leave his patients until he was good and ready, the police be damned. Whether Godfrey Price was guilty or innocent, news of his arrest would distress his wife and possibly destroy his surgical career, which would be a loss to the hospital as well as the patients who relied on him; but, unless he could conclusively prove his innocence, the repercussions were unavoidable.

Sebastian pushed the watch into his waistcoat pocket and turned back to Colin. "I must go to Essex to speak to James Harrow, Jacob Harrow's cousin. James was paying him as well."

"Think you'll learn something?" Colin asked.

"I sincerely hope so," Sebastian said, and took his leave.

## TWENTY-NINE

Elm Tree Road wasn't very long, nor did it have many homes, which made Gemma's task considerably easier. She could knock on every door and ask after Emma Harrow, or she could do the sensible thing and look for visible signs of mourning to narrow down the possibilities. There were three houses displaying black bows, and, although the protocols for mourning differed based on the closeness of the relationship, they were not different enough to tell which house was in mourning for a son-in-law. Gemma decided to try the nearest house first. She approached the door and knocked, inwardly apologizing for disturbing a family in grief.

A middle-aged woman opened the door. She wore widow's weeds and a black lace cap that covered most of her hair. Her eyes were puffy and red-rimmed, and she had the dead-eyed look of someone who no longer cared about anything.

"Yes?" she said, staring at Gemma but seemingly not really seeing her.

"I'm sorry to disturb you, madam, but I was looking for Mrs. Harrow."

"Mrs. Harrow?" the woman repeated blankly.

"Emma Harrow. Her parents reside in this street."

"Number three," the woman said, and shut the door before Gemma had a chance to thank her.

She approached number three, with its modest black bow and curtains that were tightly drawn against the light. Gemma felt a pang of guilt for intruding, but reasoned that she was doing this to help Emma as well as Sebastian. Understanding what had happened went a long way toward helping one cope; she could personally attest to that, although losing one's husband was probably even more devastating than losing a brother.

The door was opened by a young maidservant who wore a black armband over the light blue sleeve of her dress.

"Good afternoon. My name is Miss Tate, and I am looking for Mrs. Harrow," Gemma said.

The girl nodded. "I'll tell Mrs. Harrow you're here."

Breathing out a sigh of relief, Gemma stepped inside and waited in the tiny entryway while the maid went to announce her. The maid returned, took Gemma's cape and directed her to the parlor, where two women, both dressed in black, sat by the fire. The lamps had not been lit, so the only light came from the hearth, and the room was not only dim but overly warm and stuffy. The ormolu clock on the mantel had been stopped, and the mirror was swathed in black crape. The scent of lilies that stood in a vase on the mantel was overpowering.

The older woman, who was stout and had ruddy cheeks, had been reading from the Bible, while the younger woman, who was pale and appeared to be shivering despite the warmth, was staring into the flames. They both turned when Gemma entered the room, and the older woman set her Bible aside.

"Good afternoon, Miss Tate," the older woman said. "I'm Mrs. Jonas, Emma's mother."

"Pleased to meet you, ma'am," Gemma replied.

Mrs. Jonas shot Gemma a quizzical look, then turned to her daughter, who still hadn't said a word. "Emma, do you know Miss Tate?" Mrs. Jonas asked kindly.

Gemma stood awkwardly before the two women, heat rising in her cheeks. She expected to be asked to leave, but Emma Harrow surprised her by saying, "Yes. Miss Tate is Victor Tate's sister."

Mrs. Jonas's eyes widened in recognition of the name, and she nodded sympathetically to Gemma.

"Please, forgive the intrusion," Gemma said, "but Victor always spoke fondly of Mr. Harrow, and I wanted to pay my respects." She hoped the lie was justified, but was honest enough with herself to acknowledge that her invasion of Emma Harrow's privacy was unforgivably gauche.

"Please, sit down, Miss Tate. It's so kind of you to call," Mrs. Jonas said. "You're the first visitor we've had," she added bitterly. "Except for the journalists, of course."

"I'm sorry," Gemma said again. "It must be very difficult for you."

"I expect you understand what poor Emma has had to endure," Mrs. Jonas said. "You are so recently bereaved yourself, and in such similar circumstances."

"I do understand."

"It must be a comfort to you to know that your brother's killer has been apprehended. It won't bring Mr. Tate back, but knowing that justice will be served does help one sleep at night."

"It does," Gemma agreed.

"Would you care for some refreshment?" Mrs. Jonas asked, remembering her manners.

"Please, don't trouble yourself."

"Nonsense. It's no trouble at all. Tea is just the thing on

such a cold day. What about you, Emma? You barely ate anything at luncheon. Will you take a dish of tea?"

"Yes, Mama," Emma replied woodenly.

Mrs. Jonas set aside her Bible and went from the room, leaving Gemma alone with Emma Harrow.

"Did you know Jacob well, Miss Tate?" Emma asked. "He was fond of Victor and was very upset when he died, especially since he happened to be there..." Her voice trailed off. "Forgive me, Miss Tate. I didn't mean to bring back painful memories."

"It's quite all right, Mrs. Harrow."

"You must miss your brother very much," Emma said.

"I do. Every single day." Gemma felt her eyes misting with tears and looked away, willing herself to remain stoic in the face of Emma Harrow's sympathy. "I'm very sorry for your loss. It must have been a terrible shock," she said, desperate to bring the conversation around to the current murder.

Emma nodded. "It was as if my whole world fell apart in a matter of moments. I really don't know what I will do without Jacob. And the manner of his death," she went on, her voice catching. "I can't conceive of who would do such a thing."

"Have the police uncovered anything?"

"I don't know. I expect Inspector Bell will come to see me once he has news." Emma's expression became slightly more hopeful. "Jacob said the inspector was rather dogged when investigating the death of that poor woman at Highgate. I hope he will try as hard to get justice for Jacob."

"I'm certain he will," Gemma replied. "He's an excellent detective."

"You know him, then?"

"He investigated Victor's murder," Gemma said. "Did Mr. Harrow not mention it?"

"Jacob didn't really talk to me of such things. I used to ask Judith, our maid, to tell me what was going on. She read the papers once Jacob threw them away. A nosy, sullen girl, but she had her uses."

"Will you be returning home soon?" Gemma asked.

Emma shook her head. "I don't think so. I can't imagine living there on my own. Perhaps my father will find tenants for the property. I never imagined I would be leaving our home." Emma dabbed at her eyes with a lace-trimmed handkerchief. "Jacob loved that house. He handpicked every piece of furniture and every painting."

"Did he display any souvenirs from his time in Crimea?"

"Souvenirs?" Emma echoed, her feathery brows lifting in obvious surprise.

"Some people brought back keepsakes from the war and their time in Scutari. It's in Turkey," Gemma added, in case Emma didn't know where the wounded had been transported for treatment.

"Jacob had an ornamental dagger that he kept in his study. I believe it was Turkish."

"What about charms? Evil eye charms are very popular in that part of the world. Might you husband have brought one back?"

"I very much doubt it. Jacob was a devout Christian. He would never put stock in such things."

Emma appeared to be losing patience, so Gemma instantly changed tack. "How long were you and Mr. Harrow married, if you don't mind me asking?"

"Just two years. We met nearly five years ago but only married when Jacob returned from Crimea. We were so happy," Emma wailed, and her hand instinctively went to her stomach.

"Forgive me for asking, but are you expecting?" Gemma asked.

Emma nodded. "Jacob was thrilled. He couldn't wait to be a father. He was certain we'd have a boy. Now he'll never get to meet his son."

"I'm very sorry," Gemma said.

"Thank you. It brings me comfort to know that he's left something of himself behind."

Emma began to cry again, and Gemma reached out and laid a hand over her arm. The poor woman had clearly been besotted with her husband and was gutted by his death. There was no way to know for certain, but Gemma didn't think Emma Harrow knew anything of what her husband had got up to, and she hoped she'd never have reason to find out what a despicable man he'd been. But if the case came to trial, the details would emerge, and then Emma's memories of her husband would be tainted by knowledge of his deeds. Gemma only hoped that the scandal would die down by the time their child was old enough to ask about his or her father.

"I'm sorry, but I really must go," Gemma said, and stood.

Just then, Mrs. Jonas bustled back into the room, the maid-servant with the tea tray right behind her. There was a plate of tea sandwiches, and mourning biscuits that were wrapped in white paper and sealed with black wax. The gesture seemed a bit out of place, but, given that there was no body to view, perhaps the family felt they needed to acknowledge Jacob Harrow's death in other ways.

"Won't you stay and take tea with us?" Mrs. Jonas asked.

"I'm sorry, but I must get back to work," Gemma said.

Mrs. Jonas nodded. "It's not easy for a woman on her own, is it?"

"No."

"Kindly leave your address, and I will be sure to send you an invitation to the funeral, Miss Tate," Mrs. Jonas said.

"Thank you. It would be my honor to attend."

"Thank you for your thoughtfulness, Miss Tate," Emma said. "I hope you will come again."

"Emma is in need of a friend just now," Mrs. Jonas said as she walked Gemma to the door and made sure to take down her address. "We won't be receiving after the funeral, but maybe in a few months, once Emma is ready for some unassuming company."

"I will be sure to call then," Gemma promised. She would come back—she liked Emma Harrow and would gladly offer her support—but just then she was wondering how to get a message to Sebastian.

# THIRTY

Sebastian caught the next train to Brentwood and shared a compartment with two officers who were on their way to Warley Barracks. Once pleasantries were exchanged and comments about the weather exhausted, the conversation petered out and the officers took an opportunity to enjoy a bit of quiet, one reading a penny dreadful he'd purchased at the station and the other snoring gently as he fell into a doze.

Sebastian looked out the window at the passing country-side. The bleak landscape matched his sullen mood. He would call on Gemma before returning to Scotland Yard. Lovell and Godfrey Price would have to wait.

News of Lydia's death had been in the *Telegraph* this morning. How on earth had the papers got wind of the murder so quickly? Daniel Haze wouldn't sell the story to the papers, even though plenty of coppers weren't above feeding useful tidbits to reporters and lining their pockets at the expense of the victims and their families; and the driver of the wagon who'd transported the body didn't know enough to make the connection to Jacob Harrow's death. So it had to be one of the lodgers, or the landlady. The fee would have been substantial since they could provide the sort of details that would titillate the public. By the time the evening edition hit the streets in a few hours, new information would have emerged, and speculation would be rampant.

Women were murdered more often than anyone realized, and the papers rarely carried the stories, especially if the victim was a prostitute or some poor wretch no one cared about. But when a woman who'd been a nurse in Crimea and was just this side of respectable was strangled in her bed days after a man she might have known had met his hideous fate, there was money to be made.

Sebastian went cold all over as a rogue thought wormed its way into his brain and became lodged there for what he knew would be the duration of this investigation. What if Gemma's association with Lydia was mentioned in the papers and became public knowledge? If the killer thought Lydia had confided in Gemma, they might decide she had to be silenced in order to keep their secrets safe. By the time the train pulled into Brentwood Sebastian's worry had blossomed into full-blown fear for Gemma's safety, and for a moment he even considered returning straight to London and sending someone else to speak to James Harrow. But he was already here, and it would be remiss of him not to speak to James. He was not only a relation but also quite possibly a lifelong confidant of Jacob's. And Gemma had promised she would keep away from the investigation. Hopefully, the killer wasn't aware of the connection between the two women and would find no reason to target Gemma, since she clearly didn't know anything.

Brentwood station was hardly more than a short platform, and the town seemed tiny after the sprawling vastitude of London. Sebastian began with James Harrow's bank, which was on the high street and reminded Sebastian of the American frontier towns he'd seen depicted in a newspaper once. The phrase *one-horse town* came to mind as a horse-drawn phaeton appeared at the end of the road and made its way unimpeded down the nearly empty street. There were a few pedestrians, and a wagon loaded with kegs passed by, the driver spitting a gob of chewed tobacco over the side of the conveyance, but after the chaos that was London the town appeared quietly quaint.

The bank was empty, its only customer having passed Sebastian on his way in, and Sebastian had no difficulty obtaining James Harrow's address from the clerk, who seemed awed by Sebastian's warrant card even though it did not grant him authority in Essex. Perhaps the man didn't realize that, and Sebastian saw no reason to enlighten him. The helpful clerk even explained how to find the address and he thanked the man politely.

The house was a three-story cottage on a wide side street. It conveyed a sad air of neglect and could have used considerably more than a fresh coat of paint on the window frames and door. The stones in the path were cracked, there were tiles missing from the roof, and the front garden looked overgrown even in December, when it was hardly more than bare sticks. The woman who opened the door had to be in her mid-fifties. Although she was still attractive, the unrelieved black of her gown, the widow's cap neatly tied beneath her chin, and the grief stamped onto her features told their own story.

"Mrs. Harrow?" Sebastian asked gently. She nodded.

Sebastian hated to impose on the woman when she was in mourning. Although he had no way of knowing precisely when Mrs. Harrow had suffered a bereavement, the dead-eyed look in her eyes made him think that the loss had been quite recent. Sebastian wondered if Mrs. Harrow had been widowed, or maybe James's brother or sister had passed.

"I'm sorry to intrude on your grief, but I was hoping to speak to James," Sebastian said apologetically.

"My son is dead," Mrs. Harrow said flatly. "Whatever business you have with him no longer matters."

The pronouncement brought Sebastian up short. It wasn't uncommon for young men to die. Perhaps James had been ill or had met with an accident, but given his connection to the investigation and the fact that his cousin and Lydia Morton had both been murdered suddenly introduced a new possibility. As much as Sebastian wished he could leave Mrs. Harrow to grieve in peace, he had no choice but to question her. He had to find out precisely when and how James had died and use the information to determine whether James's death had bearing on the case. His demise might be completely unrelated, or he might have been the third victim of the same killer.

"I'm very sorry for your loss, Mrs. Harrow," Sebastian said. "I'm Inspector Bell of Scotland Yard, and I'm investigating the murder of Jacob Harrow, and—"

"Jacob is dead?" Mrs. Harrow exclaimed.

"Murdered."

She yanked the door open. "Come in, Inspector."

The house was as shabby on the inside as it was on the outside. The furniture and carpet had seen better days, and the curtains were faded and threadbare. The fire in the grate burned so low as to give off almost no heat. Sebastian removed his coat and hat and accepted a seat by the fire.

"Would you care for some tea?" Mrs. Harrow asked.

"Thank you. That's very kind."

"I won't be a moment."

Sebastian didn't really want tea and was worried about wasting time he didn't have, but he got the impression that Mrs. Harrow would feel more comfortable conversing in a social rather than strictly professional manner, and tamped down his impatience. He took a look around the room but saw nothing of interest. An embroidered sampler hung on the wall. A few books were stacked on a small table, and a stuffed bird sat perched on a spindly branch beneath a glass dome that could use a thorough dusting.

Once Mrs. Harrow brought in the tea tray and poured out, Sebastian could no longer delay.

"How did your son die, Mrs. Harrow?"

The woman went even paler than she already had been, her gaze straining toward the staircase visible through the door.

"James hanged himself. Up there." She pointed to the upstairs landing. "I was the one who found him."

"I'm very sorry," Sebastian said, and she inclined her head. She had probably heard the phrase more times than she could remember and knew it would do nothing to either bring back her son or ease her suffering. "When was this?"

"Nearly three weeks ago." Mrs. Harrow had the look of a woman who had nothing left to live for.

"Do you know why he did it?"

She sighed heavily, her shoulders slumping under the weight of her grief. "He was unhappy. He told me a few days before that everything he loved had been taken away from him. To be frank, I thought he was being melodramatic. I wish I had taken him more seriously."

"Do you know what he was referring to?" Sebastian asked.

"James was always different from the other boys. He was quiet and sensitive. He dreaded going to school and begged us to get him a tutor so he could remain at home. He had difficulty making friends, and when he did he lavished so much love on them that he inevitably scared them off." Silent tears slid down her papery cheeks. "He worshiped Jacob and would have happily followed him wherever he went. That's why he enlisted. He wanted to be with Jacob."

"So, they were in the same regiment?"

"Yes. West Essex 56th Foot. James was so excited. He thought he could finally prove himself to his fearless cousin."

"And did he?" Sebastian asked carefully.

Mrs. Harrow shook her head. "I don't know. He was different when he came back. Even more sullen and moody than usual. He and Jacob had fallen out, and James became upset every time I mentioned him."

"Mrs. Harrow, did you know that James was sending his cousin money every month?"

She looked genuinely shocked. "No, I didn't. What for?"

Before learning of James Harrow's death, Sebastian had believed that the man may have been repaying a loan, but now he thought it more likely that James had been one of his cousin's victims.

"It is my belief that Jacob Harrow was blackmailing your son."

"With what? James lived a blameless life."

"Perhaps something had happened in Crimea that James wished to keep private."

"You mean some act of cowardice?"

"I didn't say that."

"You didn't have to. I know James wasn't cut out to be a soldier. He would never have gone out there if it weren't for Jacob." She shot Sebastian a wary look. "What happened to Jacob?"

"He was brutally murdered, Mrs. Harrow, then hanged from Traitors' Gate, and his tongue severed."

Mrs. Harrow's shock was evident. "I never cared for that boy, truth be told, but no one deserves that."

"James wasn't the only one Jacob blackmailed."

"There were others?"

"Three people that I know of. It's very likely there were others as well."

"And you think one of his victims finally snapped?" Mrs. Harrow asked.

"It's very possible. Did James ever mention Lydia Morton?"

She looked thoughtful. "Yes, he did."

"In what context?"

"He said she was an angel," Mrs. Harrow said with a wistful smile.

"Was he in love with her?" Sebastian asked.

"He may have been. He often said that she was the most beautiful woman he'd ever seen."

"Did James ever go up to London?"

Mrs. Harrow nodded. "Yes, he did. Several times a month. I asked him once if he was going to call on Jacob, and he became angry with me."

"So, he went to see someone else?"

"Yes, but he wouldn't say who."

"Did he have many friends in London?"

"There was someone he mentioned. They met in Crimea. I believe he lives in London."

"Would you have a name?"

Mrs. Harrow's brows knitted in concentration as she tried to remember. "Captain Bertram Hadley. Yes, that's the name."

"And would you know where Captain Hadley lives?"

"Somewhere near the Strand. Or maybe in Southwark. I'm afraid I'm not very familiar with London. I've lived in and around Brentwood my whole life."

"Would it be all right if I looked in James's room?" Sebastian asked.

He thought Mrs. Harrow would refuse him outright, but she took a moment to consider, then nodded resolutely. "Perhaps you can help me to understand why my beautiful boy had to die."

"I will help in whatever way I can."

"I lied, you know," Mrs. Harrow suddenly confessed.

"Lied about what?"

Mrs. Harrow's gaze went to the door, as if she feared someone might overhear them. There might be a maidservant about, but Sebastian hadn't heard anyone. The house seemed empty aside from the two of them.

"I cut James down and hid the rope burn on his neck beneath a cravat. Then I told the vicar that he fell down the stairs. I had to make certain my son received a Christian burial. I didn't think the vicar would believe me, but he didn't even bother to check. Since James was already fully dressed, he was simply laid in a coffin, and the lid was nailed shut. It was all so quick. One minute I had a living, breathing son, and the next his casket was being lowered into the ground, the dirt shoveled on top by men who wanted nothing more than to be finished with the unpleasant task and go for a well-deserved pint."

Mrs. Harrow dabbed at her eyes and went on. "That night, as I lay in my bed, I prayed for God to take me. I had nothing left. My husband was gone. My son was dead. Even the maidservant left me when I failed to pay her on time. But God saw fit to keep me alive. Perhaps to punish me for my perfidy."

"Or perhaps so that you could help me find James's killer," Sebastian said. This poor bereft woman needed reassurance, and it didn't cost him anything to offer a word of comfort that she so badly needed.

"I will do what I can," Mrs. Harrow said, a look of determination coming into her eyes. "And as far as the lie, I don't care if I'm condemned for my crime on Judgment Day. James lies in consecrated ground, and that's all I care about."

"I don't think anyone would judge a grieving mother," Sebastian said. "Things done for the love of one's child can never be a crime."

"Do you have children, Inspector?" Mrs. Harrow asked, looking at him more closely now.

"No. But I came very close to becoming a father."

"I'm sorry."

"I'm sorry too," Sebastian said, and pushed to his feet. "I promise to leave everything as I find it."

James Harrow's room was as spartan as a monk's cell. There was a neatly made bed, a wardrobe, and a rolltop desk with a warren of cubbies and drawers. Sebastian was surprised to find the wastepaper basket full of crumpled sheets of paper and pencil shavings. Perhaps Mrs. Harrow just couldn't bring herself to throw away things James had written. He emptied the cubbies and drawers one by one and examined every piece of paper. There were several articles pertaining to current events, news stories cut out from the London papers and pasted into a thick notebook, all the bylines proclaiming Jacob Harrow as the author. There were several keepsakes that meant nothing to Sebastian, and, hidden between the pages of a book of poetry, a letter from Bertram Hadley.

Sebastian scanned the pages covered in neat, spidery script. Bertram talked of his life in London, reminisced about their time in Crimea, and mentioned that he had renewed his acquaintance with Lydia Morton, who sent her regards to James and hoped to see him again soon. The letter was signed "Faithfully, Bertie."

Was that what had driven James Harrow to suicide? He had been in love with Lydia Morton, but his friend had been the one to gain her affection? Was Bertram Hadley the man Barbara Wicklow had seen Lydia with, and could he be the father of Lydia's child? That was mere speculation at this stage, but, if Bertram and Lydia had been planning to marry, the news might have driven James to take his own life. A plausible theory, but how did it tie in with Lydia's and Jacob Harrow's murders?

Sebastian's gaze fell on the wastepaper bin and he decided to take a look through James Harrow's rubbish. Mostly it was just fiction stories he'd started to write and given up on, but there was one item that caught Sebastian's attention. It was a half-finished letter to Bertram Hadley. Sebastian folded the letter and put it in his pocket along with an article he'd come across in the bin, made sure he left the room tidy, and shut the door behind him.

Sebastian thanked Mrs. Harrow and promised to write as

soon as there were any developments, then hurried back to the station. A train to London was due in ten minutes, and he intended to be on it.

As Sebastian claimed an empty compartment and settled his hat on the seat beside him, he reflected once again that all roads seemed to converge in Crimea, and all the players in this devastating drama had crossed paths long before meeting again in London.

Exhaling deeply, he fixed his gaze on the countryside beyond the window. It looked prettier in the gathering twilight, and what had appeared bleak and barren before was now bathed in lavender light, the first stars of the evening glowing like glow-worms in a darkening sky. He hoped Gemma was still at the Foundling Hospital, where she was safe.

# THIRTY-ONE

The night was cold, and there was the pale cast to the sky that usually foretold snow. Gemma hurried down the crowded street, hoping to catch Barbara Wicklow just as she was leaving for the day. The two women had met once, a few months ago, and Gemma hoped that the brief encounter would be enough of an incentive for Barbara to speak to her. Barbara Wicklow was a no-nonsense woman in her early fifties, whom Lydia had regarded as something of a maternal figure, so perhaps Lydia had shared something with the older woman that she would not dare tell Gemma and that Barbara had been reluctant to tell the police.

Barbara Wicklow was just leaving the hospital and looked none too pleased to be hailed. Gemma thought she seemed frightened. Barbara studied Gemma with a puzzled expression that made her mouth droop at the corners and her brows knit in a way that caused a vertical groove to appear in the middle of her forehead.

"What can I do for you, Miss Tate?" she asked warily.

"I need to speak to you about Lydia."

"I must get home." Barbara began to walk rather briskly, but Gemma kept pace, refusing to be dismissed.

"I won't take much of your time," she promised.

"I know Lydia was your friend, but why are you involving yourself in this, Miss Tate?" Barbara asked.

"Because I want to find her killer."

"Don't you think you should leave that to the police?" Barbara snapped.

"Some people don't trust the police and will not tell them what they know," Gemma countered. "Lydia is dead. Strangled in her own bed." She didn't mean to sound accusing, but that was how it had come out.

"You don't need to remind me of that, Miss Tate. God only knows when I'll feel safe again."

"You will feel safe once the killer has been apprehended," Gemma replied.

"And if he isn't?"

"Mrs. Wicklow, please tell me what you know. Lydia confided in you. She might have shared something important."

Barbara sighed and slowed her pace. "There was a man."

"What man? Someone she met at the hospital?"

It was every nurse's dream to become a doctor's wife, but those dreams rarely came true. Some doctors were eager for a dalliance, but they had no desire to marry women who spent their days taking out chamber pots and changing dressings. They preferred sheltered, pliable young ladies whose only concern was the comfort and happiness of their husband. But a doctor would know how to cleanly sever a tongue, so the repercussions of an affair gone sour couldn't be discounted, especially if Lydia had threatened to denounce him to his colleagues or wife.

"No. It was someone she met in Crimea," Barbara admitted. "Someone she'd fallen in love with."

"What happened?" Gemma asked.

Lydia had never mentioned anyone, which was not to say that she couldn't have engaged in a secret romance. The sheer chaos and soul-crushing agony of the wounded and dying had left most nurses and doctors numb with shock and unable to look beyond getting through another day filled with untold suffering and endless death, but there were some people whose desire to feel something life-affirming was born of the fear and hopelessness that had paralyzed others. A few stolen moments of reckless passion got them through the worst of their despair and gave them something to hold on to.

"Lydia's hopes were disappointed, he had no wish to marry her. And why would he?" Barbara asked bitterly. "A woman who's seen men at their most vulnerable will be more likely to recognize that vulnerability in her husband and question his judgment, sometimes openly. Men don't want wives who imagine themselves their equal, but they don't have the same reservations when all they're interested in is an affair. They were still seeing each other," Barbara added. "Lydia admitted as much when she came to my room for a drink one evening."

"Do you know the man's name?" Gemma asked, praying that Lydia had let the information slip in an unguarded moment of female camaraderie.

"No, she never told me his name. No amount of gin would render her that indiscreet."

"Was he married?"

"I expect he was, or maybe he was already engaged to someone else. Otherwise, there'd be no need to keep the relationship secret."

"Did she say anything about him at all?" Gemma tried again.

"No. Actually, she did say she'd unexpectedly run into him at your brother's funeral and had to pretend they'd never met. Told it to me like it was a hilarious joke."

"Why didn't you tell the police?" Gemma demanded, her

heart squeezing painfully as the memory of that day washed over her. "It must have been Jacob Harrow. This proves there was a connection between them."

Barbara Wicklow stopped walking and turned to Gemma, angry spots of color rising in her cheeks. "And why would I tell them anything?"

"Because Lydia deserves justice," Gemma exclaimed.

"Lydia was trouble, Miss Tate. Respectable women don't get murdered in their beds. Whatever she was involved in got her killed, and I'd be very foolish indeed to draw attention to myself when the killer is still on the loose. For all I know, it was her other suitor that'd murdered her and her secret lover."

"What other suitor?

Her anger spent, Barbara began to walk again, her breath coming in rapid puffs. "Lydia said she'd had a letter from another old acquaintance from Crimea and that he had asked to see her on her afternoon off. I saw them together."

"How long ago was this?"

"About a fortnight."

"Can you describe the man you saw?" Gemma asked.

"Fair, clean-shaven, and well-proportioned. At the time, I thought he was very handsome," she added.

"Age?"

"Mid-twenties. Maybe thirty."

"How did Lydia seem after her meeting with this man?"

"She was quiet. Pensive."

"Do you think she was worried?" Gemma asked.

"Not worried, exactly, but she did seem withdrawn, and perhaps more watchful than usual."

When the two women arrived at the boarding house, Barbara said, "If the police don't make an arrest soon, I'm going to move."

"Inspector Bell will solve the case," Gemma said with unwavering certainty.

Barbara peered at her from beneath a furrowed brow. "Know him well, do you?"

"Well enough to know that he will not let this rest until he sees the killer behind bars."

"At the end of a rope, you mean," Barbara said bitterly and walked up the steps, entering the building without bothering to say goodbye.

Coming from anyone else, that statement would seem odd, more so because Lydia had been a friend and not just some random woman who had been murdered elsewhere, but Gemma understood Barbara's resentment toward the police. She knew from Lydia that Barbara's husband had been hanged for murder some years back. The killing had not been premeditated—the fatal blow had been the result of a drunken brawl—but the sentence had been the same. Death by hanging.

Gemma didn't like to think of people being executed, especially when there were extenuating circumstances, but that was the law. You kill, you die. Sebastian wasn't the one to condemn anyone to death. The accused did that themselves when they decided to take someone's life, be their actions justified or not. There was written law and moral law, and the two did not always converge, but it was up to the judge to make that determination. A policeman followed the evidence and brought criminals to trial. Their fate was not on his conscience.

In truth, a quick death was probably more humane than spending decades in prison and dying a little more each day. The prisoners hardly saw the light of day, were barely fed, and received hardly any medical care if they fell ill. The only way out was in a pine box, and Gemma supposed there were plenty of convicts who longed for the sweet release of death. Even those who weren't sentenced to death and had been shipped to Botany Bay instead didn't fare much better. She'd heard tales of famine, disease, and natives who resented the presence of the

British and wanted them gone from their land. And who could blame them?

Gemma and Victor had engaged in their share of discussions about colonialism, and Victor had been vehemently opposed to occupying other lands. He'd thought the government should focus on problems at home instead of conquering other peoples and creating more unrest abroad that usually led to armed rebellions where more British lives were lost, but it was an unpopular opinion and one he hadn't shared with anyone but Gemma. But Victor's political opinions had nothing to do with Lydia's death, except for the fact that Gemma thought of Victor all the time and wondered what he would make of this, given that he'd known both Jacob Harrow and Lydia Morton. At night, when she was alone in her room, she talked to Victor in her head, and, although she had no illusions about the finality of death, she sometimes thought she could sense his answer. Or maybe it was just her own answer based on what she knew of her brother and his views of the world.

Victor had not been a harsh person. If anything, he had been too soft-hearted at times, but he had been wary of Jacob Harrow, and he hadn't wholly approved of Gemma's friendship with Lydia. He had never said anything disparaging, but his expression would change whenever Gemma mentioned Lydia, his mouth pursing with disapproval. Victor had understood Gemma's need for female companionship but had expressed his desire that Gemma find a more suitable friend, not an easy proposition for a woman who had been labeled as unsuitable herself. Gemma had made several new friends since returning to England, but just now she had to concentrate on the connections she'd made in Scutari. There was one woman in particular, Fenella Lawson, who Gemma thought was worth speaking to if she hoped to help Sebastian solve this case. Gemma had never cared much for Fenella, whom she thought grasping and venal, but Lydia had been close with Fenella, partly because they had shared a tiny, drafty room in the barracks. Fenella had always been unapologetically out for herself, and her efforts had paid off, since she had married a doctor she'd met through her position at an infirmary where she'd found a position after the war.

Gemma had never met the man and couldn't speak to the relationship between husband and wife, but she couldn't help but wonder if Fenella had married him for love or if he was simply a means to an end. Fenella was one of those women for whom love was a bonus but by no means a requirement for happiness. As Gemma spent money she could ill afford on a cab, she thought she was about to find out.

# THIRTY-TWO

The Lawsons lived in Camden Town; their house was only two streets from the newly constructed railway station. Gemma heard the train rumble past and thought that it had been a long time since she'd traveled anywhere. She suddenly missed the sense of excitement one felt when embarking on a journey, even if one were setting off for a war zone. What she wouldn't give to see some of the places she'd read about, like Italy, France, and maybe even America. The very word sounded thrilling. It conjured up images of vast open spaces, bustling towns, and frontier encampments where people mined for gold and lived like outlaws. Perhaps she wouldn't like to see that, but Sebastian had spoken to her about New York and Chicago and had told her of his plan to join the Pinkerton Detective Agency if he was dismissed from the police service.

His position was secure for the time being, but Gemma had seen the faraway look in his eyes and knew that the dream of America was never far away. Sebastian wasn't the sort of man who could remain still for long. He needed stimulation, both mental and physical, and grew easily bored with people whose lives were bound by convention and routine. He'd been miserable while recuperating from his injury, and champing at the bit to get back to work. Disturbed as he was by the murders, he was also entirely in his element, and, although he looked tired and wasn't eating properly, this was the most himself Gemma had seen him in weeks.

Gemma alighted from the hansom and walked up to the door. The house wasn't grand, but it looked solid and welcoming, the evergreen hedges that lined the path neatly trimmed and the brass knocker gleaming with polish. The door was opened by a very young maidservant, who wore a stuff gown of dark gray, a crisp, white pinafore, and a starched cap. Fenella had certainly come up in the world, and Gemma was genuinely pleased for her. The maidservant seemed surprised by the appearance of a visitor and instead of inquiring waited for Gemma to state the reason for her call. Perhaps the Lawsons didn't entertain much, or maybe Fenella wasn't at home.

"My name is Gemma Tate. I'm here to see Mrs. Lawson," Gemma said. "We know each other from the war."

The maidservant gave her a look that said *What war?* but didn't bother to ask.

"Wait here, miss," she said, and shut the door in Gemma's face.

It was windy and cold, and after a few minutes Gemma had begun to wonder if the maidservant had forgotten all about her. But then the door finally opened and Gemma was invited to come inside. The maid took her cape, bonnet, and gloves, and showed her to the parlor, which was wonderfully warm after the windswept street.

Fenella was dressed in a tartan gown of green and blue that brought out her auburn hair and blue eyes, and her complexion glowed with good health. A dainty lace cap sat atop her curls, and, although it was early days, the small mound beneath her skirts was visible enough to confirm to Gemma that the other woman was expecting.

"Gemma, how nice to see you after all this time." Fenella's gaze was guarded and the smile less than genuine, but that was to be expected given that they hadn't seen each other in two years. "Do sit down. Shall I call for tea?"

"Tea would be lovely. Thank you."

Fenella got up and yanked on the bellpull, then resumed her seat. "You must be frozen, though," she said as Gemma held her hands out to the fire and discreetly moved her feet closer to the hearth. The thin soles of her boots did little to keep out the cold, and she was still shivering.

"It is very bracing," Gemma agreed. "Not my favorite time of year."

"And you must feel absolutely desolate, what with your brother's recent death. I'm sorry for your loss." Fenella's gaze was probing, the question in her mind obvious. Why was Gemma paying social calls when she was meant to be in deep mourning?

"Thank you. Losing Victor was a terrible blow," Gemma admitted, but offered no explanation for her sudden visit.

Fenella rushed to fill the silence. "And you had to give up your house. It's bad enough to lose your only remaining family, but to be evicted from your home—" She smiled in what she probably thought was a sympathetic way.

"I wasn't evicted," Gemma corrected her. "I simply did not renew the lease."

"Well, you couldn't afford to, could you? Not on your own. And what would you do with all those rooms anyway? I wouldn't want to live on my own either. It's so lonely, especially when you don't even have a maidservant to look after you."

As if on cue, the maidservant arrived with the tea tray. She must have had the kettle already on the hob. There was a jug of milk and a silver-plated dish of sugar lumps, but no cake or tea sandwiches. There was either nothing to hand or Fenella didn't want Gemma to stay too long. Gemma thought it was the latter and wondered if Fenella had conveyed that to the maidservant before Gemma had been shown in.

Fenella poured out and handed Gemma her cup. "How do you find living in a boarding house?" she asked.

Lydia had clearly been keeping Fenella up to date on Gemma's situation, and it rankled more than she cared to admit. It wasn't a secret that she had to work for a living and was now renting a room in a modest boarding house, but it was none of Fenella's business. Her sympathy was nothing more than a thinly veiled attempt to remind Gemma of her place in the world.

"I'm getting used to it. And how are you keeping?" Gemma asked, eager to change the subject. "You look well. Do you recommend married life?"

"Oh, yes," Fenella replied, smiling widely. "If only for the sheer pleasure of having my own hearth and home. And not having to work for a living anymore," she added spitefully. "To be one's own mistress is absolute bliss."

Gemma didn't comment on Fenella's pregnancy, but the woman placed a hand on her belly, as if to draw Gemma's eye. "We're anticipating a happy event."

"My most sincere congratulations," Gemma said. "When is the child due?"

"Mid-April. I do hope it's a boy. But if it's a girl, we'll simply try again," Fenella said airily. "Such is the lot of the dutiful wife, isn't it? I have always longed for motherhood. A half-dozen children, a doting husband, and a comfortable home. What more could a woman ask for?"

Gemma took that as a rhetorical question and decided it was time to turn the conversation toward the true purpose of her visit. She couldn't stay much longer than it took to drink her cup of tea, and Fenella's comments were beginning to grate on her already raw nerves.

"Fenella, have you heard about Lydia?"

Fenella looked blank. "No. Has something happened?"

Gemma had hoped that Fenella had seen the papers, but, as a self-proclaimed dutiful wife, she probably didn't so much as glance at the headlines when the morning paper was delivered for her husband for fear of causing him upset.

"Lydia is dead. She was murdered."

Fenella's hand flew to her generous bosom. "That simply can't be true. Who told you that?"

"It was in the *Telegraph* this morning."

"No," Fenella cried. "Poor dear Lydia. I shall miss her so."

"I want to help bring her murderer to justice."

"And how could you do that?" Fenella asked, staring at Gemma as if she had just announced that she would begin wearing trousers and a top hat.

"By assisting Inspector Bell."

"Are you working with the police?" Fenella exclaimed. "How very sordid, Gemma."

"I'm not working with the police, but I happen to know Inspector Bell."

Fenella's eyes narrowed with suspicion. "You mean you're secretly courting." Her lips curled in a sly smile. "Do tell. I always did say you were a dark horse, Gemma Tate. Never took you for someone who would welcome the attentions of a policeman, though. Such a louche profession. But I must admit, I have been known to find a ruffian attractive. Is he handsome, your inspector?"

"He is not a ruffian, and we're not courting."

Gemma tried to mask her annoyance with Fenella by adding another lump of sugar to her tea and stirring it until it was fully dissolved. Fenella was more interested in Gemma's personal life than she was in the death of her friend. It was clear that she felt superior to Gemma and Lydia now that she was married and had attained a higher social status, but her lack of genuine feeling was chilling.

Fenella's gaze was triumphant. "Really, Gemma, think of what this will do to your reputation. First your brother gets himself murdered, and now, when you should be in mourning, you're spending time with a policeman and involving yourself in a murder investigation."

"I am in mourning, Fenella, but Lydia was my friend, and I would like to see her murderer brought to justice."

"Is that what this is? A quest for justice?"

"Yes," Gemma replied defensively.

She hated to admit it, but Fenella had struck a nerve. Gemma had no business meddling in a police inquiry, nor would she be associating with a policeman if she hadn't volunteered to look after Sebastian during his convalescence and withdrawal from opium addiction. They would have said their goodbyes at Victor's funeral and never seen each other again. Did her involvement smack of desperation? She wasn't sure she wanted to know the answer to that question.

"I don't suppose Lydia will ever get to America now," Fenella said with feigned regret, immediately snapping Gemma out of her self-recrimination.

"America?"

"Lydia was going to leave. In February. Did she not tell you? I thought you two were such good friends."

"I'm afraid she didn't share her plans with me," Gemma replied. "I hadn't seen her since Victor's funeral."

"Oh, yes," Fenella went on. "She wanted a fresh start, and what can be fresher than New York?" she quipped. "A city populated by upstarts. I would never leave England myself, but I suppose I can understand the appeal. Besides, I daresay Lydia wouldn't have much choice by then."

"How do you mean?"

Fenella looked like a cat that had got the cream and shrugged mysteriously, but Gemma didn't think she'd be able to resist sharing Lydia's secret for long. Whatever loyalty she had once felt was long gone, replaced by the shock of Lydia's murder and the desire to distance herself from any whiff of scandal.

"Lydia was with child."

Gemma stared at Fenella and set down her cup before she could drop it. "Are you sure?" she asked, even though she didn't think Fenella would make something like that up. That would be vicious, even for her.

Fenella nodded sagely. "She was going to leave before anyone realized and tell everyone she was a widow once she arrived in New York. Easy enough to lie when no one knows you."

"Do you know who the father was?" Gemma asked.

"Lydia said it was someone she'd known in Scutari, but that was all she'd say. She was very secretive about the whole thing. I expect he is married."

"I see," Gemma said. "Fenella, did Lydia ever tell you anything about Jacob Harrow?"

Fenella's expression grew coy. "She may have."

"What did she say?"

"She was in love with the man. Don't you know anything? You always were oblivious to the feelings of others, Gemma," Fenella added snidely.

"Perhaps Lydia didn't tell me because she thought I'd disapprove," Gemma replied.

"And you would have. You were so prim and proper in those days. A right old saint. Not so saintly now, are you?"

"I can't afford to be."

"Life brings us all to our knees, albeit in different ways," Fenella said, and Gemma heard a note of bitterness beneath the seemingly innocuous statement.

"Fenella, you have to tell Inspector Bell what you know."

"I will do no such thing," Fenella exclaimed. "I finally have the life I've always wanted. I have a kind, generous husband, and a child on the way. Why would I involve myself in something so squalid? Besides, my husband would never permit me to speak to a policeman."

Gemma sighed, and some small part of her wished she could slap Fenella, both for her callousness and for her obtuseness.

"Fenella," she said with as much patience as she could muster, "you were privy to Lydia's secrets. And plans. And if whoever killed Lydia figures that out, you could be next."

Fenella's face turned the color of ash, and she stared at Gemma in obvious horror. "Whatever do you mean?"

"Lydia wasn't a random victim, and her death might be connected to the murder of Jacob Harrow. If the killer believes you know something that might endanger them, they will come for you next. After all, you and Lydia were very close in Scutari. And if the killer is someone who was in Crimea..." Gemma let the sentence drop, but her meaning was clear.

Fenella's face twisted with anger. "I was safe until you decided to come here and drag me into this," she screeched.

"Were you? You weren't difficult to find. And if I made the connection, so will someone else. Lydia had met with someone she'd known in Scutari recently. Did she tell you about that? This man could be behind these killings, and he might know of your friendship with Lydia."

"Get out, and don't ever come back," Fenella snapped, her face white with fury.

"Will you speak to Inspector Bell?" Gemma demanded as she stood to leave. She towered over Fenella, who sat slumped on the settee, her hand on her belly, her chin practically on her chest. "It's the only way you can make sure you're safe from harm."

Fenella nodded but didn't look up. "I said get out," she reiterated, but there was no heat in her voice this time.

"Goodbye, Fenella."

Fenella didn't answer, but Gemma had got what she'd come for, and she couldn't wait to tell Sebastian what she had learned.

# THIRTY-THREE

Sebastian was there, standing beneath a lamppost, when Gemma got back to the boarding house, and she was once again struck by his thoughtfulness. He had chosen that spot to make certain she could see his face and not become frightened by the silhouette of a strange man lurking outside her door. He looked tired and tense, but his face was transformed by a warm smile when he saw her.

"Sebastian, I wasn't expecting to see you. Has something happened?" Gemma exclaimed. She had just realized that he had to be there for a reason.

"Can we go somewhere?" Sebastian asked. "I'd rather not talk in the street."

Gemma looked up at his drawn face and sunken eyes. She could almost make out the skull beneath the skin. He was pushing himself too hard. "You look exhausted. I wager you haven't eaten."

"I haven't had time."

"You promised me you would take better care of yourself."

Sebastian smiled ruefully. "You mustn't worry about me. A few missed meals will not cause me any permanent harm."

Gemma studied his expression. "But you were worried about me. That's why you are here, isn't it?"

"I missed you at the hospital, and then Mrs. Bass said you didn't come back at your usual time. Where were you, Gemma?"

Gemma threaded her arm through Sebastian's and drew him away. "Let's get you something to eat, and I'll tell you all about it."

The wary look on his face warned her that he suspected her of interfering in his investigation, but she didn't care. She was glad to finally have something to share with him.

"Where are we going?" Sebastian asked.

"There's a chophouse a few streets away," Gemma said. "I've never been inside, but it's always busy."

The atmosphere at the chophouse was lively, the dining room nearly full. It was warm inside, the lamps glowing brightly and the smell of meat and potatoes permeating the air. Most of the tables were occupied by men, who had likely come in for a hot meal and a bit of company if they had no one to go home to. A number of patrons seemed to know each other from previous visits, and exchanged banter and the latest news while awaiting their food.

Sebastian and Gemma found a table in the corner, where they would be able to speak privately and without interruption. It wasn't lost on Gemma that most people who saw them would take them for husband and wife out for a meal together at the end of the workweek. How comforting it would be to have someone to come home to and share one's thoughts with once again, Gemma reflected as they perused the rather limited menu. It was either beefsteak or mutton chops, both options served with roasted potatoes and buttered peas.

Sebastian ordered the beefsteak, while Gemma chose the chops. Her landlady rarely served such decadent dishes, opting instead for cheaper fare such as boiled cod, pies that were thin on filling, and stews that hardly had any meat. Gemma hadn't had chops since Victor had been alive and they'd splurged for their weekly Sunday dinner.

Once the waiter took their order and left, Sebastian fixed Gemma with his probing gaze. "Where were you, Gemma?"

"I went for a walk," Gemma replied evasively.

"I'm worried for your safety."

"Well, don't be. I'm perfectly all right."

"It shames me to admit that I have no idea who killed Lydia or Jacob Harrow, but if any of this goes back to Crimea you might be in very real danger."

Sebastian had just echoed what Gemma had said to Fenella but, even though she knew it to be true, she rushed to reassure him. "Perhaps this is terribly naïve, but I don't think anyone would have reason to kill me, Sebastian. I don't know any secrets. It would seem I was completely oblivious and believed everyone I worked with to be trustworthy and moral," Gemma said bitterly.

"But they might *think* you know something," Sebastian insisted. "You were friendly with Lydia."

"Lydia kept up with everyone. That was simply her nature. I doubt anyone would wish to pick us all off one by one on the off-chance that we knew something incriminating. But there is someone you need to speak to."

"Really? Who?"

Gemma waited while the waiter set their plates before them. She inhaled the wonderful smell, her mouth watering. She hadn't realized just how hungry she was. But she couldn't eat until she conveyed what she knew.

"Lydia was particularly close with one of the other nurses. Fenella Hodgson. Lawson now. She recently married. Lydia and Fenella shared confidences and had remained close friends."

"And you think Fenella Lawson might know something?" Sebastian asked, going directly to the crux of the matter.

"I do. I went to see Fenella after my shift. And Barbara Wicklow."

"You did what?" Sebastian exclaimed, then instantly lowered his voice. "Gemma, for the love of God, you may as well have painted a bullseye on your forehead."

Gemma brushed aside Sebastian's outrage, too eager to share what she had learned to argue with him. Focusing on the case was the only way to keep the grief at bay.

"Lydia was in love with Jacob Harrow and continued to see him once they had returned to England. And Barbara saw Lydia with another man. Lydia told her he was someone she'd known in Scutari."

"Did she give a name?" Sebastian asked tersely.

"Barbara didn't know his name, but she said he was young, fair, and handsome."

"Was Lydia having an affair with him?"

"Fenella didn't say so outright, but she could have been. Lydia was always partial to handsome men, and she was definitely involved with someone."

"How do you know?" Sebastian asked.

"Because it ties in with what I learned from Fenella."

"Which was?"

"Lydia was planning to leave England and go to America."

Sebastian's expression was pained. "Lydia was with child, Gemma. She might have wanted a fresh start someplace she could have a chance at respectability."

"Yes, I know. Fenella told me," Gemma said a tad defensively. She should have realized that Sebastian would know about the pregnancy as soon as Colin had shared the postmortem results, but it would have been nice if he'd told her.

"I didn't want to upset you," Sebastian said softly.

"I know," Gemma said, absolving him. Sebastian wouldn't

want her to grieve the child or think less of Lydia, but at this stage, nothing about Lydia's private life could surprise her.

"Don't you see, Lydia would have needed funds to travel to America. And those funds most definitely did not come from her job at the hospital," Gemma said.

"And you think Lydia was going to finance her escape using the money she earned through blackmail?"

Gemma nodded. "I don't know where she kept her savings, but I'm certain she put aside enough to last her a few years at the very least."

"Lydia had gold nuggets in her stomach. Colin Ramsey found them during the postmortem."

Gemma shuddered at the thought of Colin Ramsey emptying the contents of Lydia's stomach, but had to admit that Lydia's hiding place was effective.

"After Jacob Harrow was murdered, Lydia must have feared that someone was coming for her and decided to hide her loot until she was safely aboard the ship," Sebastian said. "And gold would be easier to convert into dollars."

"Do you think she was murdered because she wouldn't give over the stash?" Gemma asked.

"I'm not sure, but whoever killed her didn't seem open to negotiation. Gemma, please, don't go out on your own after dark. I beg you."

"I promise I will be careful," Gemma said. "You have no reason to worry."

"But I do," Sebastian said brusquely. "Whoever did this might think you know where Lydia kept her savings."

Gemma chuckled. "Anyone who knew Lydia would also know that she'd never tell a soul. Lydia was friendly and helpful, but she didn't trust anyone completely, and her helpful nature was a means to collect favors she could call in."

"And did you owe her a favor?"

"No, but I would have been glad to help had she asked me to."

"You really are too trusting," Sebastian said.

"And you're too jaded," Gemma replied, amused by his obvious surprise.

"Am I?"

"Do you even have to ask?"

"Yes, I suppose you're right," Sebastian conceded. "Still, I wish you would take my warning more seriously. Whether you like it or not, you're now involved in investigating this case." He took a sip of his water and set down the glass. "Does Fenella know who the father of Lydia's child was?"

"I don't believe so, but it could have been Jacob Harrow."

"Or the fair-haired man she was seen with."

"You're a fair-haired man, and people might see me with you," Gemma pointed out. "That doesn't mean we're..." Her voice trailed off, and she felt heat rising in her cheeks. "Well, you know," she muttered when she saw Sebastian grinning at her.

"You're correct. Just because she was seen with a man doesn't mean he was her lover. But she was involved with someone. The existence of the child proves that."

"It could have been anyone. Or no one," Gemma said.

"What do you mean?"

"You're assuming the man was her lover, but perhaps the child wasn't the result of an ongoing relationship. It could have been a one-time thing. A mistake."

Sebastian shook his head. "Lydia was a nurse. She would have known how to terminate an unwanted pregnancy. If she chose to keep the child, she must have cared about the man."

"I'm a nurse, but I wouldn't know how to bring on a miscarriage. I never had cause to." Gemma suddenly felt very warm. This conversation had grown too intimate, and she found that she was embarrassed.

Sebastian seemed to sense her distress and changed the subject. "What else did Fenella Lawson say?"

"She wouldn't tell me anything, but she realizes she has good reason to be frightened. She'll speak to you. I know she will."

"Give me her address, and I will call on her first thing tomorrow."

"Thank you." Gemma recited the address. "There's something else," she added. Now that Sebastian had admitted that she was part of the investigation, he couldn't very well get angry with her. "I called on another nurse I knew in Crimea. She works at Clerkenwell Prison now. She was friendly with Agnes Frye."

Sebastian looked slightly apoplectic but clearly decided not to rebuke her.

"Agnes followed her lover to Ireland and died in childbirth. So she couldn't have been involved in the blackmail, at least not recently."

Sebastian scoffed. "Godfrey Price will be pleased to hear that he no longer has two wives. May she rest in peace," he added hastily when Gemma gave him a reproachful look.

"I also paid a condolence call on Emma Harrow."

"You did what?" Sebastian exploded.

"It's a perfectly natural thing to do. I knew her husband, and he came to Victor's funeral. No one would think anything of it."

"How did you even find her?" Sebastian asked. Gemma thought that, despite his disapproval, he was just a little bit impressed with her ingenuity.

"You told me where her parents live, and I knocked on a door that displayed a black bow." She didn't bother to tell him that she had blundered the first time.

Sebastian shook his head in dismay but couldn't hide his smile. "And? What were you able to discover?"

"Emma was besotted with her husband and had no reason to contract his murder. She's also expecting a baby. They were happy, Sebastian, at least as far as she was concerned."

"Well, I suppose it's a relief to be able to rule her out. I do hope she will be safe."

"She has no plans to return to the house she shared with her husband. She thinks her father can let out the property."

"Probably for the best," Sebastian replied.

Gemma was gratified to note that color had returned to his cheeks, and he no longer looked so worn out. Beef was good for the blood, and she hoped his landlady fed him meat several times per week.

"Did you speak to James Harrow, as you'd planned? Was he able to shed any light on his cousin's activities?" she asked.

"James Harrow hanged himself a few weeks ago," Sebastian said quietly. "Did you know him?"

Gemma felt a wave of pity wash over her. "Yes. Very briefly. He was wounded in the leg. His injury wasn't terribly serious, but he was frightened. Lydia took pity on him and sat with him during the night."

"He called her his angel," Sebastian said. "Might Lydia have become romantically involved with him?"

"I doubt it. She was simply being kind. And James was hardly more than a boy."

"What about Captain Bertram Hadley? Does the name ring a bell?"

Gemma set down her knife and fork. "Bertram Hadley?"

"Yes."

"How is he involved in this?"

"He had come by the newspaper office to speak to Jacob Harrow, and he was also a close friend of James Harrow. Captain Hadley wrote to James, informing him that he had renewed his acquaintance with Lydia Morton."

"I wasn't aware Lydia and Bertram knew each other."

"How did you know him?" Sebastian asked, his gaze fixed on Gemma's face, his food forgotten.

"Captain Hadley's younger brother, Paul, was wounded, and he came to visit the boy. The hospital didn't allow visitors, but Captain Hadley managed to sweet-talk Miss Nightingale, and she allowed him in for a few minutes. Mostly because she thought it might help the patient."

"Did Paul Hadley recover?"

Gemma shook her head. "He developed gangrene."

"Did Lydia Morton nurse Paul Hadley as well?"

"I don't believe so. No, he wasn't on her side of the ward."

"But Bertram Hadley and Lydia Morton clearly knew each other."

"And he's fair," Gemma said. "Like you."

Sebastian seemed to file this away, then reached into his pocket, pulling out several folded sheets of paper. "I took this from James Harrow's room."

"What is it?"

"It's essays he wrote about his time in Crimea."

"What of them?"

"I read them on the train, and they sound an awful lot like the articles written by Jacob Harrow."

"What are you suggesting, Sebastian?"

"There was a reason James Harrow was paying his cousin every month. Something happened during his time in Crimea that he needed to keep secret."

"But he was paying less than the others. Perhaps he was paying off a loan," Gemma suggested.

"I think he was paying less because that was all he could afford, but I'm certain Jacob Harrow was blackmailing him."

"And you think that it had something to do with these essays?"

"No. I think it was something much more shocking."

"What are you saying?"

"Don't you think it odd that all these people are still connected, years after the war ended?"

"I was still friends with Lydia, and she was friendly with most of the nurses she'd met in Scutari. I don't think there's anything strange in that."

"But this wasn't just friendship. James Harrow's mother said that James and Jacob had fallen out. James refused to even mention his cousin's name. Lydia was murdered a few days after Jacob Harrow, and James Harrow hanged himself a few weeks before his cousin was murdered. There's a common thread running through these events, and I'm sure they're connected."

Gemma nodded. "Yes, I think they might be."

"Why didn't you remain friends with Fenella Lawson?" Sebastian asked, almost as an afterthought. "I expect there was a good reason you didn't remain in contact."

"I didn't trust her."

"Why?"

"For one thing, she was always a bit spiteful, the sort of person who said the most hurtful things under the guise of concern. And for another, I saw her take things."

"What sort of things?"

"Things that belonged to patients who died in her care."

"Did Lydia know?" Sebastian asked.

"I think so."

"Was Fenella ever caught?"

"No."

"Is it possible that Lydia helped herself to valuable items as well? Perhaps that was how she built up her little nest egg."

Gemma sighed. "To be honest, I don't know. I didn't immediately believe that Lydia would ever blackmail anyone, but I don't think she would see anything wrong with taking something that would otherwise wind up in a mass grave."

"Did patients normally have valuables on them?"

"Most didn't, but there were those, particularly officers, who wore jeweled rings or had a watch. Some men wore a medallion or a crucifix for protection, and many wore wedding rings."

"Do you think Fenella Lawson brought these items back with her?" Sebastian asked.

"My guess would be that she fenced them."

"But you would trust the information provided by this woman?"

"Fenella always had a healthy sense of self-preservation. She will tell you whatever she knows for her own benefit, not because she wants to help the police."

"Fair enough," Sebastian said.

Gemma nodded, pushed her empty plate away, and reached for her reticule, but Sebastian forestalled her. "My treat."

Gemma smiled. "Then the next time is on me."

Sebastian chuckled. "You are a very modern woman, Miss Tate."

"You don't know the half of it, Inspector Bell," Gemma replied playfully, and was shocked by her own boldness.

"But I'd like to find out," Sebastian replied with a grin. "I'll see you back to the boarding house," he added when Gemma stood to leave.

He paid the bill while Gemma put on her cape and adjusted her bonnet. She was glad not to have to walk back alone, and fervently hoped that her information would lead to a break in the case.

## THIRTY-FOUR

It was past seven o'clock by the time Sebastian returned to Scotland Yard. He would have gladly gone home, but Godfrey Price had been cooling his heels in the cells for hours, and Sebastian was eager to have a chat. The building was quiet with nearly everyone gone for the day. Only two people would remain to cover the night shift and keep an eye on Godfrey Price if Sebastian decided to charge him, since it was too late to arrange to transport him to Newgate or Coldbath Fields, where he would be incarcerated as he awaited his trial.

"Has Price said anything?" Sebastian asked Sergeant Woodward when he entered the duty room.

"No. Quiet as a mouse. I thought he might have topped himself, but he was sleeping when Constable Meadows brought him a mug of tea. His conscience must be clear if he can sleep in a police cell."

"Either that or he's exhausted," Sebastian said, having recalled what Godfrey Price had said about staying up all night with the boy whose foot he'd amputated. If he sent Price down, the hospital would lose a dedicated surgeon.

Sergeant Woodward shrugged. "Do you want someone to sit in?"

"No, I'm fine. Please have him brought to interview room one."

"I'll fetch him myself," Sergeant Woodward said, and reached for the keyring.

When Sergeant Woodward escorted Godfrey Price into the room, Price no longer resembled the capable, self-assured surgeon Sebastian had met at Guy's Hospital. In his place was a man who looked defeated, unkempt, and frightened. Sergeant Woodward handed Sebastian the keys to Price's cuffs and left him to it.

"Why are you keeping me here?" Price cried as soon as they were alone. "My wife must be going out of her mind."

"Don't worry, Mr. Price. Your wife was informed of your arrest and knows where you are."

"But she'll be frightened," the surgeon persisted.

"I'm sorry about that."

"You have no right to hold me," Price said warily. "You have no evidence."

"But we do," Sebastian replied patiently. "Mr. Price, you knew both victims."

"Both?"

"Lydia Morton was murdered on Wednesday night. Her tongue was severed, and then she was strangled."

The surgeon looked horrified. "And you think I did that?"

"Jacob Harrow was blackmailing you over your ill-advised marriage to Agnes Frye, and Lydia Morton was well acquainted with all three of you. You admitted as much yourself."

"So what?" Godfrey demanded. "I knew all the nurses at Scutari. Am I to be held accountable for what happens to them now they're back in England?"

"You are if they're trying to ruin your life and then

suddenly wind up dead," Sebastian replied. "Where were you on Wednesday night?"

"I was at home. I never left the house once I returned from the hospital. My wife can vouch for me."

"Was your wife awake and watching you the entire time?"

"No, but she would have known had I left. She's a very light sleeper. She's in the final months of pregnancy and isn't very comfortable. Please, Inspector," Godfrey implored. "I didn't kill anyone. I'm sworn to uphold life."

"Mr. Price, one of the questions I ask myself when investigating a murder is who would profit by the victim's death," Sebastian explained. "There's no doubt that you will profit from the deaths of Jacob Harrow and Lydia Morton. Not only will you gain peace of mind, but you will also be able to stop paying ten quid per month, a veritable fortune for someone who's so inadequately compensated."

Godfrey Price went white to the roots of his hair. "My wife and son will perish without me," he whispered. "Joanna has no money of her own, and once her parents hear..." He couldn't go on, and fumbled for his handkerchief, not an easy feat when wearing cuffs.

Once Price regained a modicum of composure, he faced Sebastian, an air of resignation radiating from him, his shoulders slumped with defeat. He knew he would be charged and hanged if found guilty, but he would still make his case. "Tell me, Inspector, why would I murder Jacob Harrow and Lydia Morton in such a way? It's a bit extreme, wouldn't you say?"

"So, how would you have killed them?" Sebastian asked.

Price looked torn between replying truthfully and trying to absolve himself of guilt, but the need to defend himself won out. "I would poison them."

"Why?"

"Because there's no way to trace the poison to the poisoner if it takes time to act. And I wouldn't have to watch them die,"

Godfrey choked out. "And if I was to kill those two, I would have done it years ago."

Sebastian considered this. There had been only a handful of times during his tenure as detective when his reason hadn't squared with his instinct, and this was one of those occasions. On paper, Godfrey Price was the obvious suspect. He had a strong motive, was the only one who knew all the players, and would know not only how to sever a tongue cleanly but how to penetrate the heart with a single stab without the knife encountering bone. He was also young, healthy, and strong enough to take down Jacob Harrow and subdue Lydia Morton.

But Sebastian's gut instinct rebelled at the thought of charging him with two murders. Godfrey Price did not strike him as a killer, nor was he foolish enough or so brazen as to kill his tormentors in such a public way. Some would argue that that was the whole point—that he'd done the unexpected to confuse the police—but Sebastian really couldn't see this intelligent, dedicated surgeon resorting to such savagery. If he were to murder them, he'd do it in a way that was efficient and could never be traced back to him. Rowing out to the Tower and hanging Harrow with a meat hook or clambering up a drainpipe to climb into Lydia Morton's bedroom just didn't fit.

Sebastian took the key out of his pocket, leaned across the table, and unlocked the cuffs. Godfrey Price stared at him, uncomprehending.

"Go home, Mr. Price," Sebastian said.

"You're letting me go?"

"Against my better judgment, I am," Sebastian replied.

"Why?"

"Because I don't believe you did it."

Sebastian's gaze never left Price's face—he wanted to see his reaction—but there was no smugness or glimmer of triumph. There was only relief and gratitude.

"And Mr. Price," Sebastian said as the surgeon stood slowly and turned toward the door.

"Yes?" Sebastian saw renewed fear. Price thought Sebastian was toying with him.

"Agnes Frye died in childbirth."

Sebastian expected Price to display something akin to relief, but what he saw was sincere grief. The surgeon's eyes glistened with tears.

"God rest her troubled soul," he said, and then he was gone.

Sebastian stared after him but made no move to rise. Tomorrow he would have to explain his decision to Superintendent Lovell, and that meeting was not going to go well, not unless he could offer Lovell an alternative solution. Pushing to his feet, he left the interview room.

"You let him go?" Sergeant Woodward asked, staring at Sebastian as if he'd gone completely mad.

"I don't think he did it."

"I hope you've thought this through, Sebastian."

"I have," Sebastian replied. He didn't owe Woodward an explanation.

"What if he disappears in the night?'

"He's not going anywhere," Sebastian said, and walked out before Sergeant Woodward could raise any more objections.

# THIRTY-FIVE

## SATURDAY, DECEMBER 18

Sebastian would have liked to start his day by calling on Fenella Lawson, but, if he hoped to still be employed by the end of the day, he had to give Superintendent Lovell the courtesy of an explanation. Lovell was already at his desk by the time Sebastian arrived, so Sebastian walked right in and sat down without being invited.

"I should sack you on the spot," Lovell said. There was real hostility in his gaze, and Sebastian knew he was skating on thin ice.

"I don't believe he's guilty."

"Price has all but admitted to the murders."

"He has not," Sebastian countered. "He's a flawed, terrified man, but he never stopped proclaiming his innocence."

"And you believed him?" Lovell scoffed.

"I believe in facts," Sebastian replied calmly. "We don't have any physical evidence to link Godfrey Price to either murder, and he has an alibi for the night Harrow was killed."

"A rather flimsy alibi. You said so yourself."

"It's an alibi, nonetheless, provided by a woman who

commands respect and the nurses in her charge. It will stand up in court. A non-guilty verdict will embarrass the police service and remind the public that the real killer is still out there."

"So, you took the word of a man who's been living a lie for years and let him go? You've always been reckless, but I never took you for a fool. I have a good mind to take this case away from you before you make us a laughingstock. The vultures are circling, Sebastian, and by Monday they will be picking over the bones of this station."

"Grant me one more day, sir," Sebastian said.

"Do you have any viable leads?" Lovell demanded.

"I might."

"Might is not good enough."

Lovell cocked his head to the side as he considered Sebastian's request. An arrest would save the police service embarrassment, but to charge the wrong man would make Lovell the butt of endless ridicule and the press's new whipping boy. Lovell was savvy enough to see that, and the realization seemed to give him pause. He was a man who preferred to err on the side of caution, especially when it came to his own reputation and his career trajectory. If Lovell hoped to be made commissioner after Sir David retired, he'd have to keep his eye on the prize and not make any hasty decisions. Angry as he was, he knew Sebastian had a valid point, except he would have preferred to keep Godfrey Price in the cells until he was proven either guilty or innocent.

"Very well," Lovell said at last. "You have until the end of today to wrap up this case. In the meantime, I'm going to put a watch on Price. To allow him to abscond will make us look like the clueless clodhoppers the press wants us to be. It's better to have a less-than-solid case than to have no case at all."

"Is it?" Sebastian fired back.

Lovell fixed him with a baleful stare. "Inspector, can you

say with one hundred percent certainty that Godfrey Price did not murder Jacob Harrow and Lydia Morton?"

"I cannot," Sebastian admitted.

"Then there's your answer. Now, get out of my sight."

"Yes, sir."

## THIRTY-SIX

When Sebastian arrived at the house in Camden Town and the maidservant showed him to the drawing room, he was surprised to find two little boys seated before the hearth, their cheeks pink with the heat of the fire. They were playing with a wooden horse on wheels, and gawked at Sebastian when he walked in. The mistress of the house looked on, her brows knitting in displeasure, and possibly embarrassment.

"Inspector Bell, ma'am," the maidservant said.

"Take them away," Fenella Lawson told her imperiously, and the woman shepherded the children out the door as if they were stray sheep.

"Mrs. Lawson," Sebastian greeted her.

Fenella Lawson nodded and indicated a chair. Sebastian made himself comfortable and waited for her to speak, since she appeared to be debating how much to tell him.

"My husband's children," she said at last. "He was widowed in the spring."

Dr. Lawson had married Fenella Hodgson shortly after his wife's death then, while he was still in mourning for his sons' mother. That certainly put a new slant on the marriage, and

Sebastian realized that Fenella had probably hoped that Gemma would never learn of the children's existence. That would make it easier to pretend this was a love match rather than what it really was, a widowed man desperate to find someone suitable to take care of his children. To marry was vastly more practical than to hire a nursemaid, for myriad reasons.

"I'm sorry for your loss," Sebastian said.

"I'm not grieving my predecessor," Fenella replied scornfully.

"I was referring to your friend, Lydia Morton."

"Oh. Thank you."

"I understand you two were quite close."

"We were close in Scutari, but once we returned to England our lives moved in different directions."

"But you knew Lydia was with child, and that she was planning to leave England," Sebastian pointed out.

"We did see each other from time to time. And I invited Lydia to my wedding. I needed someone to sit on my side of the church," Fenella said with obvious bitterness.

"Did Lydia tell you the name of her lover?"

"No, but he couldn't have killed her."

"Why not?"

"Because he was already dead," Fenella replied.

"Speak plainly, Mrs. Lawson," Sebastian ordered. "If you don't know who the man was, how could you know he's dead?"

"Lydia didn't have to tell me his name," Fenella exclaimed, two bright spots of color blooming in her pale cheeks. "I knew who it was as soon as she told me she was with child. There was only one man Lydia would have let down her guard for. Jacob Harrow."

"What makes you so sure?"

"Because I know love when I see it, Inspector. And it shines that much more brightly when you've never felt it yourself or been loved for the right reasons."

Fenella's eyes glittered with tears when she realized just how much she had revealed of her own life and her feelings toward her husband and his toward her, but it was too late, so she gathered the tattered ends of her pride and tied them together to form a protective mantle.

"We all choose our path, Inspector," she said haughtily. "Lydia chose to follow her heart and look where it got her."

"Tell me about Lydia Morton and Jacob Harrow."

"Unless Gemma Tate has told you of her experiences, you can't begin to imagine the conditions in Scutari. The horror was indescribable, for the doctors and nurses as well as the patients. We all live with death, but this was wholesale slaughter, Inspector, the men dying by the thousands not only on the battlefields but afterwards of their injuries and postoperative infections. Each day we lost dozens of men. Their bodies were taken out and buried in mass graves."

Fenella had a faraway look in her eyes, as if she were seeing those pits of death, and Sebastian knew she'd tell him what he wanted to know. Like all those who had come back, Fenella was scarred by her experiences and needed someone to talk to. Sebastian doubted she had ever told her husband of that time in her life, probably for fear of driving him away with the scope of her worldliness. After all, Dr. Lawson wanted a mother for his children, not a self-proclaimed angel of death.

"You find things to help you go on, to hold on to," Fenella whispered. "I found solace in my friendship with Lydia and some of the other women, but Lydia had allowed herself to develop feelings for a patient. It happened to us all from time to time. It was only natural given the pressure we were under, but Lydia began to build her dreams for the future around Jacob Harrow."

"Did anyone else know of the affair?"

Fenella Lawson shook her head. "Lydia didn't want anyone to know, especially Gemma. She didn't think Gemma would approve. She was always so high and mighty," she added spitefully. "Some women are born to become old maids."

Sebastian let that go unanswered. "Did Jacob Harrow return Lydia's feelings?"

"I warned Lydia that he was toying with her and would forget about her as soon as he was released from the hospital, but Lydia said he loved her and would ensure they had a good life together. The fool even bought him a gold watch once she had returned to England, and had it engraved with her initials."

"A pocket watch with the initials M.L. was found on the body," Sebastian said.

"That's the one. Lydia's full name was Melinda Lydia Morton. She didn't like the name Melinda, but Jacob thought it lovely."

"How could Lydia afford a gold watch?"

Fenella Lawson shrugged. "I reckon she bought it off some fence for a fraction of the price. She would have given her last farthing to make Jacob happy."

Sebastian thought there was another way to get one's hands on a gold watch, but didn't say so. He had no proof that Lydia had stolen from dead men and saw no reason to accuse her at this stage.

"Was Jacob Harrow badly wounded?" he asked instead.

"He was shot in the stomach, so he remained on the ward for several weeks. Long enough to snare a trusting young woman."

"Why were you so certain he was stringing Lydia along?"

"There was just something about him," Fenella said, her gaze narrowing. "Something false. He put me in mind of my uncle."

"Your uncle?"

Fenella nodded. "My uncle is the sort of man who focuses

all his attention on the person he's speaking to. He makes them feel valued and important by asking them questions about themselves and praising their accomplishments. If the person is foolish enough to confide in him, he uses what he's learned to his own advantage."

She sighed and rested her hand on her rounded abdomen. "Lydia became angry with me when after we returned to England my prediction about Jacob Harrow came true and he married another."

"So why do you think he was the father of Lydia's child?" Sebastian asked.

"Because they still saw each other. Lydia admitted as much to me."

"Did he know about the child?"

"I doubt it. Lydia was too proud to beg him to leave his wife, but she would always have the child to remind her of their supposed love. It was once she discovered she was pregnant that she decided to go to America. She intended to leave in February and get settled before the child was born."

"Mrs. Lawson, Jacob Harrow was blackmailing several individuals. Was Lydia involved in his scheme?"

Fenella shrugged. "Possibly. He could have talked her into anything. And she needed the money."

"Did you know James Harrow?" Sebastian asked. "I believe he was wounded as well."

Fenella brightened. "Yes, I remember him. He was a charming boy. He took a bayonet to his side. The blade entered between the ribs and exited through the back. It was a miracle he survived. He was with us almost until the end of the hostilities."

"Did anyone visit him?"

"Visitors weren't allowed on the wards, but Miss Nightingale sometimes made an exception for patients who were dying. It comforted them to see a friendly face. Captain Hadley visited

James. He was permitted to see his brother, who died of gangrene, and while he was there he stopped by James Harrow's cot to offer good wishes for his recovery. They seemed to know each other well."

"What gave you that impression?"

"He kissed James on the forehead before he left. He had done the same with his brother."

"Did Captain Hadley ever come back?" Sebastian asked.

"He wasn't allowed to come inside, so he asked Lydia to pass James Harrow a notebook, pencils, and a pear."

"Why did he need a notebook?"

"Oh, James was always scribbling. He said that writing about his experiences helped him to make sense of it all."

"And did it?" Sebastian asked, recalling the essays he'd taken from James's room.

"I don't know. I never saw him again."

"Captain Hadley said in a letter he sent to James Harrow that he had renewed his acquaintance with Lydia. Did Lydia mention him to you?"

Fenella looked taken aback. "No, she didn't."

"Could Captain Hadley have been Lydia's secret lover?"

Fenella glanced toward the door as if afraid someone would overhear the conversation, but there was no one in the house save the children and a maidservant, who was preparing luncheon in the kitchen. Vegetable soup, if Sebastian guessed correctly.

"There were rumors about Captain Hadley," Fenella said, keeping her voice low.

"What sort of rumors?"

"The sort that lead to pistols at dawn." Fenella's eyes sparkled with mischief, and Sebastian realized she couldn't wait to share what she knew but wanted to draw out the suspense as long as possible. "It seems Captain Hadley was conducting a rather scandalous love affair."

"Who with?" Sebastian asked.

Fenella's lips quirked at the corners, and she leaned closer, her eyes dancing with amusement. "Wouldn't you like to know."

"I would, as it happens, so I suggest you tell me, Mrs. Lawson." *Or you'll find yourself in the cells in place of Godfrey Price,* Sebastian thought viciously. He didn't like this woman and could see why Gemma had kept away from her both in Scutari and in London.

Fenella's smile grew wider. "I don't know exactly, but what I do know is that it wasn't with someone suitable."

Sebastian sat back and considered this new information. Was it possible that the woman in question was Mrs. Wallace? She could have lied about her lover dying. That would explain the blackmail, but, unless Fenella Lawson could confirm the name of Captain Hadley's lover, it was nothing more than supposition.

"Have you ever seen one of these?" Sebastian asked, taking out the evil eye charm and showing it to Fenella.

"Yes. They were everywhere in Turkey."

"Jacob Harrow had it on him when he died."

"Maybe he had a guilty conscience and thought the silly little charm would protect him," Fenella said nastily.

"Please remain vigilant, Mrs. Lawson," Sebastian said as pushed the charm back into his pocket and stood to leave.

"Am I in danger, Inspector?" Fenella Lawson cried, her fear palpable.

"Until the killer is behind bars, everyone who was privy to Lydia Morton's secrets is a potential target."

*And the list keeps growing,* Sebastian thought morosely as he took his leave.

## THIRTY-SEVEN

Having learned all he could from Fenella Lawson, Sebastian consulted the return address on the letter from Captain Hadley and instructed the cabbie to take him to St. Martin's Lane. Although the house was modest from the outside, the interior looked spacious and was tastefully furnished and welcoming. The man himself, when he came forward to greet Sebastian, fit a similar description. Captain Hadley's manner was genial, and he was well groomed and tastefully attired despite the early hour. With thick fair hair, warm brown eyes, and a well-maintained physique, Bertram Hadley fit the profile of the man Barbara Wicklow had seen with Lydia Morton, and he was a more likely candidate than Reginald Pickering. Reginald was too young to take an interest in someone like Lydia and seemed to have no reason to seek her out, whereas Bertram Hadley and Lydia Morton had recently been in contact.

"To what do I owe the pleasure, Inspector?" Captain Hadley asked once they were seated in the parlor, which was decorated in scarlet and gold.

It was an ostentatious room, worthy of royalty or a high-end brothel, but Captain Hadley seemed to fit right in; his manner was rather high-handed. A merry fire burned in the grate, an open book lay face down on the occasional table at Hadley's elbow, and a chessboard stood in readiness on the walnut sideboard next to a half-full decanter surrounded by several cut crystal glasses.

"I'd offer you a drink, but the sun is not yet over the yardarm. I do try not to start drinking too early in the day. Not very good for one's health, I find. I could ring for tea. Or coffee, if you prefer it."

"Thank you, but there's no need," Sebastian replied, even though he would have welcomed a hot drink after the cold ride. "That's a beautiful sword," he remarked of the basket-hilt sword displayed above the sideboard. "A claymore, I believe."

"Yes. It belonged to my grandfather. He took it off some Highlander after the Battle of Culloden. That was during the Jacobite Uprising of '45. Primitive fellows, but they made fine swords."

"Have you ever used it?" Sebastian asked. The sword looked heavy, the basket hilt awkward but probably very useful for protecting one's hand.

"No, I prefer the saber. To me, fencing with a saber is instinctive. It's almost like an extension of my own arm."

"Do you fence often?"

"At least twice a week. I practice with a fencing master. I feel it's important to keep fit."

He shot Sebastian a loaded look, possibly meant to imply that he looked neither fit nor particularly agile, despite being of an age with Captain Hadley. Perhaps once his shoulder healed completely, he should consider some sort of sport. He didn't fancy bare-knuckle boxing, but fencing would probably bring him a sense of satisfaction. He would check with Gemma when it might be safe for him to attempt it.

"Was there something you wished to ask me, Inspector?" Captain Hadley asked politely.

"I wanted to speak to you about James Harrow."

Hadley's expression turned stormy, his jaw tightening with anger. "What about him?"

"You were friends."

"We were."

"No doubt you've seen the papers. James Harrow's cousin, Jacob Harrow, was murdered a few days ago."

"Yes, I'm aware. But what does that have to do with me?"

"It has come to my attention that Jacob Harrow was blackmailing his cousin. Did you know about that?"

Bertram's anger seemed to dissipate, and he looked nonplussed. "Was he? What could he have found to hold over James's head? James was the kindest, most generous man I've ever met. He was also a complete innocent."

"That's what I'm trying to discover, Captain. What could young, sweet-natured James have to hide?"

"James had nothing to hide, Inspector, but Jacob Harrow accused him of cowardice," Bertram Hadley said, the anger flaring once again. "It wasn't as if Jacob had covered himself in glory on the battlefield, but he taunted and belittled James at every turn, until he managed to completely break him down."

"How did this cowardice manifest itself?" Sebastian asked.

"James had followed Jacob into the army because he idolized his cousin, but once he found himself in the midst of a real war he realized he wasn't cut out for combat. James refused to fire on the enemy or use his sword for anything other than self-defense. He confided in his cousin that he had considered deserting."

"It would not be an easy thing to desert a foreign war. How would he find his way home to England?" Sebastian asked.

"To be frank, I don't think James ever thought that far. He only knew he had to get away before he lost what was left of his sanity."

"James Harrow was paying his cousin a substantial amount

for a man who didn't appear to have any income. I find it difficult to believe that the risk of exposure was as real as it might
have been when both men were in Crimea."

James Harrow would have been executed if he had tried to
desert, but at the time he killed himself he was no longer in the
army, and the threat had been nullified. Had he been so worried
for his reputation even as a civilian that he'd been willing to take
his own life? It didn't seem likely since suicide was one of the
most shameful acts an individual could undertake, one that
would tarnish the family's reputation for generations. It was no
wonder Mrs. Harrow had lied to the vicar to ensure her son
received a proper burial. She understood what such a legacy
would entail—not that there was anyone left to carry on the
family name. Now that both Harrows were dead, it seemed
only James's mother and Jacob's wife were left, unless Emma
Harrow was delivered of a healthy boy.

Bertram Hadley leaned back in his chair and crossed his
legs, his elegant hand resting on his knee, his elbow on the
polished armrest. He was the picture of a gracious host, but
Sebastian was aware that anger wasn't far from the surface and
could boil over at any moment. He had clearly cared deeply for
James and still felt insulted on his behalf.

"James was very young when he followed Jacob to Crimea,"
Captain Hadley said. "He had just turned seventeen. He was
frightened and naïve and believed that the truth about his fears
would destroy whatever future he might have. Jacob went so far
as to imply that he would pen an article about desertion and
would mention James by name."

"Was that what led James to take his own life? He could no
longer bear the threat of exposure?"

Sebastian watched Captain Hadley's reaction carefully, but
the man made no attempt to deny the fact that he knew the
truth of James's death.

He nodded. "In part. James felt hopeless and trapped. And

terribly ashamed of the possibility that British soldiers might have died because he had refused to fire his weapon. He told me so when I saw him at the hospital in Scutari." Hadley's eyes blazed with anger. "I didn't know Jacob was making him pay as well. I can't begin to understand how he could be so cruel to a boy who loved him like a brother."

"You lost your own brother, I believe. I'm sorry," Sebastian said.

Hadley nodded. "The surgeon, Mr. Price, operated on him, but it was too late. The infection had spread. I was most grateful to Miss Nightingale for allowing me to say goodbye."

"You knew Mr. Price?" Sebastian asked.

"We met briefly," Bertram Hadley said with a one-shoul-dered shrug.

"Captain Hadley, someone murdered Jacob Harrow and cut out his tongue. Then they murdered Lydia Morton and cut out her tongue as well."

"And you think I might know something about that?"

"You knew all the actors in this drama, including Godfrey Price."

"What's he got to do with this?"

Sebastian chose not to explain. Instead he asked, "Had you seen Jacob Harrow since returning from Crimea?"

Captain Hadley smirked. "I'm sure you already know the answer to that, Inspector."

"Were you friends?" Sebastian asked.

"Hardly. The man was a pompous turd, but he had the ear of the public, so he had his uses."

"What did you want his readers to hear about?"

"It no longer matters. Harrow was correct in his estimation that the public is no longer interested in anything that happened during the war. Best to move on, he told me."

"I must insist that you tell me," Sebastian pressed.

Hadley shrugged. "I wanted to expose certain individuals

who profited handsomely by redirecting supplies to those who could afford to pay for them. I assure you, the story has nothing to do with your investigation since Harrow didn't even ask me for the names."

"Whom were you going to accuse?"

"Lieutenant Wise of the 10th Royal Hussars and General Wallace, who turned a blind eye when informed of what was going on by his aide-de-camp in order to avoid embarrassment. There were others as well, but they had played a smaller role."

"And Lydia Morton? What was your relationship with her?" Sebastian asked as he filed away the information to be examined at a later date. This investigation put him in mind of the Turkish charm in his pocket. A circle within a circle within a circle. No beginning and no end, just endless questions and answers that seemed to point to the same group of individuals.

"I happened to run into Nurse Morton when I went to visit a friend at the London Hospital. I invited her to take a cup of tea with me. For old times' sake. She accepted."

"You were angry with Jacob Harrow for bullying your friend," Sebastian said, circling back to James Harrow just when Captain Hadley thought the subject had been exhausted. "And now James is dead, driven to take his own life by Harrow's threats."

"Yes, I was angry, but I wasn't aware of the extent of Harrow's malice. Had I known he was blackmailing James, I might have been able to help."

"How? Would you have lent him money or found a way to help in a more permanent sense?"

"We all have secrets, Inspector. No doubt Jacob Harrow had a few of his own. I could have stopped him had James confided in me."

Sebastian nodded. "I found a letter from you among James's things. In it you say that you had renewed your acquaintance with Nurse Morton. She was a beautiful woman. Did you arrange to see her again after your serendipitous meeting at the hospital?"

"We did not make plans to see each other again. I mentioned it to James because he had been fond of Nurse Morton and would have liked to know that she was well." Bertram Hadley smiled dolefully. "I would very much like to help you, Inspector Bell, but I really don't know anything about either murder. And I am genuinely sorry Miss Morton is dead. She was a lovely woman and was kind to James when he was in her care."

"Are you acquainted with Mrs. Wallace, General Wallace's wife?" Sebastian asked, hoping to take Captain Hadley unawares, but the man looked frustratingly blank.

"I haven't had the pleasure. Is she a suspect?" he asked, a smile tugging at his lips.

"Not at this time, but her name did come up during the course of the investigation. Jacob Harrow was blackmailing her as well."

"Oh, dear. Poor Mrs. Wallace. Perhaps she was trying to protect her husband's reputation."

"Where were you on Monday, between ten and two at night, Captain?" Sebastian asked. The man's smugness annoyed him, but Sebastian had nothing to reproach him with. He'd been forthcoming enough.

Hadley shrugged. "I was here. I'm afraid I don't lead a very eventful life, Inspector. You are free to question my servants, but they retire by eight o'clock, so I'm not sure how helpful they will be. They're a married couple, and they relish their few hours of privacy when they're not looking after me."

"Thank you, Captain Hadley. I'll take you up on your offer."

Sebastian questioned Mrs. and Mrs. Bush, but, as Captain Hadley had predicted, they had neither seen nor heard anything after they had retired to their room on Monday night. Their testimony was worthless.

I'll see myself out," Sebastian told Mrs. Bush, who was about to escort him to the door. She nodded and went back to preparing luncheon for her employer.

"Good luck with your investigation, Inspector," Captain Hadley called from the parlor when Sebastian passed by the door. "I hope you find whoever did this awful thing."

"I will," Sebastian said under his breath.

# THIRTY-EIGHT

The street was crowded with passersby and congested with afternoon traffic. An emaciated child of about ten darted out into the street with his broom, desperate to clean the crossing and earn a few pennies from the driver of the sleek carriage making its way down the street. A street vendor with a tray slung around her scrawny neck was selling pies, the girl's lips nearly blue with cold and her bare arms dotted with goosepimples beneath her tatty shawl. Sebastian bought the last two pies and saw the girl sigh with relief as she took off the tray and hurried toward a tavern at the corner, where she might spend the money on a hot meal or more likely hand it over to whoever was waiting for her before her tray was refilled. He also bought an orange and pushed it into his pocket.

Sebastian ate the first pie quickly but took his time to savor the second. He approached a cabstand, but then decided he needed to walk. His copper's instinct told him he was circling the solution, but he had yet to figure out how all the clues fit together. He was certain that Lydia Morton's and Jacob Harrow's deaths were linked, and that the motive went back to their time in Crimea. He was also of the opinion that whoever had killed them valued showmanship and was relishing the attention the newspapers were lavishing on his deeds. The story had dominated the front page for days, and, unless something monumental happened today, it would continue to garner attention into next week, by which time Sebastian would probably be off the case.

In truth, Sebastian didn't think any other detective would fare better. It was easy enough to commit an anonymous crime in a city of thousands and then melt into the night. The brutality of the crime spoke to a person who didn't fear capture and did not think they would pay with their life. Either the perpetrator was devilishly reckless or so certain of their own intellectual superiority that they didn't think they could possibly be caught. And, although Sebastian hated to admit it, they were right. There wasn't a single solid piece of evidence against any of the suspects. It was all circumstantial, and the case would fall apart as soon as it got to court.

Refusing to admit defeat, Sebastian decided he needed to talk the case through with someone who was familiar with the circumstances but could manage to remain objective. Gemma had an analytical mind and a way of making connections most people missed. And although she wanted to see Lydia's killer caught, she wouldn't be publicly humiliated if Sebastian failed to make an arrest. Gemma might think it untoward if he called on her at work, but he didn't have time to waste and, loath as he was to admit it, he needed help.

When he arrived at the Foundling Hospital, he knocked on the door and asked to speak to Miss Tate. The porter appeared surprised but said he would fetch Matron Holcombe and Sebastian could make his request to her. Matron Holcombe wasn't overly pleased to see him but did not object too strenuously since he was there in his professional capacity.

"Come in, Inspector. I can offer you the use of my office, but I would ask that you leave the door open."

"Thank you, Matron," Sebastian said.

He would have preferred to speak to Gemma privately, but there was no such thing as privacy when an unmarried man and woman needed to speak to each other in the dead of winter. It was too cold to go for a walk, and the coffeehouse was no more private than the matron's office. He followed the woman down a dim corridor, amazed that in a place filled with children there was such dense silence. He wondered if the children were ever permitted to play outside or had any free time to spend with their friends. An orphanage was a sad place to grow up, even if it was run efficiently and with the children's welfare in mind.

The matron directed Sebastian to a cane guest chair. Clearly not trusting him alone in her office, she remained on hand until the porter had delivered Gemma. Sebastian wasn't interested in the business of the orphanage, only the time that was displayed on the carriage clock on the mantel. He only had a few hours until Lovell rearrested Godfrey Price and sent him to prison to await a trial that would most likely end in the surgeon's death. And then Lovell's ire would turn to Sebastian. He didn't think Lovell would dismiss him, but he might demote him, and Sebastian didn't think he could live with that.

Gemma looked mildly surprised when she entered the office. Her voice was devoid of emotion when she said, "How can I help you, Inspector?"

Sebastian waited until the matron's footsteps had receded, then smiled. "I'm sorry to disturb you at work."

"Did something happen? Have you made an arrest?" Gemma asked as she sat down across from him.

"No, not yet," Sebastian said, and pulled out the small orange. "I brought you a gift." He handed her the fruit and watched as Gemma held it to her nose and inhaled the citrusy aroma.

"I love oranges. Thank you." She slid the orange into the pocket of her pinafore. "I'm going to share it with Lucy."

"Who's Lucy?"

"She's a little girl I've been caring for."

"And she's come to mean something to you," Sebastian said.

Gemma looked unbearably sad. "I know I'm not meant to get attached to the children in my care, but Lucy is just so..."

She didn't finish the sentence, but Sebastian could understand. Gemma was gentle and caring, and she needed someone to give her love to. To care for a child who needed her came naturally, and she had no reason to feel ashamed, but as a nurse she was meant to retain her objectivity, and one couldn't do that when one's feelings were engaged.

"I wish..." Gemma began, then shook her head, as if she were being ridiculous.

"You wish what?"

"Never mind," she said. "I assume you didn't come here just to bring me an orange. Please, tell me how I can help."

Sebastian sighed heavily. "I'm at a loss, Gemma. All roads in this case seem to lead to Crimea. Or from Crimea, I should say. Jacob Harrow, the three men he blackmailed, and Lydia Morton were all in Crimea and came into contact with one another at some stage. The fourth victim, Constance Wallace, admitted to having an affair with a soldier who was wounded during the charge of the Light Brigade, and it would seem that her husband also had something to hide."

"Did her lover die?" Gemma asked.

"Yes. But she may have lied," he said. "Which was why I thought that her lover may have been Captain Hadley, who also knew nearly everyone involved in this case."

"Why did you think he might have had an affair with Constance Wallace?"

"Fenella Lawson said that he was rumored to be involved in a scandalous relationship that might lead to a duel. A romance with a high-ranking officer's wife would certainly qualify."

"Yes, it would, and, if Jacob Harrow was blackmailing Hadley as well, that would give him motive. By killing Harrow, he would have freed not only himself but also the woman he loved," Gemma suggested.

Sebastian shook his head. "However, I don't think Constance Wallace and Captain Hadley were ever involved in a romantic relationship. Hadley was more interested in her husband's misdeeds, which tie the general to Harold Wise's criminal activities during the war. Perhaps Constance Wallace was making payments on her husband's behalf and made up the story about a secret affair to protect his reputation."

"If General Wallace found out that his wife had been making payments all this time, he might have murdered Jacob Harrow."

"But why kill Lydia too, and why now?" Sebastian exclaimed, giving vent to his frustration. "Fenella Lawson said that Lydia was in love with Jacob Harrow, but he'd strung her along and then married Emma when he returned to England. Lydia was about four months gone with child, so perhaps they had never stopped seeing each other, despite Harrow's marriage."

Gemma nodded. "There is an awful kind of symmetry here if they were in on it together."

"How do you mean?"

"To a dying man or a demoralized surgeon, a nurse is no different than a priest. There's a desperate need to unburden oneself, and who better to confide in than a woman who has shown endless kindness and understanding? I've seen it many times and heard a number of confessions myself."

"But not all those who were seriously wounded died, and certainly not the surgeons," Sebastian said.

"Precisely. These men had confided in Lydia in a moment

of weakness. They needed to get their sins off their chest and believed that the trust they had placed in their angel of mercy was sacred. Most nurses will take these confessions to the grave, but what if Lydia shared the secrets she had learned with the man she loved? She was perfectly placed since she had access to both the patients and the surgeons. Jacob Harrow, in turn, used the information to blackmail those who had returned to England."

"Which explains his lavish lifestyle," Sebastian said. "And Lydia benefitted as well, since she clearly got her cut. But she was afraid to spend the money or let on that she was sitting on a sizable nest egg. When she heard that Jacob Harrow had been hanged and his tongue was severed to signify eternal silence, she panicked and tried to protect her share of the takings, but there's nothing to suggest that she was in fear for her life."

"I can understand the victims' rage against a man who was holding them hostage with his threats, but how would they have known about Lydia's role in the blackmail?"

Sebastian groaned in frustration. He hated to admit it, but it seemed Lovell was right and Sebastian had made a terrible miscalculation. Godfrey Price had been aware of the connection between Jacob Harrow and Lydia Morton and had been the one to mention Lydia in the first place.

"I think Godfrey Price knew," he admitted.

"And he had the most to gain from the deaths of Jacob Harrow and Lydia Morton," Gemma mused. "Mrs. Wallace receives a sizable allowance from her husband, so the payments, although galling, are not a financial hardship. Even if her husband found out about the blackmail, he wouldn't know about Lydia's part in the scheme."

"Nor is he young or fit enough to climb a drainpipe," Sebastian said, recalling the heavyset, older man in the portrait he'd seen in the Wallaces' drawing room. The general didn't fit with

Harry Thayer's description of the man he'd seen by Traitors' Gate either.

"General Wallace could have hired someone to murder Harrow, but then he would be putting himself in their power instead," Sebastian posited. "Paying someone to commit murder is considerably worse than the possibility of a tarnished reputation, especially since the war's been over for several years now and no one much cares about undocumented abuses of power."

"Precisely," Gemma agreed. "And as for the rest, Harold Wise is deathly ill and, according to his sister, has not been in contact with any of his old friends. It's difficult to imagine how he might have planned the murder of two people from his sickbed. And James Harrow died several weeks ago. His only connection to the case is Captain Hadley, who, although deeply saddened by James's death and understandably angry about Harrow's part in it, claims not to have known about the blackmail. If that's true, then he had no real reason to murder two people in cold blood."

Sebastian nodded. Everything Gemma had said was correct. There was no evidence that Captain Hadley had been blackmailed along with the others, since his name hadn't come up in relation to the payments. And he'd had no reason to murder Lydia. In fact, he'd spoken quite fondly of her. Godfrey Price, on the other hand, was struggling financially and would lose his family and his position at the hospital if the truth about his marriage came out. If he believed that Lydia had been the one to tell Harrow about the secret marriage, then he would have reason to kill her, since she could have picked up where Jacob Harrow had left off and continued to bleed him.

"I let Price go," Sebastian confessed, wishing he hadn't been so hasty.

"Why?" Gemma asked.

"Godfrey Price had the most to gain by killing Jacob Harrow and Lydia Morton, but he also had the most to lose. If convicted, his wife and children will be left with nothing—and, once Joanna Price finds out that her marriage isn't legal, her reputation will be destroyed and her children will be branded bastards. I can't imagine that Price would have wanted to risk such an outcome."

"Perhaps he grew so desperate that he wasn't thinking of the repercussions. He simply needed to remove the cancer that was devouring him from the inside," Gemma suggested.

"Yes, I expect he did. But does a desperate man resort to such theatrics? He could have easily killed them and made it look like a random attack. No one would have made a connection to a respected surgeon who lives across the river."

"No, they wouldn't, but perhaps it was important to him that their reputations were destroyed, and their names were forever synonymous with something sordid."

"If it was, then it will be his pride that leads to his downfall," Sebastian said.

"You mean aside from the bigamy?"

Sebastian chuckled. "He would have got away with the bigamy, especially now that Agnes Frye is dead and can no longer make any claim against him."

"Godfrey Price sinned in the eyes of God and man, but Jacob Harrow was a horrible man, a leech who fed off the lifeblood of others. I expect there were others who were in his power and who paid not in money but in information. He wouldn't have stopped. It's a horrid thing to say, but the world is a better place without him in it."

Sebastian nodded. They both knew from a previous case that Jacob Harrow had had an MP in his pocket until the man had been forced to resign in shame and had left the country. Who knew who else Harrow would have blackmailed had he lived?

"I'd better go," Sebastian said when he heard rapid footsteps in the corridor. It seemed Matron was back and their interview was over.

"Will I still see you tomorrow?" Gemma asked before the matron got there.

"Of course," Sebastian promised. He tipped his hat to Matron Holcombe, who held a small, fair-haired girl by the hand. The child was crying and looked imploringly at Gemma as she tried to yank her hand out of Matron's grasp. Matron glared at her, then fixed her obvious displeasure on Gemma, whom she probably would have chastised if Sebastian wasn't there.

"Lucy, what happened?" Gemma asked gently as she approached the little girl.

"I felt ill and couldn't find you, miss," the child wailed.

"She was running down the corridor," Marton said accusingly.

"I'm sorry, I'm sure it won't happen again. Right, Lucy?" Gemma asked kindly. The child nodded vigorously, then as soon as Matron let go of her hand threw herself into Gemma's arms. Gemma wrapped her arms about the little girl, but Matron's icy glare wasn't lost on her, so Gemma instantly held Lucy away from her.

"Let's get you back to your dormitory," she said soothingly.

"We do not encourage personal attachments, Miss Tate," the matron rebuked Gemma, her tone as sharp as broken glass.

"I'm sorry, Matron," Sebastian heard Gemma say as he walked away, leaving her to sort out this minor crisis in private.

"You had better make sure it doesn't happen again," Matron replied, the clicking of her heels on the hardwood floor signifying the end of the encounter.

Sebastian turned and caught a glimpse of Gemma and Lucy, Gemma's voice soft and gentle as she said something to the little girl. Lucy looked up and smiled, the adoration in her eyes unexpectedly heartbreaking.

"Don't ever leave, miss," Lucy said, loudly enough for Sebastian to hear. "I can't manage without you."

Sebastian turned away and pushed open the door, Lucy's piping voice still ringing in his ears as he stepped outside.

As he made his way to Scotland Yard, Sebastian knew he had no choice but to rearrest and charge Godfrey Price. Lovell would be pleased, and Sir David would be sure to give a statement to the press and reassure the public that they were safe thanks to the tireless efforts of the Metropolitan Police Service, but Sebastian felt no satisfaction in solving the case, nor did he relish the prospect of eating humble pie. He was man enough to admit that all the evidence pointed to Godfrey Price; but, despite everything, Sebastian's instinct continued to kick him in the gut like a deranged mule.

# THIRTY-NINE

When Sebastian returned to the boarding house his room was bitterly cold and dark. He considered making a fire and reading for a while but didn't think he'd be able to focus on his book. He had arrested and charged his share of criminals over the last fifteen years, and there had been times when he had felt sympathy toward the poor mugs whose one bad decision was going to change their life forever or simply end it. There were the career criminals, who rarely felt remorse, and then there were men like Godfrey Price. He had been white-faced and silent as he was charged with two counts of homicide. It was only after he was taken down to the cells that Sebastian had heard him weep and knew that the man's heart was breaking. Not for himself, but for the wife he had deceived, the son he wouldn't see grow into a man, and the baby he'd never hold.

Not in the mood for a novel but not ready to go to sleep, Sebastian lit an oil lamp and fetched the stack of newspapers he kept on the wardrobe to use as liners for Gustav's litterbox. He settled before the cold hearth and leafed through the newspapers, searching for articles written by Jacob Harrow. He'd read a few pieces Harrow had written in the past, but hadn't paid specific attention to his opinions or writing style. Now that the man was dead, Sebastian was eager to understand something of his character and beliefs, especially as Harrow had been so readily maligned by those who had known him.

Sebastian started with the oldest article he could locate and made his way forward in time, focusing on every word and turn of phrase as if he were the man's editor and not a tired policeman scanning out-of-date stories because he didn't have anything better to do and still questioned his judgment when it came to Godfrey Price. Since the war, Harrow had toned down some of his firebrand rhetoric, but he still routinely addressed hot-topic social issues such as lack of habitable housing for the poor, the appalling conditions in workhouses and orphanages, and the lack of social reform that would help the poor help themselves rather than beg for handouts from those who cared nothing about their plight.

Sebastian found Harrow's position difficult to square with the hardened journalist whose only priority had been to get the story and grab his spot in the limelight, but he supposed that was the nature of journalism. Harrow had written about issues that were sure to get people talking, whether to agree with him or condemn his radical views and demand his immediate dismissal. It was all about grabbing the public's attention and not only maintaining but also increasing the circulation of the newspaper. Sebastian could certainly understand why Marshall Lawrence had kept publishing Jacob Harrow's pieces and had frequently given him coveted real estate on the front page.

Having read every article he could find and drawn his conclusions, Sebastian used one of the older newspapers to line Gustav's box and returned the rest to the top of the wardrobe to be used later. He carried the lamp into the bedroom and set it on the bedside table. Gustav, who must have actually missed him this week, kept weaving around his ankles and generally making a nuisance of himself until Sebastian had to scoop him up and set him on the bed. Sebastian drew the curtains, undressed, got into bed, and turned out the lamp. He would have given much for a hot brick to warm the icy sheets, but, since there was no fire, there was no brick. The cat immediately fitted himself to Sebastian's hip, a silky furball that was willing to share his meager warmth with his freezing master. Sebastian laid a hand on Gustav's head and the cat purred contentedly, seemingly also glad of the company.

Though he was physically tired, Sebastian's mind wouldn't allow him to rest. Once he'd managed to force aside his doubts about the investigation, he thought of Gemma, alone in her room, and of a child named Lucy, who was probably curled up in her cold bed, dreaming of a family she'd never have. Gemma never complained and had stoically accepted the change in her circumstances, but Sebastian had seen it in her eyes, that bewilderment that often came with finding oneself alone in the world. It was a strange thing to know that you were the last of your family. The end of the line. As a man, he had more choices, both respectable and less so, to quell his loneliness, and he acknowledged that the time had come to consider his future.

It'd been three years since Louisa's death. For a long time, Sebastian hadn't thought he could ever love anyone else, but he found his thoughts turning to Gemma Tate more and more frequently. She wasn't the sort of woman he'd been drawn to in his youth. Then, he'd valued a lusher beauty and a sweeter disposition, but Gemma was both beautiful and feminine in her own way. She wasn't a girl, like Louisa had been when he'd first met her while investigating a robbery at her father's shop, eager to pour all her emotion into her first love and build her life around the happiness of her husband.

Gemma was a mature woman whose life experiences had made her undesirable to most men. She was too smart, and too independent, to appeal to a man who only wanted his domestic needs taken care of and his ego stroked. But Sebastian found

Gemma's strength of character and intelligence appealing. He no longer wanted an innocent young girl who'd look upon him with undisguised awe. He wanted a partner, someone he could talk to, dream with, and start a family with. He wanted children, and he'd understood Gemma's longing when she'd spoken of Lucy. Loving a child in her care was the closest she would come to motherhood, unless she married some stodgy older man, like her previous employer, Mr. Gadd, who had wanted a mother for his future children and an unpaid carer for his ailing mother.

The thought of some other man marrying Gemma cut deeper than Sebastian could have imagined, and his body and heart stirred with needs he'd ignored for too long. Could Gemma Tate grow to care for him? To love him? Would she ever consider becoming a policeman's wife despite knowing what had happened to Louisa? Did he dare risk another woman's life, and did he deserve to be happy when Louisa and their child had died because of him?

Why was he even thinking along these lines? It was loneliness talking, and deep emotional fatigue. Without the sweet embrace of opium or even the equally potent elixir of alcohol, Sebastian had too much time to dwell and too great a capacity to feel. He missed the dulled senses and the dreamlike quality of his thoughts when he was in the grip of inebriation. Sobriety was desired, but oblivion was not to be discounted. These days, his only escape was sleep, so Sebastian settled deeper into the mattress, grateful that his body heat had finally defrosted the bedlinens and he was no longer shivering. His thoughts began to drift, and a welcome serenity finally descended on him.

# FORTY

Sebastian came awake with a jolt, his body tensing with the sudden awareness of danger. If the room had been cold before, it was downright glacial now, and, even though the curtains were drawn, he instinctively knew that the window was open. He remained perfectly still, his mind searching frantically for a weapon. There was nothing, aside from the oil lamp on the bedside table. Sebastian slid one arm from below the eiderdown and took hold of the base of the lamp, then lowered his arm and set the lamp on the floor within easy reach.

The curtain moved, and Sebastian caught a glimpse of the sky as a dark figure climbed in through the window and immediately drew the curtain to block the cold draft and the hazy moonlight that cast a silver pall onto the floor. The intruder was enveloped in darkness, but Sebastian could hear the slow, steady breaths and make out the dense outline of his would-be assailant. Time seemed to slow, and Sebastian found himself wondering if he was about to meet the same fate as Jacob Harrow and Lydia Morton. Then the figure moved toward him, and all random thoughts coalesced into one all-important goal—surviving the next few minutes.

Sebastian remained outwardly still and tried to keep his breathing even as he lowered his arm and wrapped his hand around the collar of the lamp. If he grabbed onto the glass shade it would crack in his hand, but, if he took the lamp by the base, the shade would break over the assailant's head but most likely not do enough damage to deter him. Sebastian needed the solidity of the base to inflict real damage. Despite the nearly impenetrable darkness that put him at a disadvantage, he was glad the lamp wasn't lit, or he might have set the intruder—or his bed with him still in it—on fire when the oil spilled and came in contact with the flame. Death by fire wasn't on his list of acceptable ways to die.

A gust of wind filled the curtains with air, and the panels parted. Light from the nearly full moon glinted off the curved knife in the man's hand. There was no doubt it was a man, but the lower half of his face was covered with a black kerchief, and a woolen cap was pulled low. A momentary glimpse of the eyes wasn't enough to identify the intruder, but it was enough to mark his position. The knife-wielding hand extended over the bed, aiming for Sebastian's throat. He had a mere moment before the steel bit into his flesh and severed the carotid arteries. Sebastian flipped the lamp and struck the man with the brass base. Broken glass cascaded all over the eiderdown with the force of the impact, the released oil seeping into the bedlinens and filling the room with a noxious odor.

An agonized roar erupted from the intruder as the metal base collided with his skull. Gustav let out a terrified yowl, exploded from beneath the eiderdown, and frantically clawed at the man's hand. The assailant dropped the knife and raised his hands to protect himself, both from another blow and from Gustav, whose back was arched, his bared teeth white in the moonlight. Sebastian took advantage of the momentary distraction to jump out of bed, but before he could tackle the man the intruder hurled himself toward the window and leapt toward the sycamore that grew behind the building, grabbing onto a sturdy branch. He hung there for a moment, then let go, landed on his feet, and ran, his silhouette melting into the darkness as a thick cloud sailed across the moon.

To go after him would be foolish in the extreme, since Sebastian was wearing nothing but a shirt and long underwear, and his feet were bare. He didn't keep a pistol or a knife in his room, so even if he caught up with the man he'd have nothing to rely on but brute strength to subdue him at a time when he wasn't fully recovered from injury.

He picked up the knife off the floor. Even in the moonlight he could appreciate the workmanship. It was foreign, probably Turkish, judging by the pattern on the ivory handle and the shape of the blade. Long and curved, just like the weapon that had been used to murder Jacob Harrow.

The fact that someone wanted Sebastian dead proved that Godfrey Price was probably not the one who had murdered Jacob Harrow and Lydia Morton, unless he had an accomplice who was daring enough to go after a police inspector and believed he could get away with it. News of Price's arrest would probably make tomorrow's evening edition, but tonight, as far as anyone knew, the case was still ongoing, and clearly Sebastian had come too close to the truth to be allowed to live.

Sebastian set the knife aside to be examined more closely later. If he didn't close the window, he'd catch his death. Drawing the curtains to keep out the draft, he found a candle and a box of lucifer matches and lit the wick. It was only once the room was filled with light that he noticed blood on the eiderdown. Gustav lay whimpering, his breathing rapid, his eyes pleading for help.

"Oh, God," Sebastian exclaimed. "Bear with me, old son," he said to the panicked cat, then carefully rolled him over. A jagged piece of glass protruded from the animal's bloodsmeared belly.

"This is going to hurt," Sebastian warned the cat. "You must be brave."

Gustav growled and clawed at Sebastian's hand, but Sebastian managed to extract the shard and grab a towel, which he pressed to the wound and kept in place until the bleeding subsided. "Just lie still," he told the cat sternly. And then in a softer tone, "You may have saved my life, you little rascal. I'm in your eternal debt."

Gustav meowed miserably but didn't protest and remained where he was, his head resting on his paws as he shut his eyes.

Sebastian sat down next to Gustav, choosing a spot that wasn't soaked with oil or covered with broken glass, and kept vigil until he thought the animal was no longer in pain and it was safe to go to sleep. Then he stretched out on the unsoiled side of the bed and covered himself with his coat before drifting into uneasy slumber.

# FORTY-ONE
## SUNDAY, DECEMBER 19

Snow had begun to fall sometime during the night, and everything was covered in a blanket of pristine white, unlike Sebastian's bed, which was soiled with blood, oil, cat piss, and tufts of black fur. Sebastian opened the curtains and peered at Gustav, who lay very still, his eyes closed against the bright light. Sebastian reached out and laid a hand on the cat's head, breathing a sigh of relief when he found it warm to the touch. He got up, rolled out his stiff muscles, and massaged his shoulder, which was throbbing painfully after the effort of hurling the lamp at the assailant's head. He didn't think he'd done any serious damage to the healing wound, but it was sore.

Now, in the morning light, he took in the carnage, which wasn't actually that bad except for the ruined bedlinens, and considered what he knew of his intruder. The man had been relatively young, strong, and fit, and this morning he was most likely sporting a nasty bruise or a cut on his head and a badly scratched hand, compliments of Gustav. Sebastian could think of only two people who fit the description and had the strength and agility to climb into his window and then escape without falling to the ground and breaking a limb. The maneuver had been quite graceful, Sebastian grudgingly admitted, and, since the man had got away almost unscathed, there was nothing to keep him from trying again, which meant that Sebastian had to get to him first. Not for the first time, he wished that an assailant could be identified by examining the weapon; but, although clearly expensive and beautifully made, the dagger could belong to anyone and didn't mean a thing unless there was a way to prove that it had belonged to Jacob Harrow.

Checking his appearance in the small mirror he used for shaving, Sebastian washed his face and hands, cleaned his teeth, and ran a comb through his hair. Then he got dressed and headed downstairs. Mrs. Poole was in the kitchen, preparing breakfast for her lodgers, and the kitchen smelled pleasantly of fried bread and bacon.

"Can I trouble you for some left-over meat or fish, Mrs. Poole?" Sebastian asked, smiling at the landlady in what he hoped was an ingratiating manner.

"You'll have to pay extra if you expect me to feed your cat."

"I will reimburse you. Today," he promised.

Mrs. Poole nodded and went to the larder. She returned with a bowl of chicken gizzards and handed it to Sebastian. "Breakfast in ten minutes. If you miss it, I won't make it for you specially."

"No, ma'am."

"And what was that racket last night? Woke me in the middle of the night."

Sebastian smiled apologetically. "Gustav knocked over a lamp. Ruined the bedlinens."

"And broke the lamp, I reckon. Evil creature," Mrs. Poole hissed under her breath. "If he didn't do such a good job of catching mice, I'd toss him out on his ear. It's your responsibility to replace the linens and the lamp."

"Of course," Sebastian agreed.

He took the bowl upstairs and set it on the bed next to

Gustav. Normally, the cat would be over the moon, but the smelly, glistening gizzards didn't excite him today. Sebastian caressed the spot between Gustav's ears that usually earned him a purr, but the animal did not respond. His eyes remained firmly shut. Taking his one remaining towel, Sebastian carefully wrapped the cat, then put on his coat and hat and left the room. His stomach growled with hunger, but he resolutely walked past the dining room and headed out into the street and toward the nearest cabstand. He instructed the driver to take him to Blackfriars.

If Mabel was surprised to find Sebastian on the doorstep before 8 a.m., she didn't show it. She invited him in and went to fetch her employer, who was predictably up and doing something unspeakable in the cellar.

"Sebastian, what happened?" Colin asked as he came upstairs. He wiped his hands on the apron he wore and reached for the cat.

"A piece of glass cut his belly."

Colin shot Sebastian a searching look, but Sebastian didn't have time to explain. "I think the cut is deep and needs to be stitched. He couldn't even eat this morning."

"I'll have to give him something to put him to sleep. Otherwise, he'll claw my eyes out."

"Do what you must."

Sebastian hadn't expected to feel so emotional over a cat he'd never wanted, but the sight of the limp black and white furball left him choked up. "Please," he added.

"I'll do my best. Leave him with me."

"Hello, Robert," Mrs. Ramsey chirped as she came down the stairs. "My, but you do call on us often. And you brought a cat."

"Good morning, Mrs. Ramsey. It's a pleasure to see you again," Sebastian said as he turned toward the door.

"Surely you're not leaving us so soon. You must stay for breakfast."

Colin studied Sebastian for a moment but seemed to conclude that the inspector wasn't injured, only worried and hungry. "Have something to eat, Sebastian. You don't look at all well," he said. "Whatever you have to do can wait a half-hour."

"Thank you. I will," Sebastian said. He couldn't go another day on a nearly empty stomach.

"Mabel, please make fried eggs, kippers, and fried bread for Inspector Bell. And set out some of that orange marmalade Mrs. Humphries brought for Mother yesterday. And a pot of strong tea, I think. And I will see to this little fellow."

Sebastian's mouth watered, and he obediently surrendered his coat and hat to Mabel and followed Mrs. Ramsey into the dining room.

"Your wife really should take better care of you, my dear," Mrs. Ramsey said reproachfully. "And I shall tell her so the next time I see her."

"She's been unwell," Sebastian replied, not wishing to explain yet again that his wife was dead.

"The poor woman. I quite forgot you are anticipating a happy event. When's the infant due?"

*Never*, Sebastian's mind screamed, but he forced himself to smile. "In a few months."

"I do hope it's a boy. A man needs a son to complete him."

"Yes," Sebastian muttered, and smiled politely as Mrs. Ramsey began to ramble about Colin when he was a boy. He was relieved when Mabel arrived with a tray, and he hoped Mrs. Ramsey wouldn't ask him any more questions about his family life.

Mrs. Ramsey applied herself to her porridge, while Sebastian wolfed down his breakfast and then pushed back his chair. He had to get to Scotland Yard.

# FORTY-TWO

"You look like death warmed over," Sergeant Woodward said when Sebastian walked in. "Memorable night?"

The building was quiet. Almost everyone was off work on a Sunday. Sebastian was grateful that Lovell did insist on a skeleton staff on the Lord's Day, in case something urgent came in that couldn't be pushed off till Monday. And someone had to see to Godfrey Price, who'd been brought in but wouldn't be transferred until Monday.

"I need Captain Bertram Hadley picked up at this address." Sebastian wrote out the address and pushed the paper toward the duty sergeant. "Send at least two men."

"What's he meant to have done?"

"He murdered two people. Now, be quick about it, before he realizes I'm on to him."

"But you nabbed Price, or is this some other set of murders I'm not aware of?"

"Still the same one."

"It's just me and Constables Bryant and Taft today. I'll have to go myself," Woodward said resignedly.

"Thank you, Albert."

"Don't mention it. Where are you off to, then?"

"There's someone I must speak to. Keep Hadley in the cells until I get back, and be careful. He's clever. Keep the cuffs on."

"Right you are, Inspector," Sergeant Woodward said with mock diffidence. "Your wish is my command."

Having issued his instructions, Sebastian flagged down a hansom and headed to McCrory's gymnasium. Perhaps he should have waited until Sergeant Woodward was back and taken one of the constables with him, but he didn't think he'd require backup. He should have listened to his gut instinct all along, but he was listening now, and he was sure he had his man. Still, he had to be certain.

McCrory's was open, but the gymnasium was empty save for Reginald Pickering, who was moving a large broom around the floor and whistling a merry tune. He turned at the sound of the door, and smiled in welcome when he recognized Sebastian.

"All right, Inspector?" he called. "Come to join the gymnasium?"

"No," Sebastian said, and walked right out, leaving a confused Reginald to wonder if Sebastian had taken leave of his senses.

Sebastian smiled to himself. He was glad to note that the boy's face was clear and his hands unblemished. He hadn't thought Reginald Pickering had attacked him last night, but he needed to rule him out since Reginald had the height, weight, and coordination to pull off the break-in and subsequent escape.

Sebastian climbed into the waiting cab, ready to return to Scotland Yard.

# FORTY-THREE

Sebastian returned to find a grim-faced Bertram Hadley pacing in his cell. He still wore his coat and gloves, and his shiny topper sat at a rakish angle on his head. Hadley gave Sebastian a murderous look when Sergeant Woodward unlocked the door and took him by the arm.

"You have no right to hold me," Hadley snapped.

"Don't I?" Sebastian asked.

"I demand to see your superior."

"I can ask him to sit in on our interview," Sebastian replied pleasantly. "But you'll have to wait until tomorrow. Superintendent Lovell is not here today, it being the Lord's Day."

Hadley did not look pleased at the prospect of spending his Sunday in a cell. "Then get him," he demanded imperiously.

Sebastian considered the demand. Normally, he wouldn't dare disturb Superintendent Lovell on a Sunday, but Lovell's wife and daughter were away, visiting a relative in Bath, and Lovell would probably be bored and restless once he came home from church. He would also relish the chance to charge Hadley.

"I'll send Constable Bryant to fetch the superintendent,

shall I?" Sergeant Woodward asked once Sebastian had relayed Hadley's request.

"If it's no trouble," Sebastian replied politely.

They left Hadley to stew and returned upstairs. "Cup of tea while we wait, Inspector?" Sergeant Woodward asked once he'd dispatched a less than enthusiastic Constable Bryant.

"Why not," Sebastian replied.

They didn't have long to wait. Superintendent Lovell strode into the duty room less than half an hour later, his coat unbuttoned, his bowler pulled low over his eyes, his muffler casually wrapped around his neck.

"What's this all about, Bell?" he demanded, but there was a gleam of excitement in his eyes. "I thought we had our man."

"I was never convinced that Godfrey Price was the killer. I believe now we have our man."

"Well, let's hear it, then," Lovell said as he shed his coat, hat, and muffler and headed toward the interview room.

"Bring Captain Hadley," Sebastian told Sergeant Woodward. "And keep him cuffed."

"Understood."

The room was cold and smelled stale, and the colorless sky and the snowflakes falling beyond the small window gave it an even more unwelcome appearance. Captain Hadley's nose wrinkled in disgust as he took in the utilitarian space, but, although the tension in his body spoke clearly of barely controlled violence, he accepted the seat without argument and crossed his legs, then laid his cuffed hands on the table before him. An expression of insolence settled over his features, and he refused to make eye contact, choosing instead to watch the snow fall outside.

"Captain Hadley, I'm Superintendent Lovell. I believe you asked that I be present for this interview," Lovell said politely once he settled across from the suspect.

"Either charge me or release me," Hadley barked.

"With pleasure," Sebastian said. "I charge you with two counts of murder and the attempted murder of a policeman."

"And which policeman am I meant to have attempted to kill?" Hadley asked, his sardonic smile making Sebastian's blood boil in his veins.

"Me. Would you mind removing your hat and gloves, Captain?"

Hadley took off his gloves, pulling on each finger one by one to heighten the suspense, while the chain between the cuffs rattled against the table. His right hand was bandaged, the linen spotted with dried blood.

"What happened to your hand?" Superintendent Lovell asked.

"I was bitten by a dog."

"Are you sure you don't mean scratched by a cat?" Sebastian asked.

"I'm sure I would recall such an important detail."

"Now your hat," Sebastian prompted.

It was obvious that Captain Hadley didn't want to do as he was asked, but he could hardly refuse, even if the hat served to hide further evidence against him. To keep one's hat on was bad form, even in a police station.

He slowly removed his top hat while giving his head a shake that caused a fair forelock to fall onto his forehead.

"I'm afraid you'll need a lot more hair to disguise that gash on your head," Sebastian said. "Made by an oil lamp, was it? Or was it the dog? Vicious creatures when they feel threatened."

"I sustained the injury during a fencing match," Hadley said.

"Since yesterday?" Sebastian inquired politely. "Which club do you fence at? I'll send a constable to verify your account once they reopen tomorrow."

"It wasn't at a club. I fenced with one of my army comrades. We duel in his mother's ballroom."

"Name? Address?" Sebastian asked, his notepad at the ready.

Hadley paused, clearly aware that he couldn't defend the lie. "I don't remember the address," he muttered at last.

"No matter," Sebastian said. "You're still bound for Cold-bath Fields."

"On what evidence?" Hadley snapped. "People get hurt every day. A scratch proves nothing."

Lovell looked to Sebastian, clearly waiting for whatever revelation was to follow, since he had no inkling of what had happened last night and what it had to do with the injuries Captain Hadley had sustained.

"Shall I tell you a story, Captain?" Sebastian asked as he closed his notepad.

"As long as it's not boring."

"This story has it all: intrigue, murder, love, and revenge."

"Ooh, sounds exciting," Hadley said sarcastically, smiling at Sebastian as if he were a right fool.

"That sounds like a story I'd like to hear myself," Lovell said.

"You're going to enjoy it, sir," Sebastian promised. "It begins with a young soldier who was shot in the stomach. He was looked after by a beautiful nurse who developed strong feelings for him."

"I suppose that's the love story you promised us?" Hadley commented. He endeavored to look bored, but Sebastian could see the pulse jumping in his jaw.

"There's more than one love story here," Sebastian said.

"Do go on, Inspector. I so love a good story."

"The wounded soldier quickly realized that men confess all manner of sins to nurses, especially when the night is long and dark and they don't think they will see the light of another morning. Many of them did die, but some survived, and those were the ones our soldier was most interested in. Not all secrets were scandalous or worthy of his attention, but some were the sort a man, or a woman, would pay to protect. And so a profitable partnership was born. Lydia Morton fed Jacob Harrow the information she gleaned, and he decided whom to extort. Mind you, he didn't embark on this enterprise until everyone returned to England, since being found out could have led to court-martial and execution while he was still in the army, and our brave soldier had no intention of endangering himself."

Lovell had grown perfectly still, his gaze fixed on Sebastian, while Captain Hadley looked like he was going to be ill, the derisive smile he'd worn only a few moments earlier now more of a grimace. The room was so quiet one could hear a pin drop, and Sebastian took a moment to relish his audience's rapt attention.

"Go on, Bell," Lovell commanded. "I want to hear how this story ends."

"Jacob Harrow was so confident in his power over his victims that he instructed them to either post the checks directly to his home or deposit the money into his account. And they would have continued to pay, because as a journalist he had the power to destroy them."

"He wasn't blackmailing me," Hadley said. "So how do you imagine I fit into this story?"

"No, he wasn't blackmailing you, because you weren't the sort of man who'd give in to blackmail, but he was leaning on James Harrow," Sebastian said.

Hadley's nostrils flared, but he said nothing.

"In fact, James was paying not only in coin but in something far more valuable."

"Which was?" Lovell asked. He looked like a child who wanted to get ahead of the story and find out what happened.

"Jacob Harrow was a passable writer, but he was nowhere near as gifted as his cousin. Last night, I read several articles attributed to Jacob Harrow, and I'm certain they were written

by two different men. The articles penned by Jacob use chop-
pier sentences and convey a more belligerent tone. Nor do they
contain certain unique phrases coined by James and used liberally in his own writing, samples of which I found at his home. I
don't believe Jacob Harrow would have secured the job with the
*Daily Telegraph* on his own merit, and evidently he realized
that as well."

Sebastian took a well-deserved breath and continued.
"Jacob Harrow was confident that he could raise the money he
needed to support his lifestyle, but he was interested in making
a name for himself. So he took possession of the articles James
had sent to the *Daily Telegraph* and several other newspapers
and presented them to the editor as proof of authenticity.
Having the same initials as he did, it was easy to pass himself off
as the writer, and there was no one to challenge him. Jacob
Harrow obtained a coveted position with a respected newspaper and wrote a few pieces on his own, but he also coerced
James into writing the more in-depth articles for him, to make
certain he remained firmly in the public eye and his editor did
not begin to question the abrupt shift in writing style."

Sebastian looked from Superintendent Lovell to Captain
Hadley, who sat with his shoulders hunched and his gaze firmly
fixed on Sebastian.

"And then he decided to write a book," Sebastian said. "Or,
more accurately, he decided that James was going to write a
book. And that was the straw that broke the camel's back."

"James didn't kill him," Hadley spat. "He was already
dead."

"Yes, he was," Sebastian agreed. "Unable to free himself
from his cousin's endless extortion, James took his own life, but
he also died to protect the person he loved, whom I expect Jacob
had promised to destroy should James refuse to write the
manuscript."

Hadley paled, his gaze showing evidence of mounting

panic. "There was a woman James loved," he hastened to explain. "And she didn't deserve to bear the brunt of Jacob Harrow's malice."

Sebastian took out a half-finished letter he'd taken from James's wastepaper basket and laid it on the table so the greeting was clearly visible. "My darling Bertie" was written in James's elegant scrawl.

"There was no woman, Captain. James Harrow loved you, and you loved him, a secret he'd confided to the caring nurse who looked after him when he was wounded and thought he was going to die. But James survived, and Lydia told his cousin that James was homosexual and in love with an officer, who returned his feelings. Imagine Jacob's glee. Now he could have the career he'd always dreamed of, with his very own author to propel him along."

Captain Hadley's eyes flashed with fury. "James had idolized Jacob since he was a child and couldn't believe his cousin would manipulate him that way. Jacob Harrow capitalized on James's talent and passed off James's unflinching observations and ability to immerse the reader in the world he inhabited as his own."

His face was twisted with anger, and he balled his hands into fists as he continued. "Jacob Harrow established a reputation based on someone else's talent, cheating James of the income he would have earned had he taken up a position with the *Daily Telegraph* or written a book in his own name. James and his mother were barely getting by, but Jacob didn't care about either of them."

Sebastian nodded. "And when James finally gave in to despair, you were so heartbroken and angry that you decided to punish those responsible. You cut out their tongues and murdered Jacob Harrow and Lydia Morton to show the world what happens to those who betray the trust placed in them.

Very biblical," he remarked. "One could even say godlike. Hanging the body off Traitors' Gate was a nice touch."

"I offered them a chance to repent," Captain Hadley retorted. "I went to see Harrow and asked him to credit James with the articles he'd stolen and hand over the earnings to Mrs. Harrow, so she would at least have enough to live out her days in comfort. He laughed in my face and threatened me with public exposure. Lydia Morton did much the same. She wasn't about to jeopardize her profitable sideline or help a mother who'd lost her only son." Hadley fixed Sebastian with a self-righteous stare. "If God won't sit in judgment of those who sin against others, then someone must."

"So you judged them, and sentenced them to death," Lovell said, clearly satisfied with the outcome of the interview. Sebastian could wager that Lovell could already see the headlines and hear the praise he would receive from the commissioner and the Home Secretary.

"And you judged me as well," Sebastian said, "and were going to murder me for getting too close to the truth—had my cat not mutilated your hand and forced you to drop the dagger."

Hadley looked away, his gaze fixed on the white world beyond the window. He sighed heavily, then turned back, an air of resignation in his tired expression. "You are smarter and more persistent than I gave you credit for, Inspector Bell. I admit, I underestimated you."

He snorted angrily.

"I removed all the incriminating evidence from Jacob Harrow's study and burned the letters and envelopes in my own hearth. That should have put an end to your investigation. No evidence, no murder weapon, no suspects. I even paid some urchin to watch Lydia's boarding house and study her routine. That way no one would be able to connect me to the murder. But you managed to piece it all together. I expect some thanks goes to that harridan, Gemma Tate, that you're so fond of. Perhaps I should have killed her first," Hadley mused. "That would have really thrown you off the scent, since she had nothing to do with any of this. Still, I don't believe in harming the innocent."

"You murdered Lydia Morton's unborn child," Sebastian said.

"I didn't know she was with child, but had I known I would have done exactly the same thing. She didn't deserve to blithely go on and live off her ill-gotten gains when James was rotting in the ground, his life destroyed by two pitiless, greedy people."

"And was it Jacob Harrow's dagger that you planned to slit my throat with?" Sebastian asked. "The maidservant said his dagger had been taken from the study."

"It was a beautiful knife, and I threw my own dagger in the Thames after murdering Harrow," Hadley admitted. "His wife had no use for it, and I fancied a little souvenir."

"I'd give it back to you, but you won't need it where you're going," Sebastian said, then drew the blue glass disk out of his pocket and held it up for Captain Hadley to see. "Is this yours?"

Hadley's eyes misted with tears, and he nodded. "James gave that to me. He said it would protect me from evil. He believed in such nonsense and wanted to safeguard those he loved."

"Why did you leave it on Harrow's body?" Lovell asked.

"Because I no longer had any use for it. The worst had already happened." Hadley sighed resignedly. "I will hang for my crimes; I know that. But at least I can die knowing that I will finally be reunited with my beloved Jamie."

"Unless James Harrow was a murderer, I doubt you'll be seeing each other again, Captain Hadley," Superintendent Lovell said, and pushed away from the table. He adjusted his glasses and straightened his tie. "Well done, Bell. Fill out the charge sheet and arrange for transport to Coldbath Fields tomorrow. I think we're done here."

• • •

"What about Godfrey Price?" Sebastian asked, once Hadley had been taken back to the cells.

Lovell sighed. "The man is a fool, but he's not a killer. I should have listened to you, Bell."

"Will you hold him on a charge of bigamy?"

"Personally, I think he should pay for his duplicity, but the ones who would truly be paying are his wife and children. I will defer charging him and allow him time to obtain a death certificate for his first wife and marry his current wife legally. If he fails to comply, then he will have to stand trial. Do you think that's fair?"

"I do," Sebastian said.

"You know, Bell, underneath that gruff exterior, you really do have a soft heart."

Sebastian grinned. "Please don't tell anyone, sir."

"And ruin your reputation?" Lovell quipped. "Never."


When Sebastian returned to Colin Ramsey's house, Mabel let him in, and smiled kindly at his worried expression.

"Gustav is fine," she said before Sebastian had a chance to dash down to the cellar. "He enjoyed some sardines, and now he's dozing by the fire in the kitchen. I don't think you should disturb him. He's way too comfortable."

"Thank you, Mabel," Sebastian said. He wouldn't have minded a spell by a warm fire himself, but before he took Gustav home he had to clean his bedroom and replace the ruined bedlinens and lamp. That would have to wait until tomorrow though, since most of the shops were closed on a Sunday.

"And Mr. Ramsey? Is he at home?" Sebastian asked. The house was unusually quiet.

"Mr. Colin and Mrs. Ramsey are just back from church. Mr. Colin took Mrs. Ramsey upstairs. She wanted to rest before luncheon. I'll let him know you're here."

"No, don't disturb him. I'll come back tomorrow and thank him properly," Sebastian promised. Colin would invite him to stay for Sunday lunch, but Sebastian had to go. He had to see Gemma, and that was one appointment he had no intention of missing.

# EPILOGUE
## CHRISTMAS 1858

The sky was clear and strewn with stars, the evening so cold that every word seemed to emerge in a puff of vapor, as if uttered by a restless spirit. Sebastian found a hansom and helped Gemma inside before joining her. It would have been nice to have a rug to pull over their legs, even a tatty one, as long as it wasn't infested with fleas, but the cab did not offer such luxuries. The leather seat was covered with frost, and the joints squeaked like hungry mice. The lack of a rug proved fortuitous, though, because Sebastian must have sensed that Gemma was desperate for his warmth. He moved closer to her, and she leaned into him just a little, propriety be damned.

She had been reluctant to accept an invitation to Christmas dinner when she was still in mourning, but, as she'd dipped her pen in ink, about to decline and thank Colin for his thoughtfulness, she could have sworn that she had felt Victor standing just behind her, his disapproval emanating from him in psychic waves. Victor would know how lonely she was and how desperate for company, especially on a day that was filled with bittersweet memories and all the more painful because it was her first Christmas without him. Victor would want her to go, and he would want her to enjoy herself, even if society decreed that she should wallow in misery and not see anyone unless she absolutely had no choice.

Deep mourning was for the wealthy, who could afford to hide away until it was deemed appropriate to come out and begin a period of half mourning until they could finally get on with their life. Perhaps if Gemma had enough money to last her a good while and a maidservant to see to her needs, she would take a few months to truly mourn, but she simply couldn't afford to remain at home. In fact, she saw people all the time. She couldn't help it. She had to work, was forced to share her living space with five other women, and very much wanted to help Sebastian in his work.

She had also attended Lydia's funeral two days before and was once again reminded of the brevity of life and the need to make the most of every day and find caring people to surround oneself with. Lydia's funeral was a sad affair, with only a handful of mourners present, and if not for the gold nugget Sebastian had appropriated it would have been sadder still. The remainder of Lydia's stash would be kept at Scotland Yard as part of the evidence and would remain in some drawer indefinitely—or until someone thought it was safe to help themselves to the loot. Sebastian had petitioned Superintendent Lovell to donate the gold to London's orphanages, where it would actually do some good. Lovell thought it a fine idea and had promised to speak to Sir David Hawkins in the new year.

Christmas dinner at the Ramseys' had been pleasant and peaceful, a gathering of strays that included Mabel, who'd cooked an incomparable meal and had joined them at the table when Colin invited her. Even Mrs. Ramsey had seemed more herself, reminiscing about Christmases past and not asking Sebastian any painful questions about his late wife.

Gemma sighed contentedly and settled back against the

leather seat that had warmed marginally from the heat of her body.

"Did you have a nice time?" Sebastian asked.

"It was kind of Mr. Ramsey to invite me," Gemma said. "If not for him, I would have spent my first Christmas without Victor alone in my room at the boarding house."

"Do the lodgers not celebrate together?"

"They do, and I know it would be terribly churlish of me to hide away in my room, but I simply couldn't bring myself to spend Christmas with near strangers. I'd rather be on my own if I couldn't be with friends."

Sebastian drew in a sharp breath, and Gemma realized that he was about to say something important. Her stomach lurched with anxiety, and she braced herself. She knew what she wanted it to be, but Sebastian had been moody and short-tempered the last time they saw each other and had cut their meeting short by claiming he had to check on Gustav. Perhaps he was angry that she had involved herself in his investigation, or maybe he simply saw no good reason for them to continue seeing each other.

Reaching out, Sebastian wrapped his fingers around Gemma's gloved hand. She wished she could feel the warmth of his skin, but this was the best she could hope for on a frigid December night, and she prayed it wouldn't be the last time they were together like this.

Sebastian took another deep breath before he spoke, his gaze firmly fixed on Gemma's face. She was thankful that he couldn't hear the hammering of her heart or sense her fear at the possibility of losing him.

"Gemma, I'm deeply sorry for the circumstances that brought us into each other's lives. You and I seem to be bound by violent death," Sebastian began, and Gemma's heart plummeted as she braced herself for goodbye. She lowered her gaze so he wouldn't see the pain in her eyes.

Seemingly oblivious to her distress, Sebastian continued. "But I'm so grateful to have met you. You have shown me that there's life after death and the possibility of love after heartbreak. Just say the word and we will never speak of this again, but I was hoping you might permit me to court you once you're out of mourning." He drew a nervous breath, and Gemma felt a tremor in his hand.

Just then, the carriage passed beneath a streetlamp, and Sebastian must have been treated to all the emotions that passed over Gemma's features as she looked up. She was surprised, saddened, hopeful, and happy all at once. She didn't need to be reminded that their friendship and budding affection had grown out of tragedy and, if they were to have a future together, those they'd lost would always be silent specters that inhabited their lives. But none of that mattered, because every couple had their ghosts. No one lived a life devoid of loss and pain. The important thing was that it didn't prevent them from feeling joy.

Gemma turned to Sebastian and smiled, and she knew that her gaze was glowing with love, because her heart was bursting. "I thought you'd never ask," she said softly.

She couldn't recall raising her face or leaning toward Sebastian. The kiss that followed obliterated all thoughts of death and loss from her mind. It was an expression of love, a testament of faith, and a promise for the future. Gemma pulled off her glove and touched Sebastian's cheek. It was cold and rough with stubble beneath her palm, but his gaze was warm and soft with longing.

"Happy Christmas, Sebastian," she said, and knew that, despite everything, it really was happy.

Sebastian lifted her hand and pressed his lips to her inner wrist, sending a delicious shiver through her whole body. "Happy Christmas to you," he whispered, and kissed her again.

* * *

Gemma was still floating on a cloud of contentment when Mrs. Bass knocked on her door the next morning.

"You're wanted, Miss Tate," she called out. "There's a constable here for you."

Gemma's heart began to race, and she had to gulp in several deep breaths before she could even think of going downstairs. There would be no reason for a constable to come for her on Boxing Day unless Sebastian was dead and someone thought she should be informed. She wrapped a warm shawl around her shoulders and forced herself to walk calmly down the stairs, all the while praying that she was wrong and there was some mistake.

Constable Bryant stood in the parlor, his hat in his hands, his gaze filled with sympathy, and his cheeks ruddy with cold.

"What is it, Constable?" Gemma choked out. "Is it Inspector Bell?"

"It is, ma'am."

Gemma grabbed onto the back of a chair for support, but Constable Bryant seemed unaware of her distress. He was looking away from her, as if he found it difficult to say the words.

"Inspector Bell asked me to fetch you, Miss Tate. There's a body that's been found. At the Foundling Hospital. One of the children. Inspector Bell would welcome your help."

A strangled cry tore from Gemma. She was grateful beyond imagining that Sebastian wasn't hurt, but the thought that one of the children was dead was more than she could bear.

"Who?" Gemma cried. "Who is dead?"

"I don't know, ma'am. All's I know is that Inspector Bell thinks it's murder."

"Oh, dear God," Gemma moaned.

She just knew in her bones it was Lucy and prayed that it wasn't, then felt guilty for wishing that one of the other children was the victim. She ran upstairs, pulled on her coat and bonnet, grabbed her gloves and reticule, and was pounding down the stairs in a most unladylike fashion a few moments later. But she felt calmer, more in control. She knew the Foundling Hospital like the back of her hand, and she knew those children. If anyone would be able to help Sebastian, it'd be her. And she was up to the task.

"Let's go, Constable. I'm ready."

# A LETTER FROM THE AUTHOR

Huge thanks for reading *Murder at Traitors' Gate*; I hope you loved Sebastian and Gemma's latest case. Their adventures will continue. If you want to join other readers in hearing all about my new releases and bonus content, you can sign up for my newsletter.

www.stormpublishing.co/irina-shapiro

If you enjoyed this book and could spare a few moments to leave a review, that would be hugely appreciated. Even a short review can make all the difference in encouraging a reader to discover my books for the first time. Thank you so much.

Thanks again for being part of this amazing journey with me and I hope you'll stay in touch—I have so many more stories and ideas to entertain you with.

Irina

irinashapiroauthor.com

 facebook.com/IrinaShapiro2
X x.com/IrinaShapiro2
instagram.com/irina_shapiro_author

Printed in the USA
CPSIA information can be obtained
at www.ICGtesting.com
CBHW010117230724
12013CB00031B/752

9 781805 081821